LOVE UNRAVELED

Honorable Intentions, Book 3

by Rose Phillips

ARE YOU SIGNED UP FOR DRAGONBLADE'S BLOG?

You'll get the latest news and information on exclusive giveaways, exclusive excerpts, coming releases, sales, free books, cover reveals and more.

Check out our complete list of authors, too!

No spam, no junk. That's a promise!

Sign Up Here

www.dragonbladepublishing.com

Dearest Reader;

Thank you for your support of a small press. At Dragonblade Publishing, we strive to bring you the highest quality Historical Romance from some of the best authors in the business. Without your support, there is no 'us', so we sincerely hope you adore these stories and find some new favorite authors along the way.

Happy Reading!

CEO, Dragonblade Publishing

**Additional Dragonblade books by
Author Rose Phillips**

Honorable Intentions Series
Love Denied (Book 1)
Love Abandoned (Book 2)
Love Unraveled (Book 3)

PROLOGUE

Promise us the sun forever as well as the night;
Yes. Forever the night. Promise me that.
—Marceline Desbordes-Valmore, "Let Us Cry"

1797

IF SOPHIA HAD not known he was coming, she would have assumed the tapping was the wind shifting the far-too-loose latch on her window. But she'd been waiting for him for hours. Truly for years. Her heart pounded ferociously against her chest. He was here now. As he'd promised.

She leaped from the bed and pressed her ear to the hall door. There was no sound other than a repeated tap, tap, tap behind her. She flew to the window and threw back the drapes, the shadow of Gaston's willowy body all she could make out of him in the darkness. She unhooked the latch and pushed at the window. Gaston caught it before it blew too far to the side and banged the pillar. He threw one long leg over the sash and pulled the window closed as he stepped fully into the room.

She reached past him to rehook the latch, catching a whiff of him as she did so. "You stink," she whispered, scrunching her nose.

"And you, *ma chérie*, smell like a garden of roses in summer."

He tilted his head to kiss her, and raindrops fell from his hat, chilling her bared shoulder.

She pushed him. "Well, you smell like a wet dog," she said even though excitement raced through her veins.

"More like a wet horse," he said but shook his entire body exactly as a dog would do, splattering Sophia even more. She laughed out loud. He stepped up to her quickly, covering her mouth with his hand. *"Fais attention,* Sophie. Someone will hear you."

Sophia bit his hand playfully, and she could see the flash of his teeth in the dim light. "There is a hook on the wall there. Hang your things." She strode to the window and closed the drapes again, then returned to her bedside, fumbling for the tinderbox she'd left there.

"Let me." His breath was warm against her ear as he took the box from her, and she regretted its loss when he leaned away from her to blow on the tinder. She set the wick to it, and the candle slowly took. After she set it on the table, she turned to look at him. *Mon Dieu.* Sophia still could not believe he had come.

"You are so beautiful my eyes hurt." Gaston ran the back of his fingers down her cheek, along her neck, and across her shoulder. Her flesh tingled in their wake.

"Embrasse-moi." Sophia puckered her lips and closed her eyes, and Gaston obliged her request for a kiss. His lips were soft and gentle, but she wanted more. She tried to probe with her tongue, but he kept his mouth closed to her. She opened her eyes, and he grinned. Sophia slapped his arm, and his grin grew bigger.

"You have not changed." Gaston chuckled and looked around the room, then pulled her toward the chairs by the fireplace.

"Non, it is too cold to sit by an empty grate. Come." Sophia tugged him in the opposite direction, back toward the bed.

"Sophie."

He said her name like a warning, and she ignored it. She did not fear Gaston. It was Gaston who should fear her. Sophia had waited three years for him, and she was not about to sit politely in chairs across from each other. She was going to be held, and for the first time in too long, she was going to be loved. She would settle for no less.

She let go of his hand and climbed onto the bed, feeling powerful, knowing he was watching her. She leaned forward, daringly showing the rise of her breasts, and patted the bed.

Gaston shook his head.

"But we must speak quietly," she said, tapping the bed again. "And I am chilled," she added, tugging at the counterpane and pulling it over her lap as proof.

Gaston sighed heavily. He perched on the edge of the bed and removed his boots before crawling in beside her. She was disappointed he stayed on top of the coverlet, but it did not defeat her. She would woo Gaston before night's end, and they would be bound together forever.

"I should not stay long," he said, taking her hand in his and running his thumb over her palm. "It would not do for me to be caught here in your bedroom."

"It would not do for you to be seen anywhere by *mia zia—ma tante*." Sophia caught herself and switched from Italian back to French, for it was the language they shared. "*Tante Giorgia* despises the French even more now that they occupy our cities."

"But you are French, *non*? She cannot possibly detest all French." Gaston squeezed Sophia's hand.

"She does not acknowledge that part of me. It is like Papa never existed, and she sees only the daughter of her sister." Sophia shrugged. "Still, she gave me a home when I had none. But I do not wish to speak of her any further. It is you and only you I want to hear about."

Gaston had suddenly appeared at the market that morning. She'd been examining a basket when she'd sensed someone beside her. She'd turned and blinked over and over. She could not accept what her eyes told her was true. He'd spoken quickly and quietly, and she'd given her address and specific directions to her bedroom before he'd disappeared into the crowd. It had felt like a dream, but it was not. For there was nothing imaginary about the warmth of his hand or his thigh pressed against hers, exuding a heat no blanket could block.

"Have you come with the army?" Sophia hoped not, for she detested the bold soldiers who considered her there for their taking. She had learned quickly not to leave the house without a chaperone and a male servant for protection.

"The only army I fight with is *le Régiment de Bourbon*. For my father. And for yours."

"Papa?" She sat straighter, all thoughts of seduction flown from her mind. She'd heard nothing from her father in months. "Have you word of him?"

"*Non, ma douce*, I have heard nothing directly. But the directory was annulled and the fair election overturned. In September. Many were shipped to Guiana. I am trying to find out if your father was among them or if he is still in Paris. Perhaps he is in hiding?"

There had been news of Napoleon's coup d'état, but she didn't see how it could affect her father. "But Papa, he is not in the government. He is writing for the paper."

Gaston turned to face her, cupping her cheek. "The royalist newspapers were shut down. Many journalists were shipped with the deputies."

"*Non.*" Sophia shook her head, fighting the tears stinging her eyes.

"I am sorry, *mon amour*. You must face the possibility. It is why I came."

"I don't understand…"

"The last time I saw your father, he made me promise to come to you should something ever happen to him."

"But why?" Sophia swallowed her agony. Surely Gaston was assuming the worst. Her father was a clever man. He had managed all the atrocities that had come before. An overturn in government could not be harder to navigate than the slaughter they had escaped.

"Because he knows nobody can love you more than he does…except me." Gaston pressed his forehead against hers. "And he's right."

Gaston held Sophia for a few minutes while she grappled with the concept of her father sent somewhere far away. She did not cry easily, and she would not cry now. Not for a maybe. A possibility. It was equally likely he was not among those banished. He might still be somewhere in France or gone somewhere else for safety. She knew for certain he would not come to *Venezia*. Her aunt might report him.

When her thoughts were composed and her emotions reined in, she pulled away from Gaston. He watched her, his brow furrowed in concern.

"I am not glass. I will not shatter." She flicked a strand of hair back over her shoulder. "And what does Papa think you might do for me?"

"Take you away with me."

"Where?" She asked it calmly, but her insides quivered with excitement. Her aunt had become intolerable. Other than trips to the market, Sophia's life had become one lonely dull day followed by another. And to be with Gaston? It was a dream come true.

"He would see you in England, if I can manage it."

"England! But it is so far. And I speak the language like a *bébé*."

Gaston ran his hand over her cheek and lifted her chin. "Then you must learn it, *ma chérie*. For you will live there until it is safe to return to France."

It was all so much to grasp. Her father gone. Her leaving *Venezia*. Gaston. "With you?" she asked.

"For a time. But I must do my part. I will return to the *régiment*."

Gaston was going to take her to England and leave her there. Alone. The past three years had taught her everything could change in a moment. She knew what she must do to ensure his commitment to her remained constant. She loved him too much to risk losing him.

"You will marry me." It was a statement, not a question, and it got a slow smile from Gaston.

"*Oui, ma beauté,* I will marry you at the first opportunity. Your father has given me his permission." He leaned in and kissed her, and this time, the kiss was not chaste. She was panting when he pulled away.

"I don't remember you kissing like that," Gaston said.

"I was a child. I am a woman now." She smiled at his scowl, a sense of triumph easing the sorrow of his news about her father.

"You have practiced?"

Sophia laughed at his fierce expression and the growl in his voice. Oh yes, she had power now she had not had before. Although, in truth, she'd not tried to use it until this moment. But she was not going to tell him.

She daintily shrugged her shoulders. "Perhaps, *un peu.*" She pinched her thumb and forefinger together to show him the little bit, and he growled again. She fell onto her back, pulling him with her, and demonstrated again she was more than ready to take on the task of being his partner. When she clawed at his shirt, he pulled back.

"Sophie, *non.*"

"*Oui.*" She boldly ran her finger down his shirt and teased the band of his trousers. "We are to be married. Besides, I have always been yours. And you mine."

She tugged him to her again, confident he would surrender. And she was right. Later, lying in the afterglow of their first lovemaking, he shared his plan.

"Count Tessaro has arranged a rendezvous tomorrow night with a local fisherman. You must go about your day, act as you normally do, and pack only a few things. Dress plainly."

His chest warm beneath her cheek, he stroked her arm as he talked. She snuggled closer, drifting in contented happiness. The bed dipped, and Sophia opened her eyes. Gaston was fully dressed and pulling on his boots. She sat up, tugging the cover to her chest. How could she have fallen asleep?

"My sleeping beauty awakes." He tugged on the second boot and shifted to face her. "Midnight. Be ready. There will be no time to spare."

Excitement and fear coursed through her. She did not want him to leave but knew he must. Tears stung, and he lifted her chin so she looked him in the eyes.

"I will return. I promise." He kissed her one last time, and she watched as he opened the window and disappeared. The wind rattled the pane, and she got out of bed, the marble floor cold against her feet. She opened it and peered outside, but she could see no one. "*Je t'aime,*" she whispered into the darkness before latching the window and crawling back into bed. She held the pillow against her as though it was Gaston. His scent still lingered, and the pungent smell of the stable he had slept in was now a comfort.

A few more hours and there would be no more goodbyes.

CHAPTER ONE

*And we turn'd to the growing dawn, we had hoped for a
dawn indeed,*
*When the light of a Sun that was coming would scatter the
ghosts of the Past.*

—Alfred Lord Tennyson, "Despair"

THORNWOOD LOWERED HIS voice. "Napoleon is on the March again."

"But I understood the thorough thrashing he received on the Russian front last year had depleted his army? The expectation was for him to lie low, was it not?" Walford's eyebrows narrowed.

"He's reconnected with his old *Grande Armée*. They're on the shores of the River Saale. We are bracing for a confrontation."

Lord Walford shook his head. "I am woefully out of touch."

"You have been distracted," said Stratton. "By a beautiful baby boy," he added in his booming baritone.

Sophia cursed under her breath. She'd been straining to hear the men talking while appearing interested in what the women were saying. A feat she was admirably achieving. Now Stratton had derailed the conversation, and everyone was looking at the baby. Baby Daniel was undeniably cute, but Sophia knew the child would draw everyone's attention, and Lords Thornwood and Walford would not get back to their topic of discussion.

However, she'd heard enough to know she might be of more use back in town than the country. She far preferred the city at this time of year, anyway. The season was in full swing, and she could enjoy endless activities while keeping her ears and eyes open.

"I would like to go to London," she said when everyone had finished *oohing* and *aahing* over the baby. "Come with me, *miei amici*. It would be much fun, no?"

Sophia did enjoy their company—they were the dearest of friends—but in truth, they also made great decoys. She often hid her activities behind their presence, and she never knew when she might need them as a screen. Of course, they were unaware of her private agenda. Although, perhaps the men might be suspicious of her now, as she had been involved in their spying escapade a few weeks ago. She looked pointedly at Lord Stratton, who was usually an ally.

"I'm not weighing in until I hear Catherine's decision," Stratton said. "Not leaving my grandson for a minute, if I can help it."

Sophia swung her gaze to Stratton's daughter, and parts of Sophia softened as they always did when she watched Catherine. She was seven years Sophia's junior, and much more sedate than she, but they'd become close in the years they'd known each other. When Catherine had been waiting for her soldier husband to come home, she had leaned heavily on Sophia for comfort. It had felt good to be needed.

"*Bella*, will you come?"

Catherine looked at Walford, who simply raised his eyebrows in response. Catherine pursed her lips and frowned at him, and Sophia wondered what was playing between them when Catherine burst into laughter. "You win. You win," she said, still looking at her husband, who was grinning in return.

"He wins what?" Elizabeth asked, leaning forward and glancing between Catherine and Walford.

Sophia loved that her two friends were now friends themselves. In their company, there was a freedom she'd not experienced in years—and a sense of security unrivaled by any other relationship she'd had in over a decade.

"He wins me. And Daniel." Catherine giggled. "Nicholas has been pestering me for days. He's going to London to take care of business and wants me to go with him, but I feel it is too soon." She looked at the swaddled babe nestled in her arms.

"It's not too soon, *bella*. Motherhood is beautiful. Come shine your light on the town." Sophia was confident she had at least won the Walfords' company.

"That is what I said, although not quite as poetically," Walford said cheerfully before looking at Richard and growing serious. "Thornwood, you might want to consider joining us. Off the coast of Ireland, several merchant ships were raided and taken. As a result, there have been monstrous increases in insurance. Randall's worried about the fleet."

Richard nodded. "Yes, I received word even though my commitment to his company isn't legally signed yet. Brave of him. I could back out." Richard raised a hand before Walford could say anything. "I'm not going to, of course. It speaks well of him that he is so candid. He's also applying for privateering commissions."

"All the more reason to get those papers signed," Walford said with a wink. "Lucrative business these days. So is my end of things. With Britain at war on the continent and in the colonies, ships are in high demand. Make hay while the sun shines is what I say."

Catherine gasped, hugging the babe tight. Sophia shifted closer and squeezed Catherine's hand. Walford looked appropriately contrite as he apologized. Catherine believed her brother, Laurence, was somewhere in the colonies fighting. Sophia knew Walford was a caring husband, and since he was one of the few who knew Laurence remained in England, he likely hadn't considered the insensitivity of mentioning war in the colonies.

Still, Sophia was tempted to chastise him. War was nothing to be joked about. Sophia knew firsthand the horrors it wrought. Of course, so did Walford. He'd spent four years on the continent. She guessed everyone dealt with such dark subjects in their own way. And she needed to get back to her way—keeping busy and aiding England's cause.

Sophia turned to Elizabeth. "And you, *mia amica?*"

"I would far prefer to stay here," Elizabeth said, glancing around at the sweep of lawn and pausing at the children playing on the far side of the garden. "Are you going, Richard?"

"I'm afraid I must." He flinched slightly, but a smile lit his eyes. "Business and parliament calls. I was going to broach the subject with you after this gathering."

"Oh," she said and looked at the children again.

Sophia felt her friend's disappointment deeply. Richard had only returned to Elizabeth's side a few weeks ago. She'd worry about being apart again so soon.

"It is settled. You must come too," Sophia said, making the decision for Elizabeth. She would not allow her friend to sit in this old manse and fret. Sophia hated to simply hang around anywhere. There was nothing more darkly consuming than waiting.

Elizabeth looked back at Richard, who smiled in agreement. "And, if you'd like, we can empty some more wallets for your orphanage while we're there," he said teasingly.

Elizabeth's angelic face brightened, and her blue eyes sparkled in the afternoon sun. Sophia clapped with honest joy. The busyness of London was stimulating, but the company of her few select friends brought her true happiness.

"Then I'm decided," Stratton said, holding out his arms toward Catherine, who obliged and set the swaddled bundle in them. "I'll come be your nanny," he said, and everyone laughed.

Later, Stratton accompanied Sophia around the manor to the courtyard and her coach. He paused out of earshot of the servants.

"Nick tells me you took a tumble a few weeks ago at your

masquerade ball. A man bowled you over?"

"Walford is terrible at keeping secrets."

"I don't know about that." Stratton raised an expectant eyebrow and waited, refusing to be distracted.

"It's true. I was caught off guard and landed on my backside. It is fortunate I have extra padding, no?" Sophia said it lightly, but the incident had weighed heavily on her mind.

"And you still don't know who it was?"

"Like everyone, he was in costume. A harlequin. And his timing was fortuitous. Without him, the traitor might still walk free."

"Yes, so I've been told. It was no accident the man was there?" Stratton's brow creased, his moss eyes darkening with concern.

Sophia patted his arm. "I do not know, and I tire thinking of it. It is a mystery I'm not inclined to solve."

"Fair enough. I'll not probe any further." He covered her hand in his. "And speaking of keeping secrets, I understand my lad was there too."

"He was. And is still at Château Nouveau. He's staying at my summerhouse temporarily. If you'd like to drop by before we leave for London, I will let Laurence know you're coming. If he does not know it is you, he will disappear...like that." Sophia snapped her fingers in the air.

Happy lines creased the corners of Stratton's eyes. "I would appreciate it." He leaned in and brushed each of her cheeks with a kiss. "You're a good friend. Thank you for all you do"—he looked over his shoulder where the others were slowly following—"for all of us."

Sophia smiled, and her heart swelled too big for her chest. She'd left everything behind when she'd come to England. She'd turned her aching loneliness into purpose, but somewhere along the way, she'd found these people. And these people had become her people.

Later, alone in her great bed, she tossed and turned, awakening to the pouring rain rattling the windows. She had dreamed of Gaston again and the miserable night he'd come to her window. She thought she'd laid his ghost to rest, but perhaps she never would. The strangest things prompted memories of him. Emerald-green velvet, like his favorite *redingote*. The sound of the violinist, like *l'homme* who played in the square where they'd sat. The smell of a horse stall, the scent of it on his pillow, lingering long after he'd left.

And now she could add to her list the sight of a harlequin at a masquerade. An accidental run-in that had lasted seconds. But even with the paint, he'd been so reminiscent of Gaston she'd felt she'd been kicked, not just knocked over by him in his haste to leave. But it had been dark, and it had all happened so fast, and the man was gone. Her men had tried to find him but had not succeeded.

She groaned. Gaston was long lost to her. For certain, she'd not find him roaming her property in the English countryside. She rolled over and hugged her pillow tight. It was going to be another long night.

CHAPTER TWO

*I loved her against reason, against promise, against peace,
against hope, against happiness, against all discouragement
that could be.*

—Charles Dickens, *Great Expectations*

GASTON PICKED AT a fingernail. He should simply march up the steps of *le grand château* and demand to see Sophie. He'd been watching her from afar for too long. He'd not spoken with her since she was seventeen. Although, he had seen her once before discovering her in London. His stomach roiled, and anger lit a fierce fire in his heart. Yes, he'd seen her. As another man's wife. *Countess Tessaro.* He spit onto the ground and swallowed the remaining bile.

From his perch in the tree, he stared across the lake at the summerhouse. There was no movement. Sophie had left earlier, so there was no sense in heading to his lookout near her mansion. Besides, he could not approach her until he identified the man who lived in the summerhouse and, more importantly, what his relationship was to Sophie.

He'd not expected to run into Sophie, especially quite literally. She should have been busy hosting her masquerade, not running around her property in the dark. What had possessed her to stroll beyond her gardens? Could she possibly have known a traitor was going to be taken down? He could not fathom her involvement beyond her friendship with Lords Thornwood and Walford, and he knew, firsthand, their participation was accidental. Perhaps *accidental* was not the right word, for while Thornwood remained unaware of the fact, Gaston had strategically arranged for the man's involvement.

Perhaps Sophie had followed Thornwood that night out of curiosity. It was certainly not for a tryst. He'd been watching Thornwood for months too and knew him to be a loyal husband. Even the prostitute Gaston had used as a liaison to the man had not tempted him. So what had brought Sophie out into the woods a few weeks ago? Gaston shook his head in frustration. Too many questions were knotting and looping like ship's rope in his brain.

After the masquerade ball, he'd circled back, but she'd returned to the ballroom, and her men had searched her property. He could not risk being found, so he'd left. When he'd returned to the inn, there'd been a missive he could not ignore, so he'd had to leave the countryside for a few days and return to London. When he'd returned, this man was ensconced in Sophia's summerhouse. Gaston was determined to find out why before he decided whether to approach her.

He shimmied down the tree and strolled beyond the copse of trees, out of sight from any peering eyes on the opposite side of the lake. His legs ached from sitting like a sparrow for too long, and it was good to stretch them. Spring was his favorite season, all the promise of the splendor of summer bursting at the seams, waiting to come out. It was how he'd felt all those years ago with Sophie. He kicked the ground in frustration. *Mon Dieu!* When would he accept spring had passed him by? That his budding rose had passed him by? For an Italian count.

He heard the carriage before he saw it, its wheels grinding heavily on the drive. He hurried into his position under the large weeping willow, careful the men who roamed the property did not see him. They dressed the part, but they were no gardeners.

He'd recognized one immediately as *le garde du comte*. Even though he'd aged, he was a hulking beast of a man who would be hard to forget. He'd stood by Tessaro's side when the count had spoken of the arrangements with a local fisherman and ensured Gaston the boat would be waiting for them that night. The night that had never come.

After leaving Sophie, he'd headed back to the stables for some much-needed rest. The scent of their lovemaking clinging to him, he had drifted quickly and slept far too deeply. The stable master had awoken him midafternoon, demanding he leave, afraid of the consequences if a traitor to the emperor were found in his stalls. A deal had been cut, and *Venise* was to be given to Austria. Gaston's elation had been quickly quashed when the stable master, his body visibly shaking with fear, had insisted the French had lost their minds.

Gaston had quickly gathered his things and slipped out the back. Chaos had reigned. He'd darted between streets, determined to get to Sophie, but the canals had made it difficult to stay out of sight. French soldiers had been everywhere, and his skin had hummed with warning. He'd seen those rabid looks before. Permission to plunder was a heady, dangerous power.

It had been imperative to get Sophie out, but it would have been impossible to approach her house in daylight. Her aunt would have likely stood in the way as well. It was probably for the best, as it would not have been wise for her to be in the streets. Her beauty would have attracted attention. Instead, he'd made his way to the harbor, hoping to speak with the fisherman and ensure he remained ready to hasten them away. He'd known only the boat's name. *La Nymphe*.

Squatting between two abandoned barrels, he'd eyed the waterfront, scanning for *La Nymphe*. Like ants at a picnic, the soldiers had both followed regulated lines and scattered randomly. French ships had crowded *les Vénitiens*. Ribbons of men had boarded ships, while others had dotted the shore, demanding seamen vacate their boats.

"Bastardo!"

The shout had drawn his attention, and his stomach had sunk along with the boat that had been scuttled. *La Nymphe* was not taking Gaston and Sophie, or anyone, anywhere ever again. There had been no point hanging around and watching the carnage, so he'd slunk back into the laneways. He'd had no choice but to return to Count Tessaro and ask for his assistance.

Sophie's laughter floated on the air, drawing him back to the present. He parted the sweeping branches so he could see her. She was talking to Tessaro's man and shaking her head but smiling. He wished he were closer to hear what she was saying. To see more clearly the smile on her face. To see how it lit those dark eyes.

Instead of climbing the steps to the manse, she hooked her arm in the man's elbow, and he steered her around the side of the house. Their easy familiarity galled Gaston. Sophie had always been too free with her affection and too trusting of others, especially men. She never understood she put herself at risk. Sophie had no true appreciation for her place in society. Of course, that had always been part of her charm. Her acceptance of everyone had been learned at the skirts of her mother, and for that he would be eternally grateful. Had her mother not wed her French scholar, there would have been no Sophie in Paris. And he'd not regret knowing her then, despite what time and circumstance had wrought. He shook his head, dislodging wistful sentiment, trying to regain the anger he felt, for it was more familiar and of more comfort than warm memories.

While the sun was in descent, it was still too light to move about more freely. He should stay hidden under the willow, but jealousy and curiosity spurred him forward. Besides, Sophie was with the one gardener, and the other was in conversation with the coachman. He was fairly certain no servant within the manse would notice any movement.

Gaston eased out from under the tree, darted across the open space, and slipped in behind a hedgerow. He followed it along the perimeter of the lawn. It bordered the east side and would lead him to the back gardens where, presumably, Sophie had gone. Sophie's laughter rang out, and he froze. He could not see her, but he was now close enough to easily hear what she was saying.

"I cannot believe this of you, Raimondo. The count would be as astonished as I."

"And as amused, I'm sure," the gardener replied in Italian.

Raimondo. Gaston carefully stepped closer to the hedge. How could he have forgotten the man's name? It had been an apt one for a man charged with seeing to the safety of the count and his family. *Mighty protector.*

"*Si*, the count would see much humor in it. But we are lucky, no, that you can spend your days propagating new roses? That your knife is used for the stems of flowers and not for…"

Sophie let the sentence drift. Gaston could picture her raising her shoulders and shrugging off the weight of such a serious topic. She was never blind to the ugly side of life, but she refused to dwell on it. It was one of the many reasons he'd fallen in love with her.

He had been eleven when the riots had broken out in Paris. The *Prise de la Bastille* was forever ingrained in his memory, not only because of the chaos and confusion of the time, but also because it was the day he'd met Sophie. She'd been a child, but she'd taken him by the hand and led him away from the gunfire and shouting. She'd smiled at him and hummed off-key as they'd woven through the streets. He'd taken shelter with Sophie and her mother until her father had returned from college. Professeur Auclair had escorted Gaston home.

The next day, he'd found his way back to her. And the day after. And the day after that. And, suddenly, his eight-year-old friend had been a beautiful fourteen-year-old, and at seventeen, if they could get permission from their parents, he could marry her. But fate could be cruel and mobs crueler. He closed his eyes, wishing he could block out the images of the last day he'd seen Sophie in Paris. But he knew they would never leave him.

"You move and you're a dead man."

Memories of Paris slipped away at the cold tip of the gun pressed against Gaston's temple. He shifted his eyes to look sideways. The man from the summerhouse. Gaston sighed heavily, but a quiver of excitement ran up his spine. It would seem he would speak with Sophie today after all.

CHAPTER THREE

How like a winter hath my absence been
From Thee, the pleasure of the fleeting year!
What freezings have I felt, what dark days seen!
What old December's bareness everywhere!

—Shakespeare, "Sonnet 97"

SOPHIA ADORED THAT Raimondo was enjoying the garden. He was not required to cultivate roses, or do anything else botanical for that matter, but he'd taken to it and was much more relaxed for having done so. He, too, had walked away from everything to come to England, and he'd done it for her. For the count, really, but Raimondo did not make such a distinction with his loyalty. The count had loved her, so Raimondo protected her as though she was the count himself.

"What color will it be?" she asked, running her finger over one of the many buds.

"I am hoping this one will be a deep red. I am trying to create *scarlatto*, but it is not easy."

Sophia clapped her hands. "My favorite color." Of course, she was aware Raimondo knew scarlet was her favored shade of red, but she was genuinely pleased he wanted to make her happy.

Raimondo's face changed: a curtain drew over his indulgent expression, and a fierce scowl took its place. He grabbed Sophia and pushed her behind him. as he hunched like a lion ready to pounce, his knife was now a weapon. Sophia was not new to the unexpected, yet her heart rate accelerated as she peered around Raimondo's bulky frame. And then it stopped. She was certain it did. It stopped along with the world, and the moment froze in time.

It was not because a man had gotten so close to her. Nor was it because Laurence had a gun to the man's head. It was the man. A man she'd thought long dead.

"Gaston," she whispered, and the world spun anew, her heart now pounding in her chest and echoing in her head. "Gaston," she said again as she stepped out from behind Raimondo.

His dark eyes held hers, but she could not read his expression. They stared at each other, and then a corner of his mouth tilted into the crooked smile she so loved.

"*Oui*, Sophie, *c'est moi.*"

Sophia could not recall crossing the distance between them, but she was in his arms, and he was holding her tightly and pressing kisses to the top of her head. Her mind raced, grasping for some indication she was dreaming. A new dream, for none had ever been like this—so real she could feel the muscles on his back and the warmth of his body against hers.

He pulled back, and she was reluctant to let him go lest the dream slip away too. He brushed a stray hair off her face, tilting his head so he could see her better. "*Ma* Sophie" was all he said before pulling her close again. But she'd seen the tears glaze his eyes and was now fighting her own. This was not fantasy.

Laurence cleared his throat, reminding Sophia of his presence. She could sense Raimondo lurking close by as well. She stepped back from Gaston, keeping her eyes on him as she did so, afraid he'd disappear.

"I must assume this is a welcome intruder?" Laurence raised an eyebrow at Sophia, and a smile played on his lips. He looked so much like his sister, Catherine, when he smiled. Catherine, who for her own protection, could not know Laurence was so near. So many secrets. So many ghosts from the past. And her ghost was standing here in the flesh.

"*Si. Oui.* Yes." Her three languages tumbled one over the other, her mind scrambled. She could find no more words as she stared at Gaston, his dark gaze holding hers. It was all too much to take in and more than she was capable of explaining.

Laurence slowly uncocked his already lowered gun, put it in his pocket, and flashed a full smile. "I'll not ask any questions…now. But curiosity may triumph over my gentlemanly discretion. Would you like me to stay?"

"It is not necessary," she said, shaking her head, her eyes still locked on Gaston's.

"You know where to find me."

Laurence might have directed that at Raimondo, not her, but Sophia did not look to see. The sound of Laurence's footsteps had faded into the distance before she turned her attention from Gaston. Her emotions now under control, she turned to Raimondo.

"*Vai via,*" she said. "*Per favore,*" she added, softening the order to go away.

Raimondo grunted but did as instructed. She knew he would go tell Stefano, and they would both be nearby whether she wanted them to be or not.

"Come," she said.

Bursts of memories flashed through her mind as Gaston stepped forward and put his hand in hers. Shouting, gunfire, and a boy standing stiff as a statue. Perhaps she'd been too young to understand his fear, but she'd known he would not be safe if he'd stayed there. So she'd done the only thing she could think to do. She'd brought him home. And he'd become hers.

Her thoughts were dizzying, and she was lightheaded. *Hers.* But he'd been lost to her. Could it possibly be he was now found?

GASTON WALKED QUIETLY by Sophie's side, his mind still trying to grasp this turn of events. He'd meant to confront her on his terms, to throw her betrayal in her face, and to finally extinguish the fire of his love for her. But her face—*mon Dieu!*—her face when she'd seen it was him. His heart had stopped beating, or perhaps it had begun beating for the first time in many years.

They climbed the steps, and the door opened. The tall, thin man Gaston had glimpsed many times from his hiding place under the willow tree stepped to the side, his face impassive.

"My lady," the butler said with the stiffness Gaston had come to know in the English. The man glanced briefly at Sophie's hand clasped in Gaston's before returning his attention to Sophie.

"Harris, some privacy. We'll be in the yellow drawing room," Sophie said regally as she swept by the butler, tugging Gaston along with her.

The entrance was grand, the austerity of white marble and plaster broken by a series of colorful paintings. That was all Gaston could note before Sophie dragged him through a door on the right. She let go of his hand and turned to close the doors. "Yellow" was an appropriate name for the room. Yellow chaises, yellow wall hangings, yellow drapes. It was a field of buttercups.

Sophie returned, standing before him, looking up at his face. She lifted her elegant gloved hands and cupped his cheeks, running her thumbs over the contours of his nose and lips. When she paused on his lips, he kissed her thumb, wishing the silk did not stand between his lips and her flesh. She studied him, her eyes dark with an emotion he could not name. He had so many questions, so many things to say, but he found he wanted only to be in her presence for now.

"Gaston," she said on a sigh, and his body vibrated at hearing his name whispered invitingly from her lips. Lips he wanted to kiss but was not sure he should. There was too much between them. And, while he could not seem to find his searing anger, it would not do to imagine they could simply pick up where they'd left off.

Still, he let Sophie gently pull his face down to hers and did not resist when she brushed a kiss across his lips. Nor did he stop her when she ran her hand over his cheek and began to kiss in earnest. He was beyond stopping her when her tongue begged entrance. He pulled her close and devoured her as a starving man at a banquet. He tasted and feasted and lost himself in the feel of her. *Mon Dieu*, she knew what she was doing.

The realization was like throwing a bucket of cold water over two mating dogs. He pulled away abruptly, putting a few feet between them, and swiped at his mouth. *She knew what she was doing.* Gone was her innocence. Gone was his Sophie. He'd been kissing a mirage. The reality before him was not his young lover. It was Countess Sophia Tessaro—a traitor to his heart.

CHAPTER FOUR

Rage and lust pulled her heart, as with two strings, two different ways.

—Henry Fielding, *Joseph Andrews*

S OPHIA'S HEART POUNDED so hard she was certain Gaston must hear it from where he stood. Why had he withdrawn so abruptly? She'd wanted to keep hold of him, get lost in him, not let the dream slip away. And she did not mistake his response, his desire, nor could he have possibly misread hers. Yet he wiped at his mouth as though he'd been licked by a dog. Anger quickly replaced longing.

"Was my kiss so repulsive?"

"What? *Non*, not repulsive. In fact, it was enticing."

The right words but the wrong expression. Gaston was scowling. What was wrong with him?

"And much different from what I remember. As though you've had much practice."

"Ah," Sophia said, her anger softening, the problem dawning on her. "Gaston, it has been sixteen years. You could not have expected to find the girl of seventeen again."

"*Non.*"

It was clear he was still struggling with it. Well, she was digesting his existence, so surely he could manage her years of experience.

"I suppose you have been a paragon of virtue throughout the years. Is that what you've been doing? Where you've been? Seeking sainthood at a monastery?" Sophia tugged at the fingers on her gloves, keeping her eyes on the emotions stampeding across Gaston's face several times in as many seconds. She tossed one glove to the table and yanked off the second. "Sit."

She did not look to see if he obeyed her command as she strolled to the sideboard, trying to disassemble her thoughts. Gaston had finally come. It had not been her imagination—he *was* the harlequin from the masquerade. Why had he been lurking? Why had he not come to her door and made himself known? Where had he been? Why was he repulsed by her kiss? It surprised and maddened her, but it was an insult she must push beyond if she was to stay calm and make sense of the situation. Her hand shook as she pulled the stopper from the crystal decanter and poured two cognacs. She took a deep breath and turned.

As stubborn as he'd always been, Gaston was still standing where she'd left him. Let him stand. It was all too much, and she was going to sit before her legs gave out on her. She set his cognac on the table beside a chair, then took a seat on the sofa across from it. She cupped the cognac in her hands and rested it on her lap. She did not want him to see her shaking.

At thirty-six, Gaston was still a handsome man. If anything, he was more attractive than ever. Always lanky, he'd filled out. His snug-fitting jacket and trousers outlined his form, and it was clear there was muscle where once he'd been reed thin. She could see no gray in his coal-black hair, and the new lines around his mouth and his eyes drew attention to both of those features—his lips sensually full and, from this distance, his eyes still as dark as midnight. She tamped her body's response and thrust her chin toward the chair.

"We are not children," she snapped in French. *"Assieds-toi."*

This time he did as she directed, dropping onto the chair with a grunt. He grabbed the cognac and raised it in the air. *"Santé."*

Sophia repeated his toast and took a sip. A small sip. She needed to keep her head straight if she was to sort this out. Whatever *this* was. Gaston. Here in her drawing room. She'd start with that.

"What were you doing out there?" She waved her hand toward the window, where the sun was slowly setting.

Gaston brushed at his trousers, eyeing her from under his ridiculously long lashes. "Watching you," he finally said.

"Yes, but you are stating the obvious, no?" she said, irritated that he was toying with her. "Why were you watching? Why did you not simply call on me?"

Gaston shrugged a shoulder and took another sip. Sophia waited for an answer.

He rested back against the chair, his glass dangling between his fingers. "I was trying to assess the role of the man in your summerhouse."

"Laurence?"

Caught off guard, she'd said his name. Gaston could not possibly be familiar with English society, so there should be nothing to worry about. Still, as a spy for the Crown who worked on the perimeter of the law, Laurence could easily put many people in a dangerous position. She'd not cared about her own welfare, hadn't for years. Not since she'd lost Gaston. But she was not immune to fear on behalf of others and usually spoke with caution.

"Laurence?" Gaston repeated the name, nudging her to respond, the scowl back on his face.

Once again, it made her heart soften slightly. He'd been wary. Perhaps even jealous. It was an emotion she could accept. And one she liked after all these years. For one could not be jealous of something one did not want.

"A friend who needed a place to stay. He will be gone soon."

Gaston studied her, his brow finally relaxing as he took another sip of cognac.

Sophia watched him, expecting him to say something, but he did not. "Where have you been?" she finally blurted out, hurt and confusion melding into one emotion. She was happy he was here. He was alive. But what of the years in between? The long, lonely years?

Gaston leaned forward in his chair as though to speak, and a tap sounded at the door.

Sophia wanted to scream at Harris, but she did not. Instead, she put her glass down, stomped across the room, and yanked the door open. Harris's expression was appropriately startled, then instantly contrite, and Sophia calmed. She would not direct her anger at him nor at Raimondo and Stefano, who hovered in the background and, in all probability, had put Harris up to interrupting them.

"The day is fading, my lady," Harris said, quickly recovered. "May I light the lamps?"

He was, as always, right. The room was growing noticeably gloomy. The days were not yet long enough for Sophia. She far preferred summer, when the sun shone for a few extra hours into the evening. She held no fondness for nighttime—except for one night.

"Of course." Sophia stepped aside so he could enter. *"Vai via nonni,"* she said, shooing Raimondo and Stefan. Despite the vexation still gnawing at her, she bit back a smile as they grumped away. They hated to be called grandpas.

She stood by the door until Harris was done, watching Gaston stare at the contents of his glass. In the wavering lamplight, he seemed a chimera, a fabrication of her imagination. If she pinched herself, would she awake to find him gone?

"Shall I set the fire, my lady?"

"No, it is warm enough. That will be all. I will ring if I need anything."

Harris nodded and moved to step past her.

"Oh, you can keep my men out of my hair, no?"

"Yes, my lady," he said without batting an eyelid.

How did the English do it? Keep such a wooden countenance? She could paint on an expression if needed for subterfuge, but she could not live like a marionette. No, she could not be a puppet for anybody. She'd pulled her own strings for years and would not hand the controls to anyone. She stared at Gaston. *Anyone.*

Sophia strode back to the sofa and sat, casually adjusting the folds of her dress, taking her time as though it was the only thing of importance to do. When she looked up, Gaston's dark eyes peered into hers.

"I believed in you. In us." She held his gaze, wondering if he could sense the pain behind her neutral tone. "Why did you not come back for me?"

CHAPTER FIVE

What did I feel that night? You are curious. How should I tell?
—Alfred Lord Tennyson, "Despair"

S OPHIE WAS AIMING for nonchalance, but even after such a length of time apart, Gaston could see the torment in her eyes, hear it in her voice. It was a knife in his heart. How many days had he pictured her ready for him by the window, the hours passing, the bitter disappointment she must have felt? Her distress. Her hurt. How many nights had he dreamed of making love to her, holding her, only to wake and find his arms empty?

"I do not know where to begin," he said, running a hand through his hair. So much was embedded in his brain, but much was lost as well.

"I should think where we left off would be appropriate." Sophie rested back against a cushion. Her finger tapping lightly on the arm of the sofa was the only indication she was not as indifferent as she was now trying to appear to be.

"*Oui*," he said. "*Où nous nous sommes quittés*," he said, repeating Sophie, his mind racing. How could he possibly convey all that had happened since? He could not relax like her. Instead, he set his glass down and perched on the edge of the chair. "After I left you the night we…" He struggled to put delicately into words the memories of that night. He cleared his throat. "The night we were together, I returned to the stables. I awoke in the morning to find out the news that Austria was to take *Venise*. It seemed a good thing until I stepped into the streets. Napoleon's men were raiding, destroying everything they could not take with them."

"I know this."

"*Naturalmente.*" He waved away Sophie's interruption. "I say it only to remind you of what was happening that day."

"I need no reminders. I lived it, no?" She swiped at her dress as though irritated, then looked back up at him. "And not for a day. Too many days. It was a time of great fear, and I faced it alone."

She was more than irritated. The fire of fury flashed amber in her eyes. It was an anger he understood well. To believe someone you trusted, someone you loved, had abandoned you? It was the worst feeling, a dark pit with no light. There were times he'd wished she'd been taken from him rather than have given herself away, so freely, with no thought of him.

"Shall I speak? Tell you the tale, or would you prefer to tell me?" Gaston's anger sparked too easily, but it was painful to look at her and know she'd chosen another.

Sophie looked as though she was going to say something further but changed her mind. She kicked off her slippers and tucked her stockinged feet under her derriere. It would have been sensual, her limbs outlined as she'd shifted, if it weren't so infuriating. Sophie angry with *him*. The gall.

She pressed her lips together, and his anger drained away. He wanted to forget everything. To slide onto the sofa beside her and taste her once again. To push aside the years and start anew.

"Well?" she prompted, tilting her head to one side.

"I went to the harbor to ensure the boat would be ready for us," he continued, ignoring all foolish longing for things to be different. He'd used to be a dreamer, but he was a realist now. "I watched it sink. *La Nymphe.* It was gutted and sank along with others. It was our way out, and it was gone. I did not know what to do."

"You could have come back to me."

"And what would you do with me? Hide me? Even if you managed to keep me from the soldiers, how could you keep my presence from your aunt? And she hated the French. She would have reported me."

"But she hated all French equally," Sophie said. "Why would she turn you over to French soldiers? She owed them nothing."

"Because she hated your father most of all. And I was there to do exactly what your father had done years ago with your mother. Take you away."

He could see Sophie's mind turning it over, but she made no comment.

"I did the only thing I could do with soldiers swarming all around *Venise*. I went to see Count Tessaro again. He had no alternative plan for us but promised to devise one. He would not house me while he hatched it. He gave me the address of a man friendly to *les Bourbons* and told me to return after dark. I never made it to the safe house."

Sophie leaned forward. "What happened?" she whispered, her brow now furrowed in concern.

"I don't know. I had slipped out of the count's house and was headed along a narrow lane, and that's the last I remember. I awoke a day, or maybe two, later, a prisoner *en route* to Paris." Gaston took a long sip of his cognac, letting Sophie digest his story.

"You truly have no idea…?" she finally asked.

"For certain? *Non*. But the count was agitated I'd come. He was reluctant to help. He'd managed to keep himself out of the foray for years, and he made it clear he had no wish to become embroiled in it. It might be a coincidence; it might not."

Sophie quickly unfolded from the sofa and sat board straight, her eyes widening in disbelief. "Are you insinuating Carmine had something to do with it?"

Carmine. Merde! Gaston wished the count were still alive so he could slay the man for stealing his life. He swallowed hard, forcing his anger back into the pit where it dwelled. He scanned Sophie's body from head to toe before meeting her eyes and holding her stare.

He swallowed the bile souring his throat and shrugged a shoulder. "He benefited greatly from it, did he not?"

CHAPTER SIX

The passion of love is to be conquered only by flying from it.
—Miguel de Cervantes, *The History of Don Quixote*

SOPHIA REFUSED TO accept what Gaston was suggesting. Not that he'd been taken away from her against his will, for she did not think he would lie about such a thing, but that Carmine had anything to do with it. It could not be.

"*Impossibile!* He was heartbroken for me."

"I bet he was," Gaston said dryly, easing back in his chair, his cognac once again dangling casually from one hand.

Sì, he could relax now that he'd stirred her blood. Who was this man who looked so much like Gaston but oozed with such bitterness? She, too, had lost everything, but she did not see villains where there were none.

"I do not accept it. You did not know him like I did. Carmine was distraught I had been abandoned." Although, Carmine never mentioned Gaston had come to him. Doubt wiggled in, and she pushed it away. She'd been married to Carmine for four years, and he'd been nothing but kind. He would not have deliberately hurt her in such a way.

Gaston's expression did not change. "Why don't you ask Raimondo? He can confirm I came to the count for help. He knows what happened."

Sophia did not hesitate. She was never one to shy away from a truth. She strode to the wall and pulled the bell cord. Soon there was a light tap at the door. Harris knew better than to walk into any room without a direct invitation, bell or no bell.

She pulled open the door, startling Harris for the second time. "Find Raimondo." Movement drew her eye, and she spotted him lingering by the stairwell. She should have known he would not be far away. "Raimondo, *vieni qui.*"

Raimondo did as instructed and joined her at the door.

"Come in. I have some questions."

Raimondo's face was impassive. Despite his large size, Sophia did not find him intimidating. She knew what he was capable of, but he'd loyally taken care of her for too many years for her to fear his strength would ever be used against her.

"Raimondo, do you recall the plans Count Tessaro had for Gaston and me?"

"*Sì.*"

"Can you tell me about them?"

He raised his shoulders, seeming puzzled by the question. "The count had arranged with Monsieur Lavigne to take you under cover of night. *La Nymphe* was to—"

"*Sì, sì*, I know about those; it is the others I do not. Did Gaston return after the *La Nymphe* was destroyed?"

Raimondo looked from Sophia to Gaston and back again. Sophia did not look at Gaston. She kept her eyes on Raimondo, searching for the truth in his face.

"*Sì*," he said slowly. "He spoke with the count the following morning."

"And what happened next?"

His eyebrows came together, and he looked much like a perplexed eagle. "Next? Nothing." Raimondo thrust his chin in Gaston's direction. "He never returned."

"And why was that?" Gaston stood and walked over to them. "Why did I not return?"

"*Non lo so*. You tell me." Raimondo threw his shoulders back, bristling at the challenge in Gaston's tone.

Sophia scowled at Gaston. "Silence! Do you want the truth or would you like to continue to spin tales with invisible threads?"

Gaston's nose flared, but he remained quiet. Sophia turned her attention back to Raimondo, who was equally heated. They were like two bulls ready to charge each other. Men. Always ready to battle. The world should be run by women. It would be a kinder, gentler place.

"Raimondo, did the count make alternate plans for Gaston and me?"

"He sent me to check the harbor. There was no hope of escape from there. And the roads were blocked."

"So you decided to turn me over instead?" Gaston took a step forward, and Sophia raised her hand to stop him.

"Did you turn Gaston in? Raimondo, did the count ask you to intervene and ensure Gaston was taken by the soldiers?"

Raimondo's face said it all, and her growing apprehension slipped away. Raimondo could remain stone-faced, but he could not fake his emotions when they did surface. He was appalled by the accusation.

"*No, la mia contessa, no.* He would never do such a thing. Not to you. We were sent into the streets to look for *him.*" Raimondo's glance at Gaston was none too friendly.

Gaston guffawed unpleasantly.

"We risked ourselves for you, *signore.*" Raimondo glared at Gaston.

He was fuming, and Sophia put her hand on his arm to steady him. Raimondo angry was like a hungry bear, and she had no energy left to deal with him too. "*Grazie,* Raimondo," she said quietly.

"What plan did the count concoct?" Gaston said it like he was throwing down a gauntlet.

Sophia sighed and squeezed Raimondo's arm to let him know she believed him. It seemed to work, as the tension in his muscles eased somewhat.

"The count had no solution," he said, looking at her. "He intended to leave Monsieur Armand at *la casa dei bourbon* for another night while he worked on it. I went there to tell him to stay put until we had a plan, but was told he'd never arrived." He looked to Gaston, who was frowning in disbelief, shaking his head from side to side. "We assumed you were hiding somewhere, so we waited for your return. When you did not show, we scoured *Venezia* for you throughout the day and waited a second night. The count hoped you were temporarily waylaid." Raimondo covered Sophia's hand with his big paw. "By the third night, he knew he must tell you."

Everything Raimondo said fit with her memory of those days. After three nights of waiting for Gaston, Carmine had called at the house, asking to speak with her in private. Her aunt had been more than anxious to accommodate his request, hoping he was there to court Sophia. Eventually, he would but not until years later. He did not tell her of the destruction of the boat or of Gaston returning to see him. He told her Gaston had disappeared. That he had looked for him but could find no trace. Carmine was a protector, and she could only assume he'd withheld information to keep her safe. In those days, it had been easy to say the wrong words to the wrong person and find yourself in trouble.

"*Grazie*, Raimondo, for then and for now. You may leave."

He hesitated for a moment as though he was going to say something further, looking from her to Gaston and back again, but in the end, he was an obedient man, whether he liked his orders or not.

"Satisfied?" she asked.

Gaston stared at the closed door before looking at her. "He could be lying."

"He could be. But I assure you, he is not."

She grabbed her glass, strolled to the side table, and poured some more. Gaston could get his own. After all this time apart, for Gaston to have begun with a ludicrous accusation was unacceptable. Carmine had taken her in when her aunt had died and had ensured her safety from the ever-changing political climate. Gaston had been gone three years when the count had suggested marriage. She owed him her loyalty, even in memory. What did she now owe Gaston?

She turned around and leaned back against the table, eyeing him over the rim of her glass. He stood where she'd left him, and her heart skipped a little at the sight of him in her drawing room, something she'd never imagined she would see. He had been taken. He could not help that. She must forgive him her abandonment. But sixteen years had passed. The pain of loss mingled again with rising outrage. Sixteen years.

Sophia set her glass on the table and crossed her arms. "It was not your fault you did not return that night. But you appear to be a free man, and you did not come back to me at all. It is not Raimondo who should be cowering under questioning; it is you. Where have you been?"

CHAPTER SEVEN

O! never say that I was false of heart,
Though absence seemed my flame to qualify.
As easy might I from myself depart
As from my soul, which in thy breast doth lie.

—Shakespeare, "Sonnet 109"

GASTON DID NOT know whether to laugh or take Sophie into his arms and teach her who was in charge. She'd never been a dormouse, but she'd become a formidable woman. One who was confident she had full control of this reunion. She was wrong. He would tell her what he wished her to know. And he would make her see the injustice of her behavior.

"I was dragged along with the army for months, but I would serve no man except one who was rightfully on the throne. Eventually, I was left at the fortress, *Bitche*, where I rotted for two years. With the help of a guard sympathetic to the cause, I escaped with a British officer and came with him to England."

Sophie's mask dropped, her chocolate eyes growing rounder before narrowing. "You have been here all along?"

"*Non.* I returned to the continent."

He said it casually and strolled toward her, watching her face to see if she'd known he'd returned to *Venise*. If she did, she was a remarkable actress, for he could see no sign of it. She stiffened as he neared. He paused, her scent washing over him, so close he could smell the cognac on her breath.

"Veuille m'excuser," he said, reaching past her to the decanter on the table. He took a clean glass and poured a generous amount. "I find myself thirsty." His arm brushed against hers, and she shuddered. He smiled. She was not immune to him.

She marched away. Gaston turned to watch her as she settled back on the sofa, her haughtiness evident even from the back. No, she was not immune, but she was resisting it. And what of him? His desire for her had not abated, but nor had his anger at her betrayal. He, too, would resist. He would say his piece and be done with the memory of her. Of them. Finally.

Gaston took a large sip and sauntered back to his chair, not looking at her until he was comfortably seated. He, too, could play the game of insouciance. He crossed his legs and settled his glass on the side table. He'd yet to meet a more beautiful woman than Sophie. Her thick ebony hair, shining in the lamplight, was twisted elegantly up, but he'd seen it down, run its silky strands between his fingers, and his body burned at the memory. Her skin, so like her mother's and so unlike the English's penchant for paleness, was flawless. Age lines so thin he'd only seen them when he'd stood face-to-face. Time had been kind to his Sophie. *His?* She was not his, may never have been, and he'd best not forget it.

"Are you through taking inventory of me?" she asked.

Oh yes, Sophie was definitely no dormouse, but nor was she the tigress she perceived herself to be. There was vulnerability in her eyes, a shifting uncertainty. Did she fear a confrontation? Had Carmine told her he had finally come for her? Would she admit it if he had?

"I returned to the continent." He had not forced Raimondo to tell her of his return, for he wanted to assess her reaction himself.

"Yes, you have said so," she snapped. "But not to me." She, too, set her drink aside. "Not to me despite the fact you promised. You promised, Gaston!"

He sat forward in the chair, holding her stare. "Au contraire, I returned directly to *Venise* at the first possible moment. I kept my promise to you…" He let the sentence dangle, his implied meaning clear.

Sophie abruptly sat forward. "When? Why did you not come see me, talk to me?"

It took every ounce of self-control for Gaston to keep his tone dispassionate. "I could not. You had given yourself to another. What would be the point in it?" He glimpsed doubt in her eyes. Did she think he would lie about such a thing? Anger pricked at him, and his nonchalance slipped away. "Over three years, I dreamed of you. My memories of our one night together sustaining me. How could you do it, Sophie? How?" He'd not meant to expose his pain, had not intended to show her she'd had the power to hurt him.

He watched the play of emotion on her face before she, too, schooled it into indifference and sat back against the sofa. "*Non*," she said. "I do not accept the guilt you are handing me. You are the one who left me to believe you were dead."

"You had a husband to comfort you," he said, grabbing his glass and swallowing the contents whole, the burning of his throat more acrid than warming. "You'd no need of me."

He'd been so grateful to make it back to *Venise* and, with the Austrians in control, had had no need to hide. He'd gone directly to her aunt's house only to find strangers living there. They'd told him she'd died and the niece had married Count Tessaro. He'd been convinced they were mistaken, so he'd made his way over to the count's house.

Count Tessaro and Sophie had been going out for the evening. Swathed in the height of fashion, all signs of the girl he'd once known gone, the woman, Countess Tessaro, had clung to her husband's arm. She'd laughed lightly, and Gaston's ears had rung with the familiar sound. The count had leaned in and whispered something to her, and her responding smile was seductive. The ringing in Gaston's head had grown. When they'd settled into the gondola, Sophie had leaned over and kissed the count on the cheek. Gaston's head had resounded with his fury, with his hurt, and he'd known he must leave or he would do something he'd regret.

He had returned later and confronted the count, who, unruffled, had claimed he offered Sophie a life Gaston, a penniless traitor, could not. He'd calmly pointed out the point was moot anyway, as they were irrevocably wed. When Gaston had argued, the count had had Raimondo escort him from the property. He would have returned were it not for the intimate scene he'd witnessed between the count and Sophie. She had gone on with her life. Gaston had meant nothing to her.

"Non, non, non. You will not do this to me. You will not make me feel guilty for living. I waited for you, Gaston. I waited for three years. And you did not come. You did not write. There was no word at all about you. Aunt Isabella was dead. As far as I knew, you were too. What was I to do?"

He'd not expected her anger, and he'd not accept it. "The same thing I have done my entire life. Keep my heart only for you." Gaston did not mean those words lovingly, for he was tired of the weight of the memories of Sophie, of the dreams he'd once had. It was why he'd decided to find a way to approach her. To confront her would be cleansing, and he could finally put the past behind him.

Sophie flew to her feet, pointing at him. "Only for me? Is that why you were hiding in the bushes? Holding on to my heart? *Ridicule!* I did what I had to do, and I'll not apologize for it. But you—" Sophie paused, catching her breath, her chest heaving with emotion. "Carmine has been dead ten years. Ten years, Gaston! You, so brokenhearted at my loss, have had ten years to find me. To talk to me. To claim your love for me. I ask you again. Where have you been?"

Gaston swallowed, his mind a whirlwind. He could not tell her the truth, but he would not lie either. So he simply shrugged.

"Get out of my house," Sophie said through gritted teeth, the color in her cheeks deepening with her anger. "I never want to see you again." She turned and walked regally out of the room.

Gaston had never wanted her more.

CHAPTER EIGHT

My tongue will tell the anger of my heart,
Or else my heart concealing it will break.

—Shakespeare, *The Taming of the Shrew*

SOPHIA FOUGHT THE urge to run up the stairs, to bury her face in a pillow, to scream. Or to cry. No, she would not cry tears for someone who did not deserve it. She'd been in love with a memory. This man was not her Gaston. He was forever lost to her.

Raimondo stepped out from behind the staircase. "See him gone," she said as she walked past him, toward the back of the house.

She strode through the ballroom, stopping in the middle of the room as the thought struck her—Gaston had been here a few weeks ago when she'd held a masquerade. He'd not said a word, had deliberately not revealed himself. Had he not accidentally run into her, she'd not even know he'd been here at all. How long had he been watching her?

She muttered to herself, cursing him in three different languages, as she made her way in the dark to the saloon and on through to the conservatory. It was her favorite room, and she could easily navigate it without light. Still, she lit the lantern by the door and slipped it off its hook. When the fog had rolled into

Venezia and the winter days had grown dull and gray, she had longed for the smell of fresh flowers. She'd promised herself, if she ever lived in the country, she would have such a room built. She'd had it added to the back of the house a year after she'd moved in.

The smell of oranges filled the far corner, and she went to them, leaning in and slowly inhaling their scent. It helped to settle her anger but not enough for her to sit down. She set the lantern on a table and paced along the bank of windows looking out toward the gardens. The moon was behind clouds, so she could see nothing but shadowy shapes, real or imagined, she didn't know. She paused. Something had moved. She scanned the darkness but could see nothing further. It was probably Stefano doing his night rounds. If it had been Raimondo, she'd have recognized him. Even in shadow, he was hard to miss.

Sophia pulled at the pins in her hair and set them on the ledge, shaking her head so her hair would fall free. She massaged her temples, trying to chase away a growing headache. Gaston. Returned to her at last. Her initial burst of euphoria now extinguished, there was no longer joy in it. Why had he not come to her sooner? If Laurence had not found him skulking, would he have come to her at all?

The news he'd been taken prisoner had not come as a surprise. Carmine had proposed such a theory. He'd also bluntly told her rebels, loyal to the old ways, did not often survive capture. She'd held on to hope, knowing Gaston was wily and clever. If anyone could escape, it would be him. But she'd heard nothing from him or about him. Nor about her father. Carmine had assured her he was seeking information where he could, and she'd had no reason to doubt him. Should she question his integrity now?

Sophia could not imagine the level of betrayal Gaston was suggesting. The count had been kind and patient in those years after Gaston had disappeared. His presence in her life had ensured her safety among the many men who vied, often forcefully, for the hands of young Venetian women. He was a man who'd known how to appease those in power yet manage to maintain his own. When Aunt Isabella had died, Carmine had taken her in for her own protection. They'd grown close, and marriage seemed a logical step. She would have the protection of his name as well as his guards.

She could not accept the count would do anything to hurt her. Even in death, he protected her. When he knew he'd not long to live, he'd contrived a plan to see her leave *Venezia*. There were rumors Napoleon would return, and Carmine had not wanted to leave her vulnerable. Her French father had long been shipped away, and all her mother's family were dead. He'd decided England would be the safest place for a woman on her own, since fighting did not seem to land on Britain's shores. Carmine had been all she'd had left, and she'd been numb with his impending loss, so she had not cared where she went. Anywhere there weren't memories.

It was only after she'd arrived in England that she realized he'd been planning her escape for years. Money was here. The town house in London was already in her name. A man who'd planned so far ahead for her safety could not possibly have stolen the only thing she cared deeply about. He would not have arranged for Gaston's capture. He would not.

She rubbed her temples again, those early years in England rushing back in. Carmine had easily established financial security for her, but he'd understood money only bought so much in society, especially when you were a foreigner whose paternal country was at war with your newfound country. So he'd sent her with secrets. She'd presented them to the Foreign Office as instructed. In exchange, they did not pursue her history or question the past she'd fabricated for herself. Not truly invented though, for she never lied. She simply created an illusion by omitting details of her life.

The Home Office called on her still, and she was more than happy to oblige. It had become a goal over the years, a quiet revenge for her lost life. She volunteered information she garnered while socializing. Men talked easily in the company of a woman, and she became privy to many secrets she did not solicit. If she thought it would help England defeat the little emperor— the man who'd stolen her father and her love from her—she passed it on. It was seamless. Men from the Home Office came and went from her home with ease. Who would suspect a beautiful, self-centered Italian widow of anything except liaisons?

She'd built a good life here and had grown content. If she'd never stopped dreaming of Gaston, it was because the young girl in her longed for the boy. Not the man who was here today. The man who could still ignite her emotions and light a fire within her with a simple word or look. *Basta*! Enough! She would not hang around the countryside and lament. She'd planned to go to London in a few days; she'd move it to tomorrow. In London, she'd have a purpose. And her friends would soon be there.

She would leave her memories and Gaston behind.

GASTON WATCHED SOPHIE through the window. Raimondo had made the mistake of letting Stefano escort Gaston off the property. Stefano was not rigid like Raimondo, nor was he energetic. He had walked Gaston only as far as the entrance gate, then ambled back up the drive to the house, assuming Gaston would cooperate and leave. It had been easy to slip through the back gardens. A light in the *conservatoire* had drawn his attention, and he'd crept closer.

Sophie paced like a caged animal. He was pleased with her agitation, for it reflected his own. Apathy would have ended his desire, but this restlessness she was displaying only fired it further. He groaned when she took the pins from her hair. He longed to reach out, entwine those thick strands through his fingers, and pull her close. When she rubbed her temples, his heart ached a little. He wanted to massage away any hurt he had caused.

She'd been angry and composed in the drawing room, but he saw none of that now. Watching her when she did not know she was being observed shifted something in him. He cursed himself for a fool, but years of yearning could not be dismissed with the wave of her hand. Gaston still believed the count had been involved in his disappearance, but he was now certain Sophie was unaware of it. There was comfort in that. For his own sanity, he must discover if she'd loved the count. More importantly, Gaston must find out if she'd ever stopped loving him.

CHAPTER NINE

These are certain signs to know
Faithful friend from flattering foe.

—Shakespeare, "The Passionate Pilgrim"

"I'M SORRY I'M late," Catherine said, her naturally flushed cheeks far more attractive than any rouge Sophia had seen applied on the ladies attending this evening. "Daniel had a fussy day, and I didn't want to leave until I knew he had settled."

"You are always late, *bella*. But you're a good mama." Sophia kissed both those rosy cheeks.

"I'm not," Elizabeth said as she followed suit and brushed a kiss across Catherine's cheeks. "A good mama, that is. I must confess, I am enjoying these days without the boys. The freedom! I'm glad Richard insisted we not interrupt their new governess so soon. She's only begun to set routines."

"Those four will not even notice you are gone, especially with a new soul to torment." Sophia was happy to see Elizabeth smile at her teasing. They both knew the children, while relentless in energy, were well-behaved boys. Elizabeth and Richard were actively involved in their little lives, and it showed. "They will grow to be independent men, not mama's boys. It is what you want, no?"

"There is some merit in what you say. At least, I shall grant it credence as a sage observation when I am overcome by guilt." Elizabeth grinned.

"I thought this was to be an intimate gathering?" Catherine glanced around the small ballroom. "It seems a great crush."

Sophia found it overcrowded as well, but it was exactly what she needed. There was no time to think at a gathering like this one. There was also ample opportunity to listen to conversations. She'd only been in London a week, but she'd heard nothing so far, only that Napoleon had crossed the River Saale. Of course, she shared none of this with her friends.

"There is so much competition at this time of year. Many fear their affairs will be underattended. Perhaps they sent out extra invitations to ensure a good turnout and then, *voilà*, everyone appears. In truth, we were not to be here. I had to work my magic." Sophia waved an imaginary wand in the air.

"You mean work your duke, don't you?" Elizabeth said, and Catherine giggled.

"Maybe." Sophia pursed her lips and looked away, pretending she was offended, but it was exactly what she'd done. They had many events in the coming weeks thanks to the duke's influence. And hers. But she did not delude herself. Her presence was desired by many, but she did not hold the same power as the Duke of Salinger.

"Speak of the devil…um, duke," Elizabeth said, and Catherine laughed again.

This time, Sophia swatted her lightly with her fan. "Cease. You are having fun at your good friend's expense."

Catherine sucked in both lips, trying to look contrite, while Elizabeth raised a knowing eyebrow. Sophia smiled at the two of them, winking playfully before turning her attention to the Duke of Salinger.

"My lady," he said, taking her proffered hand and bowing slightly. "I saw you the moment I walked in. You light the room."

Sophia dipped her chin in acknowledgment of the compliment but did not comment on it. The duke was always ready with plaudits, but she recognized the hollowness in his flattery. She was no fool to fall for his shallow accolades. The man wanted one thing from her—her money. She'd yet to decide whether being a duchess would be worth the struggle to hold on to her purse strings.

"My ladies," the duke said smoothly, acknowledging Elizabeth and Catherine, then immediately dismissing them and returning his attention back to Sophia. "Will you spare me a dance this evening, Countess Tessaro?"

Sophia fluttered her fan in front of her face, not because she was playing coy but because she found it irritating when he casually ignored her friends. If the liaison might not be so advantageous for many reasons, she would send him on his way. The duke played in powerful circles, including that of the regent himself. Many of her tidbits for the Home Office had come from there, especially from foreign visitors who enjoyed the regent's liquor as much as the regent did himself.

Still, if she did decide to marry him, he would need to temper his arrogance. *Gaston.* Could she marry anyone now she knew he lived?

"Countess?" The duke was frowning, and Sophia was not convinced it was out of concern. She had not meant to drift to thoughts of Gaston, and it was frustrating she had done so.

"I will consider it," she said, more tersely than she'd meant to, but she felt no remorse. The duke's skin was a thick pelt, and he'd not feel the sting of anything she said.

"Of course." He bowed stiffly and walked back into the crowd.

"I honestly do not know what you see in him," Catherine said. "I know it's none of my business, but seriously, he could be your father."

"He is handsome, no?" Sophia said it flippantly, hoping to dissuade further conversation on the topic. She did not want to dwell on the duke any more than she wanted to stew over Gaston.

"I suppose, if you like old, whiskery grandfathers." Elizabeth's angelic face scrunched in distaste.

"Have I mentioned you two are evil? Not every woman is fortunate enough to marry for love."

Both her friends blushed becomingly. Sophia could not begrudge either of them their happiness. Each had earned it. She did an exaggerated shrug and smiled at them. "He is a duke. What more could a woman want?"

"And what are you beautiful ladies smiling about this evening?" Walford asked as he leaned in and pressed a kiss to Catherine's head.

"We will reveal nothing willingly," Catherine said, her moss eyes shining brightly in the light of the candelabras. She leaned in to his ear. "I'll tell you tonight," she said, deliberately loud enough for Sophia to hear.

"*Amici.*" Sophia shook her head good-humoredly. "It is not my enemies I must fear; it is my friends."

Walford made no comment. Instead, he excused himself and pulled Catherine toward the dancers. She wiggled her fingers in a goodbye and blew Sophia a kiss before they disappeared into the morass.

Elizabeth put a hand on Sophia's arm and squeezed. "We tease because we don't know what else to do about your interest in him. We only want the best for you, and we worry his temperament is not suited to yours. We'd hate to see you with someone who would dampen your spirit."

"I know," Sophia said, covering Elizabeth's hand with her own. "I adore your honesty. Both of you. But here comes that delicious husband of yours and," she groaned dramatically, wanting to lighten the evening, "His Mighty Grace, the duke."

"Your lemonade." Thornwood handed Elizabeth the glass. "Sorry it took so long. Bentley waylaid me and Walford, insisting we join him in Lord Ander's study to taste a new cognac Ander's managed to secure. Thought we might be interested in procuring some. Of course, we all know his true motive. So he can come over and drink it."

Sophia laughed. Bentley did love being the contrast to both Thornwood's and Walford's soberness, literally and figuratively. The three men had gone to Eton together, but Bentley was starkly different to the other two. She always enjoyed Bentley's buffoonery. It was harmless and playful.

"Countess, I'm told a waltz is next. If I may?"

With a curt nod to Thornwood, the duke confidently raised his arm. Sophia put her hand on it. His expectance of obedience was nothing new, but tonight she found it annoying. She knew how to put him in his place, had done so before, but here was neither the time nor the place. Besides, she'd come here for a little fun, and the duke was an exquisite dancer.

He strolled proprietorially, steering her around the room while they waited for the next set to begin. "I sense you have been avoiding me," he finally said, clicking his tongue at the end as though correcting a child.

He was more astute than she'd given him credit for. "Not at all, Your Grace. My mind has been elsewhere lately, but I assure you it has returned to the here and now."

"I am glad to hear it. It would not do—"

The duke was abruptly cut off by a gentleman Sophia did not recognize but with whom the duke seemed more than happy to converse with about horses. The Duke of Salinger was a handsome man despite his age and old-fashioned beard. He was not whiskery as Elizabeth had suggested. His beard was neatly groomed, much like her father's had been the last time she'd seen him. Gray peppered the duke's beard and hair, giving him a distinguished look suitable to his bearing and position. His high shoulders, his stiff back, and his agility on the dance floor proved his body was aging well. And he could be entertaining when he chose to be. She could do worse.

Gaston's hair remained black as the day she'd met him as a child. He'd had a mustache for a while when he was fifteen and trying to look older. Still a child, she'd pet it and call it her *petite chenille.* Her little caterpillar. She smiled remembering his laughter.

Her father. Gaston. And there she was back in the past again, as she had been every night this past week.

"Pardon me?" she said, registering the duke was speaking to her.

He eyed her quizzically. "It does not matter," he said smoothly, although she could see the hint of censure in his eyes before he returned his attention to the gentleman. "If you'll excuse us, the next set is about to commence."

The duke led her to the front of the room even though there was no such protocol for the waltz. Was that what life would be like with him? Always doing things in the old ways? Was he truly so inflexible he could not change as the world shifted? She'd made so many adjustments throughout the years she could not fathom what it was like to stand still in time.

The first strands began. The duke raised his arm, and she mirrored it. As it was a private soiree, some couples stood much closer, but the duke kept a respectable distance. His hand guided her, and she felt light on her feet when dancing with him. Not that she was lead-footed, but the man did know his way around the dance floor. She knew all unoccupied eyes were upon them, so she kept hers on the duke, and his bored into her. The room would assume they were deeply attracted to each other. Illusions were so easily created.

The Walfords swirled by, but they took no notice of Sophia or the duke. They had eyes only for each other. A minute later, the Thornwoods whirled into view. Snugged close, they smiled at each other. They, too, were oblivious to other dancers. Sophia fought a sigh. No, she did not begrudge them their love, but she did envy it sometimes.

Sophia despised falling into melancholy, so she scanned the room to distract herself. There were some young women out for their first season and a few bachelors, but for the most part, this was a gathering of those settled into their lives. Even Catherine's old auntie was here, sitting on the sidelines, clapping excitedly at something. She was endearing in her odd way, unlike Sophia's Aunt Isabella, who had been formidable. The woman had never forgiven Sophia's mom for running off to France and had often treated Sophia as though she was the one who had committed the offense. She mentally cursed, damning Gaston for dredging up all these memories.

She smiled at the duke, and he returned it slightly, his lips pressed together. Did the man ever show his teeth? Grin? Laugh aloud? Her mind raced back through the past few months, and she could not recall a moment where he had done any of those things. What did it matter? She was not considering him out of love, nor was he looking at her with any true affection. Although, he lusted. Which was more than she could say about her reaction to him. Perhaps he would grow desirable?

The duke twirled, and she closed her eyes, throwing her head back, hoping her thoughts would fall from it and she could get lost in the movement. The duke abruptly tugged her closer, and she opened her eyes. She'd narrowly missed colliding with another couple. She laughed merrily at the stern look on his face and surveyed the room again, stumbling, her breath stalling in her throat. Had it not been for the duke's firm grip on her waist and hand, she might have tripped in earnest and tumbled to the ground.

"Are you quite all right, my dear?" he asked, his face a mixture of concern and irritation as dancers slowed around them and stared.

"I am fine," she said, hoping her free hand went unnoticed, for she could not control its shaking. She smiled at him but lowered her lashes, looking at the floor, trying to pull herself together.

"You are trembling."

"Perhaps I do need to sit for a moment."

She allowed the duke to lead her to a chair, and she sunk gratefully onto it. The duke stared at her, attentive and solicitous, aware of watching eyes. She would normally take full advantage of the moment and give the papers something to write about, but right now, she needed him gone.

"A lemonade, please," she said, her breathlessness only partially faked.

He bowed and turned, heading to the back room, where refreshments were at the ready. She was aware of eyes upon her so resisted looking the opposite direction. She pretended to watch him longingly. When she nonchalantly turned the other way, her distress became all too real. Eyes were no longer on her. They were following the course of a man cutting his way through the crowd. A man heart-stoppingly resplendent in his finery.

Gaston! Mon Dieu! He was heading directly toward her, unflinching in his gaze. What was she to do now?

CHAPTER TEN

Call me however what thou wilt—I am who I must be.
—Friedrich Nietzsche, *Thus Spake Zarathustra*

GASTON'S FATHER HAD befriended Lord Liverpool by accident. Twenty-three years ago, Jenkinson—as Liverpool had been known then—was on his grand tour of the continent when his traveling coach broke an axle. Were it not for Gaston's father, André Armand, the Marquis de Lyon, Jenkinson and his companion would have been overtaken by the gang who had set the trap to stall the coach.

As Liverpool often told the tale, André Armand had been riding in the hillside when he'd spotted the bandits. An exacting marksman, the marquis had taken the cap off the lead culprit and calmly informed him, if he continued in his pursuit of the company in the coach, he would next take off his head. Apparently, the man had needed no more proof than the hole through his cap, and he and his men had scattered back into the Italian hillside.

Liverpool and the marquis had spent the night at a local *taverna* and had become fast friends. When the riots had broken out in Paris and the slaughter had begun, the marquis had turned to Liverpool for aid, and he'd come through. He'd helped set the marquis up in Scotland. Gaston's father had quietly lived there until his death nine years ago.

Gaston's own acquaintance with Lord Liverpool had been equally unplanned. When he had finally escaped the dungeons at *Bitche*, he'd tagged along with the British officer and returned with him on a smuggler's boat to England. By that time, Jenkinson had become Lord Hawkley, had been active in parliament, and had had an eye on the Home Office position. When the marquis had introduced Gaston to Hawkley, Hawkley had been impressed by Gaston's ability to switch between French and English with little hint of an accent. Gaston had cockily switched to Italian and German too, and Hawkley had become intensely interested in Gaston's aptitude for languages.

Gaston had had every intention of returning to *le Régiment de Bourbon*, but Hawkley had insisted he would have a far greater influence in the outcome of the war through spying than he would have standing with a bayonet. Gaston was weary of fighting, so he'd not been averse to the suggestion. Hawkley had arranged a clandestine meeting with the Home Secretary, the Duke of Portland, and they'd made an agreement. Gaston could come and go from Britain, freely visit with his father, in exchange for information. He would be paid for his services, but they would not be registered. Everything he did would be off the books. In fact, in England, he did not exist.

Eventually, Gaston had answered to Hawkley himself when he'd become the secretary, and now he answered only to him as Prime Minister Lord Liverpool. Gaston was the man's secret weapon, but he was tired of being secretive.

"I'm not entirely sure what you are asking of me?" Liverpool inched forward in his chair, put his elbows on the desk, folded his hands together, and waited expectantly. He was looking older. Tired. His eyes, always exceptionally large, were growing hooded, and the pouches beneath them gave him the air of a sad hound. But Liverpool was anything but morose. The man was well able to deal with any situation put before him, which was why Gaston had decided to ask for his assistance.

"I want a piece of my life back." Gaston still stood, refusing to take a seat until there was an indication Liverpool was amenable.

"And you think you'll find a piece of it in the drawing rooms of London?" Liverpool's brow furrowed, and he shook his head slowly, still seemingly bewildered by Gaston's request.

"It will not interfere with my work. I assure you, I can keep the two separate." Gaston's pent-up frustration clawed beneath his flesh, demanding release. "You owe me." He'd said it more harshly than he'd intended, irritated more with his own short fuse than with Liverpool.

"And you owe me your father's life, but that is not what we are discussing, is it?" Liverpool unclasped his hands and waved one at a chair. "Oh, do sit, Armand. We are not enemies."

Gaston begrudgingly dropped onto the seat in front of the desk.

Liverpool sat back. "I am still waiting for an explanation for this sudden desire of yours to live a public life. What is this piece of your life you seek?"

Gaston debated lying, but there was no point in subterfuge. He didn't know why Sophie hid her full past, but he would respect it. So long as he did not reveal Sophie's French heritage, he would not be betraying her. Besides, what would it matter to Liverpool who Gaston was seeking out?

"The Countess Tessaro. We once knew each other. I'd like to regain her acquaintanceship."

Liverpool's face remained impassive.

"I would like to enter society as the marquis," Gaston explained when Liverpool said nothing.

Liverpool shook his head. "The Marquis de Lyon is dead, preceded in death by his only son. It was a sacrifice you willingly made."

"But it is a lie that can be undone. Reports of my death could be said to have been in error."

"I suspect the error would be corrected quickly. There are many who would see you dead, Armand, if they knew who you truly were and what you've been doing all these years. You've always known you walked away from your name when you agreed to spy. At least until the war is over. As for the return of your title, that rests entirely on the outcome of the war."

Gaston's skin prickled as he suppressed his irritation. "Then give me a new identity so I might approach Sophie."

Liverpool arched an eyebrow and tilted his head questioningly.

Merde, he'd not meant to use her French name. The prime minister was no fool. He'd caught it and could easily deduce Sophie might not be entirely who she claimed to be. Gaston bit his tongue before he could say anything else he shouldn't.

"I'll tell you what, let's make a deal. All debts nullified on both sides if you can do one more thing for me. I could do with a feather in my cap right now."

Gaston knew Liverpool was walking a fine line in parliament. The regent had appointed him prime minister despite the lack of support from the lower house. It was not surprising he was aging. The pressure to prove himself worthy of the position must be wearing.

"Go on," Gaston said, his irritability shifting to empathy. "What would you have me do?"

"Exposing the traitor in the Home Office was an exceptional feat, one we would not have accomplished had you not orchestrated the entire scheme to entrap him. Miller would still be undoing our work. But there has been another leak."

"You suspected there might be a second." Gaston was not surprised. Miller was no intellectual prodigy. Gaston, too, had always thought Miller had been dancing to someone else's fiddle.

"I wish I'd been proven wrong. But yes, someone is working for the enemy, and I want him." Liverpool rubbed his forehead with a knuckle before continuing. "It could be someone in the Home Office, and we're watching, but so far there are no indications of it being an insider there."

Gaston wasn't sure where he came in if they were already

watching their own. He said as much to Liverpool.

"I hope I am wrong, but the traitor may be among the nobility. It's the only thing that makes sense. Other than those who work for us, there is no access to important information except through select parliamentary committees. And the regent, of course. So far, we've been unable to narrow it down. But with your ears to the ground, so to speak, maybe you will hear something, or spot something, out of the ordinary."

"If I find out who it is, I can declare myself for who I am?"

"You can declare yourself the new emperor for all I care. Find me the traitor."

Three days later, Gaston was settled in bachelor quarters with a new identity. He'd kept his first name but had switched his last from Armand to Durand. And Gaston Durand was on a mission. To find the traitor and to claim the beautiful woman who currently looked like she might faint.

"Countess Tessaro," he said loudly in impeccable English. He bowed formally and held her wide-eyed gaze as he straightened. "May I have this dance?"

CHAPTER ELEVEN

Nothing but dissembling,
Nothing but coquetry.

—William Butler Yeats, "A First Confession"

LIKE A STONE skipping through water, Sophia's mind jumped from thought to thought. She broke Gaston's stare and looked toward the back room. The duke would not be happy to return and find her on the dance floor. But if she spurned Gaston, it would make a scene. She was used to being the center of attention, but this was different. She was not in control. She wanted to yell at him to go away, yet her body yearned to be held in his arms again. But that way lay insanity.

"I do not dance with strangers," she said, smiling for the gossips to see she was unaffected, and testing his temperament before deciding on a manageable course of action.

"Of course," he said evenly. "Let me introduce myself. Seigneur Gaston Durand, *al vostro servizio, mia signora.*" With an elegant roll of his wrist, he bowed again, smiling charmingly when he straightened and held out his hand.

Ladies nearby should be offended by his brashness, but instead, they audibly sighed and flapped their fans rapidly. Sophia's anxiety gave way to anger. She wanted to slap Gaston. At her service indeed. And his Italian was irritably impeccable. He was putting on a grand show, and now she would have to play a part in it, whether she wanted to or not. She'd deal with the duke, and her emotions, later.

She sighed dramatically. "Since we are no longer strangers, I must accept, no?" She forced a light laugh as she extended a gloved hand, far too aware of the warmth of his as he gently tugged her from her chair and led her onto the floor. The waltz set was not yet done, and unlike the duke, Gaston pulled her close.

"There is no Raimondo to see me to the door, so you might as well stop fighting me," Gaston said into her ear.

Sophia pulled her head back and smiled through gritted teeth. She did not know what bothered her more. That he had appeared tonight despite her dismissal of him, or that her body tingled where they touched, and she felt a flush of heat each time she glanced at him.

"You are too bold," she said, and he grinned as they twirled.

"And you are too beautiful for your own good." He leaned in closer and breathed lightly into her ear. "Or mine."

She pulled back, ignoring her body's reaction. "Why did you call yourself Durand?" She was not surprised he'd not used his title. It was probably gone along with his estate. However, the use of a different surname was perplexing.

Gaston raised an eyebrow. "Consider it a show of good faith. You seemed to fear a connection to me. This ensures none can be made."

Sophia studied his face. She could not detect a lie, yet she remained unconvinced it was that simple. "I have no idea what game you are playing, Gaston," she whispered, her heart beating a staccato that contrasted with the smooth, melodic notes from the orchestra, "but I'll not be a party to your fun." She smiled like a fool for the onlookers.

"Au contraire, *ma chérie*, Sophie…"

"Sophia," she snapped as quietly as possible. "Countess Tessaro to you."

The reference to the count hit its mark, and Gaston dropped his smug expression but only for the seconds it took to do a turn. He smiled flirtatiously, and curse her traitorous body, it responded.

"I wish only to be provided the opportunity to court you." He watched her from under his eyelashes, and sensual memories flowed through her mind and coursed through her veins.

"No," she said. "It is impossible."

"You will make it possible."

"No, I cannot." Sophia could not allow Gaston another opportunity to hurt her. Nor could she risk him undoing the life she had created in England. "I am taken." She'd quickly decided the duke would make the perfect excuse.

"Taken?" Gaston tilted his head sideways, and she was unable to look away. "I think not."

"I am pledged to another." He need not know she had not committed.

"Why do I not know this?"

"It is not yet public."

Doubt flittered across his face, quickly replaced by a grin far too big for the moment. "You never were good at lying to me."

"It is no lie." The orchestra was on its final flourish, and she could soon escape his arms. "The Duke of Salinger and I have an understanding."

"You will tell him you were too hasty with your decision. That you are not ready to settle for anyone at the moment."

"I will do no such thing." The last strands of music floated across the air, and she turned from him, but he grabbed her hand and tugged her close.

"You will, *Sophie*." He said her name louder and with a heavy French accent.

"Shh," she said, trying to pull away.

"You will, or I will share stories of our childhood far and wide."

Sophia shrugged as disinterestedly as she could at the idea he could bring her world crashing down around her, then turned and walked away, leaving him on the dance floor. She did not care she was being watched. It would prove to him how little she cared about his threat.

The duke had still not returned with her lemonade. Not exactly solicitous of him, but he'd never been one to dote on her. He was probably waylaid and talking horses with someone. They were a great preoccupation of his. She dropped elegantly onto a chair, adjusting her gown and tilting her legs at the right angle to show her ankles to advantage. She held her head high, facing the opposite direction to where she'd left Gaston.

Catherine and Elizabeth walked toward her, smiling. They were total opposites. Catherine was tall with hair the color of a dark claret and eyes the color of moss. Elizabeth was shorter with hair so fair it was almost white, and she had the bluest of eyes. Sophia always considered their combined beauty a reflection of earth and sky. Neither of them ever noticed the men and women who eyed them as they walked by. Those two had eyes only for their husbands.

They took chairs on either side of Sophia, leaned in at the same time, and in perfect synchronization, asked, "Who was the man you were dancing with?"

Sophia looked at her feet, unwilling to look them in the eyes and lie. "He was nobody."

"I'll try not to be insulted."

Sophia whipped her head up. Gaston was smiling charmingly at her friends, but when he looked at her, his eyes flashed a warning.

"Gaston Durand," he said, not waiting for an offer of introduction.

There was a moment of silence. Sophia knew her friends were not insulted by his boldness but were, instead, waiting for her to introduce them. When she didn't, Catherine jumped into the void and introduced both herself and Elizabeth.

"We are old friends," Catherine said, clearly trying to think of something more to say.

"Old friends are the best kind of friends," Gaston said. "In fact, the countess and I—"

"Met in *Venezia*," Sophia interjected. "Briefly," she added.

"Yes, briefly. It is my hope she will grant me more of her company this time," he said to Catherine before looking at Sophia. "I would so enjoy hearing more about your life here in England." His eyes dared her to rebuff him now.

"I will consider the possibility." She had absolutely no intention of doing so.

"We are at the theater Tuesday," Catherine said, her face radiant. "Will you be attending?"

"I will," Gaston said smoothly, and Sophia knew, until this moment, he'd not had plans for the theater.

"Wonderful." Catherine clapped her hands much like her aunt had been doing earlier.

"Please join us in our box," Elizabeth said, her eyes dancing merrily.

"It would be my pleasure."

The three of them chatted amiably for another minute, and Gaston departed after kissing an unwilling Sophia's gloved hand. It was all she could do not to yank it free. She hated that he had bested her.

"Oh, Sophia, wherever have you been hiding him?" Catherine said excitedly after he left.

Hiding? She smiled mysteriously and flapped her fan playfully. If they only knew!

CHAPTER TWELVE

Above all else, guard your heart,
for everything you do flows from it.

—Proverbs 4:23 (New International Version)

SOPHIA'S PENCHANT FOR sweets won out, and she helped herself to a third cake. She, Catherine, and Elizabeth were in Sophia's morning room, the gossip from a soiree they attended the night before as delicious as the rout cake. She must remember to thank Monsieur André. He always put in more sugar and currants than was necessary, and she adored him for it. She should consider bringing him to the country to cook for her there as well.

"It is an odd world we live in." Catherine let her pronouncement dangle while she took a sip of tea. "A riot at the theater; who would have thought such a thing could happen?"

The old fear rose in Sophia's throat and pounded in her head. A riot? Her mother's face flashed through her mind, and she blinked, trying to erase it.

"It is truly ridiculous," Catherine said. "Apparently, it was difficult to tell who were the actors and who was the audience. The stage was completely overtaken."

Elizabeth shook her head. "Oh no."

"Oh yes," Catherine said, her laugh breaking through Sophia's dread.

Sophia took another bite of the cake, trying to regain focus on the here and now. It stuck in her dry throat, and she grabbed her tea to wash it down. Catherine continued, and Sophia was relieved neither of them had noticed her momentary distress. For it was temporary. She had put those demons to bed long ago.

"Yes, Nicholas read me the account this morning. The actors playing dead soldiers got up and fought in earnest, the band fled, and that terrible actor… I've forgotten his name?"

"Mr. Coates," Elizabeth supplied, and Catherine continued, now with Sophia's full attention.

"Yes, that's it. Apparently, Mr. Coates had his finest hour onstage and managed to garner everyone's attention, calming things a bit. But it didn't last. Eventually, they drove him from the stage. Real soldiers arrived, and those sitting in their boxes had a grand time trying to sort out who was who, wagering on how it would all end."

"And how did it end?" Elizabeth asked, joining Catherine in laughter.

"With no show. The company departed, and by midnight everyone was leaving the theater." Catherine wiped at her eyes, still giggling.

"But what caused such a disturbance?" Sophia was now fully recovered and certain her friends had noticed nothing. She forced a smile at her friends' amusement but mentally cursed Gaston once again. She'd not been haunted by her past in a long time. There could be no other reason than his return.

"It was all because Madame Catalini refused to perform. Apparently, she has not been paid for past performances and will not set foot on the stage until she is recompensed."

"Then she is in the right, no?" Sophia did not like to see people taken advantage of, especially women.

"Oh, of course," Catherine said agreeably. "But surely the audience had other recourses than to create such chaos? They simply could have refused to attend until she was paid."

"This is true." Sophia thought about her options and choices in life. "But sometimes which path to choose is only clear when we look behind, *mia amica*." She could tell by the look on her friends' faces she had said too much. "Do you think we will get such a good show tomorrow?" she asked, trying to divert them from dwelling on her words.

"I'm afraid not," Catherine said, making a face. "There will be no performance of *La caccia di Enrico IV*. It's been canceled."

Sophia pouted in an effort to suppress a smile. Gaston presumed he'd won the last round, but it seemed she would be the one to triumph after all.

"How unfortunate," Elizabeth said. "I was so looking forward to it."

"And I was looking forward to more of Monsieur Durand." Catherine waggled her eyebrows at Sophia.

Elizabeth laughed. "Oh, that too."

Sophia reached for another cake, changed her mind, and sat back in her chair. "Evil women," she said, back in a playful mood now Gaston was out of the picture.

"No, curious ones," said Elizabeth. "And since you will not expand on your acquaintance, we must probe Monsieur Durand for information."

Sophia threw both hands, palms up, into the air. "Such is life. The evening was not meant to be."

"I assume Monsieur Durand will hear of the events and know it has been canceled. Perhaps we should let him know, in case he has not?" Elizabeth looked innocent, but Sophia knew she was still trying to find out how well Sophia knew Gaston. They had spent yesterday evening playing the same game, although thankfully there had been other people around to interrupt their interrogations.

"He's a big…eh…*ragazzo grande*." Sophia's brain worked in three languages, and English was often the weakest of them. Sometimes the simplest of words eluded her. "Boy," she said, snapping her finger when the word fell into place. "A grown man.

He'll figure it out. Besides, I do not know where you can find him." It was the truth. Sophia had no idea where Gaston was staying, nor did she care to know.

"Oh, but I do," Catherine said, looking far too triumphant for Sophia's comfort. "Quite by accident, we ran into Bentley during our early-morning promenade with Daniel. It seems your Monsieur Durand is staying in the same bachelor quarters as him."

The cake churned uncomfortably in Sophia's stomach. Gaston was getting far too close to her life. She smiled at Catherine. "What a coincidence," she said, but she knew there were rarely coincidences. She was certain Gaston had known the connection when he'd chosen his rooms.

"And, since we are all unexpectedly free tomorrow evening and it is too late to find another event to attend, I have decided to hold a small gathering."

"A superb idea," Elizabeth said, and they both looked at Sophia.

Catherine raised a hand as Sophia was about to protest. "Sophia, you cannot deny me my first hosting experience since Daniel's birth. Papa is here and would be severely disappointed if you did not attend."

Sophia relaxed back in her chair. She'd assumed Catherine was implying she would be including Gaston and was relieved that was not the case. She'd not realized Catherine's father had arrived in London. Sophia got along famously with Lord Stratton, and Catherine often paired them together.

"Of course, *bella*, I will join you."

"Wonderful." Catherine stood, and Elizabeth followed her lead. "Maybe Papa can find out more about your mystery man," she said as she kissed each of Sophia's cheeks. "He's always been good about drawing people out."

Sophia frowned, and Catherine laughed.

"Oh, did I forget to mention Nicholas went to see Bentley after he dropped me here? It seemed only polite to also include your monsieur."

Sophia sat staring out at the small garden long after her two friends had left. She would find Catherine's scheming amusing were it not for the subject of her games. She still had important work to do, and it was far easier to accomplish it as the Italian Countess Tessaro. She could not risk Gaston ruining everything she had built over the years—including the walls around her heart.

CHAPTER THIRTEEN

These beings have no other calling but to cultivate the idea of beauty in their persons, to satisfy their passions, to feel and to think.

—Charles Baudelaire, *The Painter of Modern Life*

GASTON HAD SEEN Lord Walford from afar on numerous occasions. When he walked, it was clear he'd once been a soldier. The rigid deportment of the military rarely left a man. Tall and broad, he might be taken as foreboding if it weren't for the smile that constantly broke his stern expression. And his friend Bentley brought Lord Walford's smile to the surface frequently. Gaston, on the other hand, found Bentley frivolous and shallow. Of course, it had worked in his favor. Gaston had chosen these rooms for just such a connection, and it had taken little effort to ensure Bentley passed on his new address to the Walfords.

Liverpool had been quick to follow through on his promise of establishing Gaston's new identity. It was always easier to stick as close to the truth as possible. He was now officially an émigré who had fled with his father during the revolution and sought refuge with the Count d'Artois in Edinburgh. The ties to exiled royalty would help allay suspicion brought about by the sudden appearance of a strange Frenchman. The count was sequestered at Hartwood House in Buckinghamshire, laid up with gout, so he was not currently in society to refute the claim. As long as Gaston kept a low profile, his lie should go undetected.

"So you'll join us tomorrow evening?" Lord Walford asked, leaning on Bentley's doorframe, ready to depart.

"It would be my pleasure." Gaston was truly pleased at how quickly he'd managed to enter Sophie's inner circle.

"Thank goodness," Lord Walford said, the grin cutting across his face once again. "Lady Walford would not forgive me if I did not secure your attendance. Prepare yourself. The women are overly curious about you."

"I'm afraid they will be sorely disappointed, my lord." Gaston was not concerned about any woman except one.

"You underestimate how easily they are amused," he said, thrusting out his hand. "Please, call me Walford."

"Walford," Gaston repeated, Walford's solid confidence evident in his grip. One could tell a lot about a man by his handshake.

"Shall I send my carriage?"

"No need," Bentley piped from where he was sprawled in the chair, brandy dangling from one hand. "He can come with me. I assume I am to join you."

If the man was offended by the lack of a direct invitation, he didn't show it. He stretched lazily, bringing his glass to his lips and eyeing Walford over its rim.

"Could I prevent you if I wanted to?" Walford asked, chuckling.

"Of course not, but I did want to confirm. I do hate it when the staff have to scramble to set an extra plate, or when I get stuck beside Lady Walford's aunt." Bentley sat up straighter. "Is she going to be there?"

Walford shrugged. "I am merely an errand boy. I didn't study the guest list. In or out?"

"Most definitely in," Bentley said, slumping back in the chair. "I suppose I will just have to take my chances."

"I will be sure to let Catherine know how excited you are to have invited yourself over." Walford grinned and tipped his hat before exiting the room.

Gaston found the interplay between the two men fascinating. They were so unalike, yet he sensed a genuine fondness between them.

"Well done, Durand. If I might say so, you were impressively quick ingratiating your way into the fold."

From another man, Gaston would have considered it an insult, but Bentley's demeanor remained relaxed and playful. He doubted the man had a serious thought in his head.

"It is due to my old acquaintance with Countess Tessaro. A simple matter of courtesy as opposed to being invited *into the fold*, as you say."

Bentley waved toward the chair opposite him. "Sit down, Durand, unless you have somewhere more pressing to be?"

"Not at all."

"Excellent." Bentley thrust his chin toward the decanter. "Pour yourself a drink and unwind. You seem a little tense."

Gaston did as directed while contemplating what about him appeared tense. He'd no patience for fools, but he knew this particular fool provided the perfect opportunity to do exactly what he was accusing Gaston of doing. Ingratiating himself. He knew from watching Sophie these last few months that she spent a lot of time with the Walfords and the Thornwoods. They were her Achilles heel, and he'd use them if he needed to, to get closer to her.

"So where did you say you met our infamous countess?" Bentley swirled the contents of his glass, appearing casual in his inquiry, but Gaston assumed Bentley was as curious as the others.

"*Venise*," he said smoothly, mimicking what Sophie had told the others.

Bentley waited for more, but Gaston said nothing further. "*Venise*," Bentley finally repeated with a decent French accent. "Oh, do tell me about it. The meeting, not Venice. Although, I've always been keen to visit it. You know, canals and gondolas and Italian passion and all that. Maybe someday, if this bloody war ever ends."

Gaston struggled to squash irritation. The man had no idea exactly how bloody war was, nor about the price people paid. Their costs were far greater than missing one's grand tour, or whatever it was he was lamenting. Gaston took a large swallow of brandy and set the glass aside. He was no longer in the mood to play along with Bentley.

"I will leave the story of our meeting to the countess," he said and stood. "If I recall correctly, she does enjoy being the center of a tale."

"You *do* know her," Bentley said on a laugh.

"I have some errands to run. I'll see you tomorrow night."

They said goodbyes, and Gaston closed the door behind him, taking the stairs at the end of the hall to his suite of rooms. If needed, he would query Bentley about Sophie some other day. He'd secured his invitation. For the moment, it was all he needed.

CHAPTER FOURTEEN

I am fearful of you and afraid of my memory
That has kept your voice and calls to me often.

—Marceline Desbordes-Valmore, "Parted"

SOPHIA HAD DEBATED sending a note to Gaston and demanding to see him but changed her mind. She didn't want him to know he'd managed to rattle her composure. She decided she would corner him at the Walfords' and send him on his way. Somehow.

Catherine had mentioned she'd included the Randalls tonight. They were a lovely couple, but more importantly, Randall tended to be a font of knowledge. His merchant ships covered large swaths of territory, and he came across various bits of information that sometimes proved helpful to the Home Office. Sophia assumed he would be an even greater source now that he was officially entering privateering. An old friend of the Thornwoods, and now a business partner with both Thornwood and Walford, he tended to speak freely at smaller gatherings. Although, Gaston's presence might impede such conversations. Another reason to get rid of him as soon as possible.

She leaned into the small mirror and adjusted her pearl-drop earring. Cara had braided Sophia's thick hair, wound it like a crown on her head, and tucked pearl-topped pins into it. Sophia liked the effect, like dew-kissed snowdrops glistening in the morning sun. She tilted her head to the opposite side and adjusted the other earring. Her mother had loved Sophia's thick hair, always cooing and singing as she'd brushed it. Her mother had had a beautiful voice, and Sophia would drift away on a happy cloud.

She shook her head and frowned at herself in the mirror. *"Basta!"* she said out loud. "Enough!" The past was coming too close these days, and it was all Gaston's fault. She pushed back the bench and stood. No one controlled Sophia Auclair Tessaro, not anymore. If Gaston thought he could step back into her life and she would fall at his feet, he was going to be thoroughly disappointed. She'd lost much through the years, and she would lose no more. She would not let him ruin the life she had created in England. She would not allow him to disrupt her newfound family.

"My apologies, *signora mia*," Cara said, coming into the room with Sophia's short robe. "It needed pressed. Had I known—"

"Sì, sì," Sophia said, holding out her arms so Cara could slip the robe on. "It is my fault, I know."

Cara had come with her to England and was used to Sophia's idiosyncrasies, including changing her mind at the last moment. It was unusual for her maid not to be prepared for any eventuality, but tonight's change of wardrobe had caught her off guard. In all fairness, the robe Sophia unexpectedly chose had been brought from the country. Cara had been forced to pack with such haste when Sophia had decided to come to London quickly that she was still catching up on her duties.

The robe was the color of an unripe mulberry, and while it was a nice contrast to the gray silk evening dress, she'd chosen to wear it because it was the darkest item of clothing she owned. She far preferred vibrant colors, but she wanted to present a somber Sophia to Gaston, to let him see his presence made the evening funereal.

Cara finished and stepped to the side. Sophia looked in the

mirror and sighed. Unfortunately, the silver crepe trimming the neckline as well as the sleeves and the flounce, the matching belt encircling her waist—pulled snug under her breasts and cinched with a pearl broach—softened the severity of the color. She should have borrowed one of Catherine's mourning gowns. She sighed again. Even if Catherine had them in London, they wouldn't fit. They'd be busting at the seams and dragging along the floor.

"You are not happy, *signora mia?*"

"No, Cara, I am not, but there is nothing to be done about it."

Sophia took the wrap from Cara, although she did not think she would need it. May was beginning on a splendid note. Well, the weather was anyway. After tonight, the rest of her life should fall back into a comfortable pace, where she was once again in control of where she went and with whom she spent time.

Raimondo escorted her to the waiting carriage and waited until she was settled. She smiled to herself when he climbed on the box seat with Charles, the carriage rocking from the sheer size of him. He would not be much good at sleuthing unnoticed. Of course, nor was she. She always attracted attention, a blessing and a curse, she supposed. It was why she did her spying in plain sight.

There was nothing to fear from a frivolous woman who simply sought a good time. It was not an unenjoyable role to play. She had always been sociable and gregarious. It had been far more difficult to repress that side of herself during her years in *Venezia* with her aunt. No, she did not detest the game she played, only the reasons. She longed for an end to the war, when the rightful heir to the throne returned to France. Only then would her mother's needless death have been avenged. And her dear papa's, for he must be dead too, or she would have heard from him.

Sophia blew out a long breath, the agony of loss suffocating. Mama, Papa, Carmine, Gaston. No, not Gaston. She would mourn him no more. She blessed the memories of the others and cursed Gaston for bringing such pain into her world once again.

Chapter Fifteen

But quickly on this side the verdict went:
His real habitude gave life and grace
To appertainings and to ornament.

—Shakespeare, "A Lover's Complaint"

Walford had not been exaggerating when he'd said the women would be inquisitive. They each took turns questioning him. It would be amusing were it not so frustrating watching Sophie avoid him at every turn.

"Yes, it is true. It was a terrible time, but I am fortunate to have found a new life here," he said.

"In Scotland, I understand. Pity it has taken you so long to find your way to London." Lady Thornwood said it innocently enough, but her quick glance toward Sophie gave away her intended implication. Angelic-looking she might be, but she was devilishly determined. It was clear she wanted to make a match between Gaston and Sophie. He'd not spurn her assistance.

"Yes, had I known the enticements of the city, I am sure I would have come sooner."

Lady Thornwood smiled triumphantly as her husband stepped up beside her. "Seigneur Durand was saying he is finding London appealing."

"Seigneur?" Thornwood asked, tilting his head. "Where were

your family's lands?"

Thornwood asked it casually enough, but his eyes were alert, no doubt assessing the stranger in their midst. Before Gaston could respond, Lady Thornwood interrupted, putting a hand on her husband's arm.

"He does not wish to talk about such things. They are lost to him forever, and he remains heartsick. In fact, he insists we not use seigneur any longer, as it represents another man altogether." She touched Gaston's arm. "My apologies for using it, *Monsieur Durand*."

Gaston nodded, schooling his face appropriately, but he wanted to laugh. He certainly had managed to woo the women.

"Indeed," Thornwood said, looking unconvinced. However, he did not pursue it. Instead, he asked about Gaston's current situation, which was almost as awkward. Fortunately, they were interrupted as Lady Walford clapped her hands to get everyone's attention. The room quickly grew quiet.

"I have a special treat for us this evening. Miss Langdon is going to play the pianoforte."

"What a treat," Lord Stratton boomed. "The girl works magic with those keys. She can put little Daniel to sleep in seconds, so soothing are her melodies."

"Well, let's hope she does not put you to sleep, Papa," Lady Walford said with a laugh. "Do help yourself to a beverage, if you don't already have one, and take a seat."

Gaston lingered, waiting for Sophie to sit, which she seemed hesitant to do. She'd always been able to guess what he was thinking and had probably assessed he was trying to get close to her. Finally, she sat beside Stratton, and Gaston quickly slipped into the chair to her right. She stiffened but otherwise did not acknowledge his presence.

Miss Langdon, dressed simply in a white gown, sat at the pianoforte and delicately slid on spectacles. She adjusted both the sequence of pages and her eyeglasses before turning and smiling at the small gathering. "I do hope I live up to Lord Stratton's praise," she said shyly.

"Oh, you will." Bentley, sitting in front of Sophie, said it loud enough for everyone to hear.

The young woman blushed scarlet. She glanced toward the doorway, and her smile grew larger despite her embarrassment. Gaston turned to see what had caught her attention. An older man stood in the entrance with an unmistakable look of pride on his face. One sleeve folded and pinned where part of his arm used to be, and his board straight back, denoted his military background. Of course, the girl's father. Gaston had done his research on the Thornwoods and the Walfords and knew Walford had kept on his batman from the army. Such loyalty spoke highly of both Walford and his man Langdon.

Miss Langdon began to play, and a gentle melody filled the room. There had not been much beauty in Gaston's world of late, and music was an indulgence long relegated to the past. As the notes grew melancholic, so did he, and he'd no wish to. He leaned toward Sophie.

"I wish to talk with you alone," he whispered.

Sophie looked straight ahead as though so mesmerized by the music she did not hear him.

"Do not make me repeat myself," he said more tersely, yet she still did not acknowledge him.

"*Ma chérie*, Sophie," he said a little louder, and her head swung toward him as Bentley turned around abruptly with a finger to his lips.

Gaston would have laughed at the man were it not for Sophie glaring at him with wide eyes. She truly was worried her friends would find out she, too, was French. Well, partly anyway. Gaston put a finger to his lips, and satisfied, Bentley returned his attention to Miss Langdon. Gaston grabbed Sophie's hand and sidled off his chair. She had no choice but to shift across and join him, or she would make a scene. Stratton glanced their way but said nothing.

Miss Langdon's father leaned back against the doorframe and

opened his eyes when they neared.

"I'm overheated," Sophie said as they slipped by him and into the hall. They were barely out of earshot when she came to a sharp stop. "Gaston," she growled in warning.

"We will walk, and we will talk." He could see the debate in her fiery eyes and knew the moment she decided it was far easier not to argue. There was no garden, nor did he want to go outside anyway. Raimondo waited for Sophie, and he might interfere. "Where can we find some privacy?"

She led him through the hall, toward the back of the house, stepping into the study, the door to which was open. He closed it behind them. While he would use it as leverage, he did not truly wish to expose her.

She spun on him instantly. "You are a beast to come here and disrupt my life," she said in rapid French, flushing with her anger. She took a deep, steadying breath. "We have nothing to talk about."

She'd switched to English, attempting to dismiss him with cold arrogance. But she'd failed. Her clenched jaw, her tight fists, and the amber flashing in her eyes told him all he needed to know. She was not indifferent. And nor was he. His body hummed at her presence, more alive than it had been in years.

"We have much to talk about but not tonight. Not here." Gaston kept his voice level as though calming an animal, for it was no different. Her survival instincts were guiding her behavior, and he needed her to see past them. "I am asking for a chance, Sophie. A chance to get to know each other again."

"You maintain Carmine deliberately harmed you. You think, perhaps, I was a party to such a thing, no? I do not know what your game is, but I will not play it."

"I play no game, Sophie. I promise. I'll admit I wanted to see you again so I could say goodbye to the memory of the girl I loved. But I find myself intrigued with the woman she has become. And I would like to get to know her." He had not meant to be so forthright, but the words were out, and they were the truth.

Sophie shook her head slowly from side to side, but she un-clenched her hands and her jaw. "There is no point," she said quietly, the anger leaving her eyes. "Let us leave the past where it lies."

"But it is still with us, and it will not disappear simply because you wish it." He stepped closer and touched her cheek. "It is a part of us, a burden we must carry, or a joy, *ma chérie*." This time, he meant the endearment, for he could see his Sophie in her eyes.

Her nostrils flared as she fought emotion, but she did not remove his hand from her cheek. "What is it you want?" she whispered hoarsely.

"Time. I want your time. With your friends. Away from your friends. I want to get to know Sophie Auclair all over again."

"Sophia Tessaro," she corrected, stepping back, the momentary connection broken.

His hand dropped to his side, and this time, it was he who had clenched fists. "Sophia Tessaro," he acknowledged, although his mind screamed, *Sophie Auclair Armand*. But that was only true in his heart, as they'd not had a chance to get married.

"With the Duke of Salinger vying for my hand, my time is not my own." Her haughtiness was firmly back in place.

He'd thought she'd exaggerated about the duke but perhaps not. He pushed away rising jealousy. "I insist you give me the opportunity to compete for your attention."

"But—"

"Sophie, I do not wish to blackmail you into it, but I will do so if you do not willingly agree." He'd barked his threat, letting his emotions get the better of him. Why did he lose control every time he was near her? He pinched his forehead with his thumb and forefinger, massaging it until he'd put his jealousy back in its place. "A chance, Sophie. It's all I'm asking. Perhaps you are right and the past should be left alone. But how are we to know, if we walk away from each other now?"

She turned and did just that—walked away from him, stopping at the window, staring out into the darkness. He waited, wondering what was running through her mind, wondering what she would do next.

"Sixteen years, Gaston," she said quietly. "We were children. You try to recapture what has long died."

He stepped close behind her, watching her reflection in the window, but not touching her. "If that proves to be the case, we will mourn the loss and move on with our lives. You owe it to me." Her shoulders stiffened, but he continued. "You owe it to yourself. You owe it to the dreams we once believed in."

He could not see her expression in the glass, but her shoulders relaxed, and she sighed heavily. "One month, Gaston. I will give you one month."

Gaston exhaled slowly through his mouth, and a chill rippled along his spine. In one month, Sophie would either be a part of his life again or gone from it forever.

⟫⟩⟨⟨

GASTON'S BREATH DANCED lightly across Sophia's neck, and she shivered. Instantly, she regretted the agreement. How was she to bear being with him? His nearness, the smell of him as he stood behind her, made her body come alive as it had not since…since their night together. She turned abruptly, but he did not move, and she found herself inches from his chest.

"You will find you are chasing a dream," she said, looking up at him.

"As I have for sixteen years, Sophie." He smiled sadly.

Sophia stepped around him and walked away. Gaston angry, she could take. Jealous? He was fun to torment. Stubborn? He'd always been, and she was accustomed to it. But sad? It was not something she was used to seeing on his face, or in his eyes. In the darkest of times, he had not betrayed such an emotion.

She spun around. "There must be parameters," she said,

needing to set aside the tug at her heart and take charge. "I decide what we do. And when. You will not elaborate about our friendship to anyone."

"What? When?" he repeated with a growing scowl. "Friendship?" he said slowly, as though turning over the word and examining it. It apparently did not pass muster, as his scowl deepened into deep furrows.

"What would you have me call it, Gaston?"

He waved his hand in dismissal and walked toward her. She held her ground even when he stepped in close and ran a finger down her cheek. Her knees weakened, but she was determined he would not see it.

"You said one month. And I concede to your time limit." He hooked his finger under her chin, gently caressing back and forth.

She held his gaze, willing herself to remain unaffected.

"And you will grant *my* conditions, or you will lose my agreement."

Sophia shifted her chin, eliminating physical contact but holding his dark stare. "And they are?"

"We will see each other every day. I will not deny you your social schedule, but I will follow along because you will invite me to join you."

He held up his palm to stop her, and she held back the angry words she was going to say.

"If you have nothing on your calendar, it is I who gets to decide what we do." He placed a finger against her lips. "Tut-tut," he said and leaned in, his warm breath against her ear heating her body. "You try to interrupt far too much," he whispered, the slight brush of his lips and the timbre of his voice far more sensual than words of chastisement should be.

Sophia took a big step back, irritated her body responded so easily to him. "And what of the duke?" she asked, pleased to see a ripple in Gaston's composure.

"I don't give a damn about the duke. Your friends don't seem to either, do they? Why would they have invited me, knowing you had committed yourself to the duke?"

She shrugged dismissively. "I have not told them."

Gaston eyed her skeptically, ran a hand through his hair, and looked at the ceiling before returning his gaze to her. "If what you say is true, you will tell him you need some time apart to consider the situation. I have seen you with him, and it is clear this is not an affair of the heart. Arrangements can be…how do you say…unarranged."

"You think you know everything. You do not. And your conditions leave me nothing."

"Nothing?" He tilted his head casually, unperturbed.

She wanted to kick his shins as she'd done when they were young and he was determined to frustrate her. Her emotions were tumbling, one over the other, and he was standing there as calmly as if they were discussing the weather. "*Oui*, nothing."

"I don't know why you hide your truth. You see how your friends accept me as an émigré. But it is clear you don't want them to know about you. About your life in France." He closed the distance between them once again and lifted her chin. "About us."

He paused. She squirmed inside at the intensity of his gaze and willed her body not to betray her.

"I will keep your secrets, *ma chérie*, for the month."

"And when the month is over?" Sophia feared Gaston was threatening eventual exposure regardless of the promise. Yet her eyes were drawn to his lips, lips coming dangerously close to hers.

"I will have my answers," he said quietly and brushed his lips gently across hers.

She wanted to pull him close, to devour him whole, to go back in time where years of heartache did not lie between them. Instead, she stiffened and turned her head to the side. She would give him this month and send him on his way.

CHAPTER SIXTEEN

How does the Meadow-flower its bloom unfold?
Because the lovely little flower is free
Down to its root, and, in that freedom, bold.

—William Wordsworth,
"A Poet! He Hath Put His Heart to School"

SOPHIA HAD LAIN awake into the wee hours of the morning, reliving the conversation in Walford's study. She should not have granted Gaston the time alone. He could not have made such a preposterous proposal in a public setting. Still, she was the fool who'd agreed to it. And that was what had bothered her throughout the night. She bowed to no man, yet she had given in to his demands. Why? For surely he would not truly expose her? Of course, there lay the biggest problem. She was not sure what he would or would not do.

In the end, she decided she would beat him at his own game. She would play along in front of her friends, feign a slight interest in him, and when the month was through, claim they were not suitable for each other. What she had yet to figure out was what to do with the duke. Luckily, she had until the evening to figure it out.

When Catherine's soiree had drawn to a close, Sophia had tried to sneak out before any further plans could be made. Gaston had intervened as she was saying a quiet goodbye to Catherine. She must give him credit for his boldness. A little too much, but she would eventually put him in his place. He'd expressed an interest in the goings-on in London, asking for suggestions, so he might spend time with Sophia and get reacquainted.

Elizabeth had come from behind and overheard his question, and both she and Catherine were on it like dogs on a bone. Sophia had stood by, smiling indulgently while steaming beneath the surface. He'd not even given her a chance to work out an amenable schedule. When Elizabeth had suggested the Exhibition of the Royal Academy, Sophia had chimed in and claimed she'd adore going to view paintings. While she did have an affinity for all the arts, that was not why she'd declared herself so passionate for the outing. It was because it was a daytime event. It would satisfy her obligation to Gaston and leave her free to join the duke, as planned, at Lord Bennet's private ball.

Catherine had begged off joining them as she'd planned on strolling through the park with baby Daniel and her father, "showing them both off," she'd said. Walford was going to be at the shipyard with Mr. Randall and Thornwood, and the reminder almost resulted in Sophia losing her jocular composure. She'd been so preoccupied skirting Gaston, she'd not managed to listen in on a single important conversation. She'd silently cursed him and smiled pleasantly.

In the end, it had worked out well. Not only was her commitment to Gaston during the day, in a crowded public venue no less, it had also been decided Elizabeth and young Miss Langdon would join them. Even better, Bentley had interceded and invited himself along as well. Gaston had spewed sweet words about flowers and bouquets, but she could see he was not happy he'd been bested. As he'd turned to receive his hat from the footman, she'd been certain he'd muttered *"épine."* Whether he was referring to Bentley as a thorn or her, she didn't care. It was delightful to have circumvented his intentions. To have gotten under his skin was an added boon.

Sophia smiled into the mirror and blew a kiss to herself before straightening and adjusting her bosom. It was frowned upon to wear a low neckline during the daytime, so it was what she often chose. It made no sense to her that what was acceptable in the evening was not acceptable in the day. Were they not the same people with the same goals, the same desires, regardless of time of day?

Of course, she also understood the power of dressing so brashly. Men were drawn like moths to a flame. And while she did not actually seek the attention they were willing to bestow, she did want their secrets. More often than not, it was that simple. The women, on the other hand? They chattered behind their fans. Some in envy, some in disdain. It made no difference to Sophia. It all contributed to the illusion that was Sophia Tessaro—a woman who did what she wanted and was impervious to rules.

She'd deliberately chosen crimson for today. Admittedly, she'd done so in part to taunt Gaston with what he'd given up, for she had not forgotten for a minute he'd had years to return to her. But she was also wary of her own reactions to him. The attention the color would draw would be another distractor from Gaston. She wished him luck in trying to maintain any semblance of intimacy with her.

"Your pelisse, *signora mia*." Cara held out a matching robe, and Sophia slipped into it. "And your reticule." She looped it over Sophia's arms. "I have put your spectacles in, in case you have need of them."

Sophia frowned at Cara. "I was about to call you a treasure, but I think I won't now."

Cara smiled and told Sophia she might require them to read the program. Sophia harrumphed and swept from the room, but she heard Cara's soft laughter follow her. It made her laugh too. At thirty-three, she must accept the signs of aging. After all, she was lucky to see them, was she not? Still, spectacles in public? She looked at the neckline of her gown, her flesh mounded and presented perfectly. No, she would let her body continue to define her, for now. It was of far more use than spectacles.

Chapter Seventeen

And mixt, as life is mixt with pain,
The works of peace with works of war.

—Alfred Lord Tennyson, "Ode Sung at the Opening of
the International Exhibition"

Gaston waited not so patiently by the arched entry to
Somerset House. Sophie had insisted she must gather the
other two women herself and denied him the opportunity to
escort her from her home. She'd won the first round altogether
too easily, but he would not let her best him again. If she thought
she could deter him from more intimate settings, including her
town house, she'd quickly learn how wrong she was.

"Durand," Bentley said in greeting as he sidled lazily up beside Gaston. "If you'd waited but a few minutes, we could have
shared a hackney."

"I had no need of a hackney," Gaston said, softening his irritability with a smile. "I walked."

"Did you?" Bentley said, looking surprised. "You are an ad-
venturous sort, aren't you?"

"One would hardly call a stroll to the Strand a daring feat,"
Gaston said, dismissing the man's foolish statement as he spotted
Sophie's carriage and waved it his way. Raimondo sat beside the
driver and frowned at Gaston as they came to a stop, but he said

not a word. The man climbed from the carriage like a great ape and lumbered to the door, opening it.

Lady Thornwood was the first to step out. Bentley eased past Gaston and took her hand, bowing elegantly over it. Bentley proceeded to help Miss Langdon, who blushed when he leaned in to say something to her. It seemed the man was an incorrigible flirt. Gaston stepped forward before Bentley could turn his charms on Sophie, who of course was the last to alight.

Her skin rich against her red dress, the sun catching the amber in her eyes, Sophie was truly the most stunning woman he'd ever known. She'd always been a beauty, but time had ripened her into a breathtaking creature worthy of any artist's canvas. She smiled at him as she took his proffered hand, and he fought excitement. With all that lay between them, he knew it was all for show, so he could not fathom how she managed to have such an effect upon him.

He offered his arm, and she hesitated. He raised an eyebrow, daring her to refuse him, and she sighed dramatically before placing her hand in the crook of his elbow. Even through the gloves, the warmth of her hand heated his body. He covered her hand with his, as though he could trap her there. He almost laughed out loud. Sophie was no butterfly to be captured. More a lion to be caged until it could be trusted not to bite.

With a woman on each arm, Bentley led the way across the courtyard. The trio's laughter floated back to them, but Gaston had no interest in what amused them. He cared only about one thing. That Sophie relax so he might uncover the truth about her feelings for him. Then and now. She had been his beacon throughout the years. It seemed he was not ready to relinquish her hold, even though he knew hope was a cruel mistress.

"You are quiet, *ma chérie.*" He spoke softly so as not to upset her with his use of the endearment.

"As are you," she said without looking at him. Instead, head held high, she looked straight ahead, walking regally without a glance at the crowds surrounding them.

"Perhaps we should have chosen a more suitable venue for an outing." His vantage point due to height gave him a prime view of her assets, and his body was responding. He wished they were in a more private setting.

"And what is wrong with this one, Mr. Durand?"

She spoke in English, and he swallowed a retort in French, hating both the language and his fake name on her lips. It would not do to constantly ruffle her feathers. Before he could answer, Bentley turned around and handed them a catalog.

"I have paid for us all."

Bentley proclaimed it as though it was a generous moment, when in fact this was not an exclusive event. At a shilling, many people could afford to attend. It was the reason for the sheer number of people pushing toward the foyer. Gaston used the crowd as an opportunity to put his arm around Sophie's waist and steer her off to the side.

"We are losing the others," she said, standing on tiptoe, trying to see over everyone.

"I know," he said and smiled at her. He loved the fire that lit her eyes when she knew she'd been bested again. He squeezed her waist. "You are safe with me."

"Am I?" she asked, her eyes lingering on his lips.

He shifted uncomfortably. The little coquette knew what she was doing. The throng thinned slightly, and he moved them toward the steep, winding staircase. People descended the narrow stairway as others ascended, so he had no choice but to let Sophie slip from his grasp and precede him up the stairs. The view from behind was tremendously enjoyable. It was difficult to resist the urge to trace the curves of her body. He wanted to put his hands on her deliciously plump derriere. He now understood why this vertiginous architectural feat was jokingly referred to as "the stare-case."

As though she could sense his licentious imaginings, she looked over her shoulder at him and promptly lost her footing. There was a collective gasp around them as she fell backward. His heart stopped for a fleeting second, but he managed to smoothly catch her while keeping her head from hitting the rail. Her eyes huge, she stared at him, gasping for air, her chest heaving. *Merde!* He could take her right here, right now.

The world around him came back to life, and suddenly conscious of the scene they were creating, Sophie wiggled. Gaston helped her stand, ensuring she was stable before he let go and instantly regretting the loss of her in his arms. "*Ça va?*" he asked, and she bristled.

"Yes, I am perfectly fine," she said and turned to continue the long climb to the exhibition room.

He sighed and followed. The others waited for them at the entrance.

"We've had a peek, but it's so crowded we decided to wait for you." Lady Thornwood hooked her arm in Sophie's before he could manage to do the same. "In truth," she said, leaning into Sophie, "I was in need of time to catch my breath after climbing those stairs."

They both laughed, and Gaston noted again Sophie's ease in the company of her friends. It reminded him of what they'd once shared. Would they ever know such companionship again?

"The pictures are numbered as they are placed in the room. The first number is over the door," Lady Thornwood continued, as oblivious to his disappointment as she was to Sophie's pleasure. Sophie gave him a triumphant look over her shoulder, and he had no choice but to follow them through the arched entrance like one of the lapdogs milling about with its owner.

The ceiling was a good thirty feet high, and the sun, shining from above through glass panes, lit the large room. His eyes tracked downward, the walls barely visible behind the vast number of paintings hung from the ceiling to about seating height. It was visually spectacular and incredibly loud. No wonder Sophie was so smug about their outing. She knew how impossible it would be to have a private moment in such a place.

He found her staring at a painting featured in the center of one wall. Lady Thornwood, standing a few feet away, was reading her catalog and glancing up periodically to scan the walls. He wedged his way in beside Sophie, but she didn't appear to notice him. He peered at the number, then flipped the pages in his catalog. The painting's label read, "148 Blind-man's Buff *D. Wilkie, R. A.*"

"I do not like it," Sophie said loud enough for him to hear.

He stared at her grim expression, then back at the painting. The focus of the painting was a blindfolded man, hands out, seeking the people in the room. The others were scattered about, some hidden, some appearing to be taunting the blindfolded man. It was a masterful composition, and he could not see why it lacked appeal, or why she was so rigid in response to it. "Why?"

"It is…" She waved her hand around and turned to him, her eyes watery. "…*chaotique*, no? The furniture overturned, the women, the children hiding. The glee in some of the others' eyes."

"But it's only a parlor game. A simple bit of fun caught on canvas."

She shook her head. "No, I do not like it."

She sucked in her bottom lip as she stared at it again, and it struck Gaston what it was she saw. *Chaotic.* She was not seeing a child's game; she was seeing a memory. The day he'd arrived in time to save her from the mobs but not in time to save her mother. He wanted to take Sophie into his arms and hold her until her hurt faded.

"Sophie," he said quietly in her ear. "I am here now. As I was then." A tremor ran through her, but she did not turn to him.

"Yes," she said, "you are."

He stood beside her, watching her as she stared at the painting. Her nostrils flared, and she let out a long breath. As she calmed, Sophia Tessaro returned as though a mask was slipped over Sophie Auclair. Or perhaps it was armor she donned?

Sophie turned away from him and waved at Lady Thornwood, smiling beatifically as though she'd not been thrown into the maelstrom of the past. He didn't follow her. He'd let her escape both him and her memories for now. But he'd seen her facade drop and glimpsed *his* Sophie in her pain. He was more determined than ever to find out which woman she really was now, and what he was to her.

✥

"OH, I DO like this landscape," Elizabeth said, standing nearer the entrance.

Sophia wanted to flee past her friend and down those stairs, but she did nothing of the sort. She'd stopped running years ago, and she would run no more. Gaston's presence was resurrecting the past. That was all. Nothing had changed. She was still Sophia Tessaro, and Sophia Tessaro was spirited and full of laughter, as Sophie Auclair had once been. *Mon Dieu!* She must let the past be.

"Do you think Richard would enjoy it? I have not bought him anything for such a long time." Elizabeth looked at Sophia. "It captures the fields on the way to Thornwood Manor; don't you agree?"

"It is lovely in a barren, cold, abject, lonely way," Sophia said and grinned.

"It's titled *Frosty Morning*," Elizabeth said and giggled. "It is rather austere, isn't it?"

Sophia scooped Elizabeth's arm. "Let us wander into a smaller room and see if we can find something livelier. You want color in your life, no?"

Elizabeth glanced around the room.

"Miss Langdon is in Bentley's good hands," she said as she steered Elizabeth through the door.

"But what about your Mr. Durand?"

"He is not mine, *mia amica*," Sophia said lightly. She wondered if he ever had been. For surely a man so committed and in love would not have taken so many years to return to her, never mind arrive with his horrible accusation.

"Oh, but I'm certain he'd like to be." Elizabeth bumped against Sophia playfully, and Sophia forced another smile.

"I will let the man dream for a while," she said, "but alas, it is far more likely I am destined for the duke."

"We shall see," Elizabeth said, dropping to a bench and pulling Sophia along with her. "One never knows how life will unfold."

Her friend did not realize how true her words were, but Sophia did. Nothing in her life had unfolded as she'd imagined. Nothing.

CHAPTER EIGHTEEN

I know her by her angry air,
Her bright black eyes, her bright black hair.

—Alfred Lord Tennyson, "Kate"

"H E REFUSES TO leave, *signora mia*," Cara said, closing the door. "Raimondo would like permission to escort him from the house," she added, biting back a smile.

Sophia set her brush on the dressing table. She'd left Gaston in the courtyard at Somerset, informing him she had a prior engagement for the evening. He'd not said a word, but she could see frustration in his face, and she'd been pleased to put it there. She'd promised him a month, and she would not tempt him to break his side of the bargain, so it would not do to let Raimondo put him in his place. She sighed heavily. She'd wanted to rest before getting ready for the ball, but it would seem she would have to deal with Gaston herself.

"Put him in the library. I will be down soon."

She had changed into a simple, unadorned day dress, with the intention of lounging alone at the back of the house. The small garden outside the morning room always brought her a measure of peace, which was what she was craving after the rush of emotions at the exhibition. She debated piling her hair back up but decided to leave it as it was. Gaston would survive her state of dishabille.

Raimondo hovered outside the library. "*Signora mia*, he is a stubborn one. I can unbend his will easily, should you want it."

"*Grazie*, Raimondo. But patience, *per favore*. He will be around for a few weeks only."

The door clicked closed behind her, and Gaston spun around from where he stood by the empty grate. Sophia squeezed her lips together to stop a smile. Oh yes, she had truly annoyed him.

"Did you honestly think I was going to let you off so easily?" His voice was steady enough, but his eyes flashed in challenge.

"Whatever do you mean, Mr. Durand?" His alias did not flow easily from her tongue, but his scowl confirmed using it had gotten the reaction she'd been seeking. "I kept my end of our little agreement."

"Hardly, Sophie Auclair," he said, walking toward her. "A crowded room with friends as a bulwark does not satisfy the agreement."

"You said you wished to participate in my socials, and it was what my friends wanted to do." She fought her response to him, tried not to react to his proximity. "What was I to do?"

"In that case, I will grant you grace this one time. And you will make it up to me. We will enjoy an evening together," he said, his gaze softening as he ran a strand of her hair through his fingers.

She could not stop the shiver that shimmied across her neck and down her arms, but she could resist the invitation in his words and in his eyes. "I have an engagement."

"Oh, do tell," he said, taking a step back. "What are we do-ing?"

"*We* are doing nothing."

She walked away and took a seat on the sofa. Sophia hated that he could rankle her so easily. She did not expand further. Instead, she looked toward the window, discreetly keeping an eye on his reflection as he strolled to the side table and poured himself a drink. The man was audacious, and she should find it unappealing, but for some reason, she did not.

Gaston strolled to the chair facing the sofa and sat, looking far too relaxed now. "Tut-tut, Sophie, a deal is a deal. Of course, *we* are doing something this evening."

"*I* am going to Lord Bennet's ball." Sophie casually wiped at her skirt, then looked back at him. "With the duke." She was well rewarded. She'd wiped the smug look off his face.

"You are breaching the terms of our agreement. You were to tell him you need time."

"I'm not entirely certain I approved such a directive." She held up a hand to stop him before he could say anything. "Regardless, even if I concede, I have not yet had a chance to tell him, have I?"

"Sophie, you are testing my patience. A note would suffice." He frowned, his drink untouched.

"Surely you would not have me do something so personal by letter? I have no wish to offend him." He nodded slowly as though in agreement. She should have let it be, but of course, she could not. "After all, I will need the man to renew his offer for me in a month's time. It would not do to run him off." She stood. "You may choose tomorrow's activity." She turned her back to him and walked to the window.

She heard his growl before he reached her, and her body hummed with anticipation, not fear, as he grabbed her hand and pulled her around, locking her against his body with his free arm. His eyes burned into hers, and she lifted her head, waiting for his lips to meet hers, waiting to taste him once again. Perversely, he abruptly let go and took a step back.

"You have won this round, Sophie. For now." Gaston turned heel and strode out the door.

She stood in the empty room, touching her unkissed lips, disappointment warring with excitement. While she did not for a minute believe they could find their way back to the love they'd left behind on the continent, she was beginning to see that this month was going to be interesting. As a cat finds pleasure in playing with a mouse, so might she have fun with Gaston.

DINNER WAS A dull event. Sophia learned nothing, nor was she been entertained. Were it not for the delicious meringues, she would declare it a complete failure. The duke was in fine form, arrogantly commanding attention, although he'd not much to say to be worthy of it. His talk of horses was growing increasingly tedious.

Retiring with the ladies was equally mundane. She did wish she'd been able to bring Elizabeth or Catherine along with her, but it seemed rude to impose upon the duke for an invitation on the night she was going to dismiss him, albeit temporarily. Others would be arriving soon, joining the Bennets in the ballroom. So there remained a slight possibility the evening would improve.

She'd already decided she was going to talk with the duke on the way home, although she still didn't know what she was going to say. Sophia wasn't concerned about breaking the duke's heart. She had no illusions. His interest was more in her purse than in her, although he was not altogether impervious to her charms. He'd never tried to seduce her. He was too old-fashioned to attempt such a thing. But she'd seen the lust in his eyes when she'd allowed him a parting kiss. Recognized the yearning in his body as he'd held her close. Unfortunately, she'd felt nothing. Could she live without passion?

Sophia had attended many events with the Duke of Salinger this season, and it had led to much speculation in the papers and among her friends. He'd tried to broach the subject of marriage, and she had redirected him each time, not ready to commit. *Yet.* She wasn't offended by his interest in her money, for most men would find her wealth an appealing attribute. And, even though he was twenty years older than her, he was somewhat attractive if not inspiring. But his rigidity made her hesitate most of all.

She'd suffered under the inflexibility of her aunt, and she'd vowed never to live under such constraints again. She'd been working to change him, waiting for a glimpse indicating it was even possible.

"Countess?"

"Oh, do forgive me," Sophia said to Lady Bennet. "I attended the exhibition today, and it wore me out. I blame my inattention on fatigue."

"Exhibition?" Lady Bennet asked.

Her voice always took Sophia aback. It seemed too high and shrill for her solid, matronly form and towering height. She should be commanding but instead consistently sounded like a frightened young girl.

"The Somerset House exhibition," Sophia said, and Lady Bennet looked lost. "The Royal Academy? Opened their doors Monday? Art?"

Lady Bennet frowned, shaking her head. Sophia glanced around the drawing room. There were plenty of paintings, many of them quality. How could the woman not know about such an important event? "You have never been?"

"Indeed, I have not. Perhaps my husband has. Oh, there he is now." Lord Bennet led the group of men entering the room. "Percival, over here." Her voice pierced the room, and Lord Bennet obeyed, followed closely by the Duke of Salinger. Lady Bennet questioned him about the exhibit, while Sophia fought the urge to roll her eyes.

"No, I did not attend it," Lord Bennet said. "Why would I? Far too plebeian. Quite distasteful."

Sophia's blood boiled at his extreme arrogance. Her mind whispered, *Patience*, even though hers was already at a minimum, and her smile felt too tight for her face. "I believe it is marvelous the show is accessible to a large swath of people. We are all capable of appreciating talent and beauty, no?"

"I would sincerely doubt that, Countess Tessaro. Besides, I far prefer admiring all beauty in private."

His lecherous scan did nothing to temper Sophia's ire. "In the dark, I would imagine, since no beauty would willingly—"

"Have you even attended the exhibition?" the duke asked Sophia, cutting her off with a stiff smile and a warning in his eyes.

"As a matter of fact, I was there today, and I thoroughly enjoyed the art and the throngs of people. It was lively. Fun. Not remotely dull like—"

"We need a bit of a stretch after such a stupendous meal," the duke said, narrowing his eyes at Sophia. "My apologies, Lord Bennet. Lady Bennet." The duke offered his hand. "Countess, a short stroll?"

Sophia was acutely aware it was a demand, not a question, but she had no desire to escalate this interlude any further. It was not worth it. So she allowed him the moment of control.

"You are behaving ridiculously." The duke's harsh whisper in her ear irritated her further as he pulled her through the drawing room, into the hall. Sophia wanted to tug free of his grip, but eyes were upon them, and she did not wish to make a scene. Or did she? She hesitated, and he continued forward as though he was tugging along a reluctant child. He stopped and glared at her but quickly caught himself and softened his expression.

"Your rudeness is surprising, my dear. May I ask what has gotten into you?" he asked, his voice almost pleasant but his eyes hard as steel.

Irked by his sense of ownership, she found her answer. She didn't care about a scene. She yanked her arm and spun on him.

"You may ask whatever you want. You are a free man." She forced another tight smile for the gapers and gossips. "And *I* am a free woman."

The Duke of Salinger feigned a smile too. "One too free with her words this evening," he said through gritted teeth. "Lord Bennet is not without some influence—"

"And what need have I of influence? I am not the one who spends too much time, and too much money, on horses."

They had never talked openly about his money issues, and his surprise was evident. Well, good. She'd no desire to finance his future losses, so he might as well accept that now.

"How dare you," he said, his smile re-pasted as he glanced around as though interested in the people now flowing around them to the ballroom.

"No, how dare *you!*" Sophia said, not making any attempt to temper her volume or lower her voice. "I am not your chattel to direct as you see fit. I will say and do whatever I wish." She turned abruptly and banged into a hard chest. "Gaston!"

Gaston did not look surprised or pleased. In fact, he looked angry as he glanced at Sophia and over her shoulder, presumably at the duke.

"Shall I take you home?" he asked quietly.

"No," she said, thrusting her chin high. "You may take me into the ballroom." She scooped his elbow and directed him forward, without a look at the duke.

Sophia knew she had overreacted. She'd been overreacting to everything since Gaston had walked back into her life. Still, it might be for the best. Now she did not need to lie to the duke. She was genuinely angry with him and his overbearing assumptions. With so many people witnessing their argument, their time apart would be attributed to their disagreement tonight. As for repairing the damage a month from now, she would worry about it come the time. If at all. She was no longer convinced she could change the duke, and she would not settle for a domineering bore.

She turned to Gaston. "I would like to dance."

His smile was reflected in his eyes, and her heart skipped a little. Sophia would let the past rest as it should and the future stay where it must—out of reach. For now, she would live in the only moment guaranteed. And she would, for tonight, enjoy being in the arms of the man she'd once loved.

CHAPTER NINETEEN

You pierce my soul. I am half agony, half hope.

—Jane Austen, *Persuasion*

AFTER LEAVING SOPHIE'S town house, Gaston had gone directly to Liverpool. The prime minister had been in his chambers and not entirely comfortable with Gaston's sudden appearance, but he did see the wisdom of securing Gaston a ticket to the Bennets' private ball. Apparently, Lord Sidmouth had dropped by earlier and informed Liverpool they were making no headway in discovering who was leaking important operations information. More than ever, Liverpool was convinced the informant was among the peerage.

Gaston had not told Liverpool his true goal was frustrating Sophie's circumvention of spending the evening with him. It was irrelevant. He was entirely capable of listening in on conversations while undoing Sophie's evening. What he hadn't expected was this reversal in her, the invitation to dance, and his own need to see the anger in her eyes extinguished. It was one thing when he put it there, a shared fire, but to know someone else had genuinely upset her was distressing.

They stood side by side and hand in hand and looked at each other. Sophie did not avoid his gaze. In fact, she seemed determined to hold it.

"He has upset you," Gaston said loudly enough for her ears only. Saying it angered him as much as seeing the man tower over Sophie had. He'd not heard their exchange, but the duke's face had made it clear it had been a heated one.

"Only momentarily," Sophie said dismissively. She turned into him and placed her left hand on his shoulder. "I would dance in the newer way."

Gaston was happy to oblige. He placed his right hand on her waist while keeping a gentle grip on her other hand.

"How did you manage an invitation?" she asked.

Gaston laughed. Sophie was always quick to recover. "I have my ways."

He turned her, delighting in her fluid movement, easily directed by a simple touch. His mind strayed to other movements he'd enjoyed with Sophie, and he had to harness it and tug it away from such memories. His need was not to bed her. It was to find out if there was anything salvageable for them. She ran her gloved thumb across his palm, and his body instantly responded. He smiled at her. Bedding her would assuredly be an added boon.

"I am happy you are here," she said, throwing back her head and laughing as he twirled within the ensemble surrounding them.

She stayed that way, and he could see the little girl in her. Sophie had always loved to spin. She would turn and turn until she became too dizzy. She'd fall to the ground in a pile of skirts and laughter. Sometimes, he would join her, and they would lie there looking at the sky, watching the clouds roll by.

They did not speak again for the remainder of the dance, but she remained rapt, her dark gaze boring into his, her smile inviting. Gaston knew she was putting on a show for anyone watching, but he could not help but get lost in it. He'd dreamed of her for too long not to yearn for the promise her facade offered. He wished it were not an act.

As the last notes lingered in the air, she touched his cheek. "Gaston" was all she said before stepping back. Yes, a performance, but it went straight to his heart, and he wanted more. He presented his arm, and she tucked her hand around it.

"Would you like a beverage?" he asked as she took a seat on one of the gilded chairs lining the edge of the dance floor.

"*Sì*, I am unexpectedly parched." Sophie ran an elegant finger along her neckline, stopping at her daringly exposed chest.

Gaston's body took note, and he turned uncomfortably in time to see the duke pivot and walk away. He must remember Sophie was playing a game right now and he was a pawn to be used. He hoped that would change, but he must not lose sight of it, or he would succumb again to a woman who would discard him. The same woman. *Mon Dieu*, he questioned his sanity.

He waited for some lemonade, listening to various conversations. Mostly mundane bits and pieces about the season and events. One gentleman referred to a game of faro being played in another room, and Gaston decided he would be wise to take his leave of Sophie for a while and focus on his end of the bargain with Liverpool.

Sophie flitted her fan playfully in front of her face when he returned with the lemonade. "I'm going for a game of cards, Sophie. I'll be back in a while should you choose to grace me with another dance."

"Oh," she said, taking a quick sip before setting the glass aside and getting to her feet. "I adore a good game. I'll join you."

"Sophie," he said, about to tell her it was no place for her, but stopping at the look she gave daring him to say it. What did he care? He held out his arm. "By all means, please do. I enjoy a good commotion."

She laughed joyously and hooked her hand over his forearm. It seemed some things did not change. Life with Sophie was never dull.

CHAPTER TWENTY

Trust everybody, but cut the cards.

—Finley Peter Dunne, *Mr. Dooley's Philosophy*

"HE MAY HAVE won the battle, but he is without cavalry. Our allies should be able to corner him now."

Sophia was instantly alert, leaving all thoughts of flirtation with Gaston behind. She did not turn to see who had spoken. Instead, she swept the room with her gaze as though tremendously interested in the goings-on. She was not the only woman in the room, but they represented just a handful, and other than a group in the corner playing whist, most were watching, not engaging in the games.

"I've heard the allies are in retreat. The emperor has got them on the run."

Sophia casually turned in the direction of the voices. Men too free with their words were the best men to engage. A forbidden game of faro. How fitting. She let go of Gaston and walked toward the men, too late realizing the Duke of Salinger was among them. He had yet to notice her.

"Sophie," Gaston said quietly as he caught up with her and presented his arm.

She wanted to slap it. The men would not talk so easily in front of a stranger. But if she publicly rebuffed him now, they would not be at ease with her effrontery. Of course, she was also assuming they had no knowledge of her earlier confrontation with the duke. Although, some of them might applaud seeing the duke quelled. He was not an especially well-liked man.

Regardless, she could no longer slip into the game seamlessly so was left no choice but to act in keeping with the expectations they would have of Countess Sophia Tessaro. She scooped Gaston's arm and visibly pulled him toward the faro table.

"My lords, I do hope you'll indulge me and allow me to join your little game." She bestowed her best smile on them and, with her free hand, flipped open her fan and fluttered it coquettishly. "Do you know how to play, Monsieur Durand?"

"I far prefer to watch," he said.

"Oh, do tell," she said with a small smirk and an exaggerated raise of her brow. Gaston in turn raised an eyebrow, and she got the response she was seeking. Sophia fluttered her fan again and allowed the men their titter. It was exactly the distraction she was trying to create so they would return to their relaxed state.

Lord Bertram slid off his stool and offered it to her. She sat and adjusted the folds in her dress, shifting her shoulders so her neckline dropped a tiny bit. She looked up to find the duke staring at her. She disregarded him by immediately turning her attention to Lord Bertram.

"I have seen it done. It is easy to play, no?"

"Of course, my lady. We are about to commence a new game. Would you care to be a punter?"

"Oh, that sounds entirely naughty, so yes."

The men around her laughed appreciatively, and Lord Bertram took some metal coins from his velvet purse. "I shall loan you some counters."

"Place your bet, your counter," Lord Bertram said, holding up the metal coin etched with his insignia and rolling it through his fingers before placing it on the two of spades, "on the card you predict the banker may draw as the winning one. Or if you'd prefer," he continued, moving the token onto the ten of spades, "on the card you think may be considered the losing card."

She studied the suit of spades set out numerically on the table and chose to place her counter on the queen. While she did not turn around, she could sense Gaston standing behind her. She could also feel the weight of the duke's stare. She deliberately tucked a pinky under her neckline and traced its edge slowly, wetting her lips as she watched the dealer take a card from a small box and set it aside. He extracted another one, a king of hearts, and set it to the right of the small box. A few men groaned, and she quickly noted the king of spades had three checks on it. The dealer drew a third, which he slowly flipped over, revealing the queen of diamonds.

"You have won the round, Countess Tessaro," Lord Bertram said cheerfully.

Sophia clapped her hands excitedly, although she could care less whether she'd won. What mattered was the men were focused on the game and not worried about her presence or, it seemed, Gaston's. She hoped it boded well for renewed conversation.

She continued to place her tokens on cards, winning more times than not. Most of the men applauded her success, but the duke grew more and more sullen. She did note he seemed to be losing the majority of rounds. She smiled, enjoying her triumph over him, and he turned from her and nodded at the dealer to continue.

It would seem she had been too precipitous in her gloating, as she lost the remaining rounds.

"Would you enjoy another game, my lady?" Lord Bertram was a pleasant man and seemed unperturbed by his own losses in the game.

"Not at the moment, thank you. I shall simply watch for a while. Please, Lord Bertram, have my seat. I shall have my man settle with you tomorrow."

She pivoted on the stool, smiling as Gaston assisted her to her feet. They backed out of the way as the banker reshuffled the deck and put it carefully in the small box while the men placed their various counters on their cards of choice. They grew louder after the first few rounds, and Sophia debated if there was any point standing around any longer. It would be impossible to overhear any conversation now anyway.

"Perhaps we should leave. It would seem my luck has run out tonight," Sophia said into Gaston's ear, although she was not referring to the game.

"You did not run out of luck. The banker cheated. Those doublets he pulled toward the end of the game were likely planted. Twice I saw the quick sleight of hand that allowed him to see the card, and when the men were more attentive to your breasts than the board, he shifted tokens."

"How did I not notice?"

Gaston raised both eyebrows. "You were busy playing your games while he was playing his. As was your duke."

"The duke?" Sophia did not doubt men cheated at gaming hells, or perhaps at Almack's or their clubs, but surely not here at a private ball among friends. And certainly not the duke. He was no rule breaker. "No, you are mistaken. No gentleman cheats at cards."

"I will not argue that." Gaston leaned in closer. "And your duke did."

Sophia was not convinced. "Why would you say such a thing?"

"Because the tokens the banker shifted belonged to the duke."

"No!" Sophia recalled the look exchanged between the dealer and the duke. She had thought the duke was merely telling the man to continue. Could Gaston be correct? Was he so resentful of her winning a silly game that he would resort to cheating?

Suddenly, the night seemed too much. The long, dull dinner. Her spat with the duke. Gaston's unexpected appearance. The entrancing dance with him. Her failure to learn of anything to help the war effort and now the duke behaving dishonorably. And the memories. So many memories.

"Take me home, Gaston. *Maintenant.*"

CHAPTER TWENTY-ONE

My soul has many wounds
That you cannot cure.

—Marceline Desbordes-Valmore, "The Flower Returned"

"TAKE ME HOME, Gaston. *Maintenant.*"

Gaston both loved and cursed the imperative. The men directly behind him had been discussing movement on the continent. If the talk of Napoleon's lack of cavalry impeding his ability to gain knowledge of the allies was correct, now was the time for strategic troop movement. Gaston knew the area between Bautzen and Berlin well and could perhaps be of some assistance.

He would like to have stayed to hear more, but Sophie's smile was tight, and the spirit in her eyes had disappeared.

"Of course," he said and escorted her from the room. He would go to Liverpool tomorrow and share what he could. Whether a messenger could even get so far east before something further happened was debatable anyway. Besides, while the men talked of things generally confined to more intimate settings, there was nothing treacherous in talking about battles past or potential. He did not sense a traitor there, which was his assignment, not assisting strategy in battle. There was nothing that would not keep until morning.

Sophie was quiet while they waited for the servants to fetch her pelisse and his hat. He remarked on the marble statue in the foyer, similar to *David*, except this well-endowed gentleman was headless, cradling the curly decapitation in his arms.

"It is difficult to know what to stare at, don't you think?" he said, hoping his joke would bring back some light to her eyes.

Sophie scanned the statue impassively, lingering on the cradled head, but made no comment. She turned from him but not before he saw her eyes glaze with tears. He cursed himself for his insensitivity. While he had seen worse horrors than the guillotine, Sophie feared her mother had suffered its fate, although he'd found no evidence to support such a fear. Her father swore she'd died in prison, and Gaston had no reason to question the man's word. But Sophie had always remained unconvinced, saying her nightmares told her otherwise.

"Your carriage, my lady." The footman bowed as they stepped out into the cool night air.

Raimondo opened the carriage door, and Gaston helped Sophie into it. Gaston hesitated, unsure whether she'd meant for him to accompany her or not, especially after his gauche attempt at humor.

"*Rejoins-moi, s'il te plaît,*" she said, patting the seat beside her before laying her head back against the seat and closing her eyes.

Gaston did not need to be asked twice to join her. He hopped into the carriage, ignoring Raimondo's scowl as he closed the door. He sat beside Sophie, unsure of what to do. He did not know what had defeated her boisterousness, but something had taken the wind out of her sails. And he'd deflated her further.

"Sophie, my apologies," he said, watching her face for a sign of what was going on behind that beautiful face of hers. Her expression did not change, nor did she open her eyes. She put her hand on his lap, and he took it in his and held it as they quietly rode the few blocks to her town house.

Gaston got out before the lumbering Raimondo could open the door, and he extended his hand back into the carriage for

Sophie. She took it, descending elegantly. She gripped his hand tightly as they walked up the steps to her home. The door opened, and her man stepped aside as they entered. She waved away a footman.

"That will be all, Harris," she said to her butler. "You too, Raimondo," she added without looking over her shoulder, where the beast hovered in the entranceway. "I will see you in the morning."

Still holding hands, they slowly continued upstairs. He had not been further than the library on the ground floor but had noted the ornate staircase leading to the first level. He was exceedingly curious about Sophie's life beyond the elaborate railing. His heart thrummed loudly in anticipation, contradicting his worry for her.

Her drawing room was richly colored in reds and yellows, the walls covered in paintings as vibrant as Sophie. Although, there was nothing currently spirited about Sophie as she pulled him down onto a large chaise at the far end of the room.

"What is wrong, Sophie?" he asked, letting go of her hand so she could slip out of her pelisse. He took it from her and set it aside with his hat.

She sighed heavily as she tugged at the fingers on her glove, and he followed her lead, removing his own. "It seems nothing is as it appears to be anymore."

Was she aware he was listening in on conversations? Did she suspect he was a spy? "I'm not sure I understand," he said calmly, despite the uncertainty swirling through his mind.

"A game of chance manipulated. A gentleman unmasked as a cheat." She turned to him, and his chest ached at the confusion in her eyes. "A man who was dead brought to life."

"I was never dead, Sophie." He took her hand again, relieved she did not suspect his motives tonight. And saddened. While his original intention was to see her hurting as much as he had, he found there was no pleasure in her pain.

"I know," she said, nodding. "But you were to me." She

sucked in her lips, then blew out a long, audible breath. "Your return has dug up memories long buried, and I must find a new place to set them. That is all. But tonight I am…" Sophie looked at the ceiling before returning her sad gaze back to him. *"C'est beaucoup trop."*

It's too much. Gaston knew the feeling well. He raised her hand to his lips and brushed a kiss across her knuckles.

"Stay with me tonight, Gaston. Hold me while I sleep."

She said it quietly, and he knew this was no invitation to her bed. Sophie pulled the comb from her hair and plucked out the remaining pins. She shook her head and ran her fingers through her long, thick locks. She kicked off her slippers and drew her legs onto the chaise, adjusting until she was comfortable on her side, watching him all the while.

Holding her gaze, he stood and shrugged from his jacket and waistcoat, laying them over the back of a nearby chair. He walked around the room and extinguished the lamps, carefully picking his way to the far side of the chaise. He sat and tugged off his shoes before curling in behind her. He wrapped his arm around her, and her scent wrapped around him.

She cupped his hand and pulled it to her breast, holding it there fast. Eventually, he could feel the steady rise and fall of the breaths of sleep. It was hours before he would follow. After years of dreaming of it, he finally had Sophie back in his arms. He wanted to savor every minute.

CHAPTER TWENTY-TWO

Falsehood flies, and truth comes limping after it.

—Jonathan Swift, "Political Lying"

SOPHIA STARED AT the sliver of light shining on the flocked wallpaper. Still hazy with sleep, it took her a minute to place where she was and why. She sat up abruptly and looked around the dim room. Gaston was not there. She touched the chaise where he had lain. It was not warm to the touch, so he'd not recently left her. The drapes remained drawn, but it was clear the sun was well risen.

She swung her legs over the side and dusted the floor with her feet until she made contact with her evening slippers. She stood and shook out her hair, running her fingers through it haphazardly. Cara was not going to be pleased with the mats. For that matter, nor was Sophia. She hated the yanking it took to unknot them.

A tug on the bellpull brought both Harris and Cara faster than expected. They must have sprinted up the stairs. Of course, ever efficient, they had probably been nearby waiting for a signal. Once Cara had ensured Sophia's decency, Harris directed in a footman who drew the drapes fully open. Sophia squinted at the contrast in lighting, her head aching as though she'd had too much drink, which she absolutely had not. What she'd had was too much emotion. Overindulging in brandy would have been preferable.

"What time did Monsieur Durand leave?" she asked.

"He did not leave, my lady." Harris's expression did not change, nor did the level tone of his voice. If he was appalled his mistress had spent the night in her drawing room with a man, he did not show it. Of course, it was why she'd kept him on even when later provided with the opportunity to have a French or Italian butler. Harris was the soul of discretion and ensured all staff fell in line. Still, even though many men came and went, this was the first to stay directly with her through the night.

"Where is he?" Sophia assumed Gaston was in the breakfast room and was surprised to hear he was sequestered downstairs in her library. She walked toward the door with the intention of heading directly down but changed her mind. She'd been vulnerable last night, and she had no wish to have Gaston assume she remained so. She could forgive herself a weak moment, but she had no intention of repeating it.

"Cara, please," she said to her maid and walked back across the room and through the far door, through her private sitting room and into the boudoir.

As Cara brushed her mess until the dark locks gleamed in the sunshine, Sophia contemplated the previous night. If the duke did cheat at cards among friends, what else did she not know about him? She prided herself on easily reading men, yet she seemed to have failed with the duke. Had the desire to belong overshadowed her good sense? She was no longer certain she could consider him at all. She remembered the weight of Gaston's arm, the warmth of his body pressed to hers. She'd felt safe. She could not imagine experiencing the same calming security in the duke's arms.

Gaston had made the horrible jest about the headless statue, and she'd almost come undone. She'd thought he'd not made the connection to their past, but when he'd apologized, it was clear he had. And his words were enough. Being with someone who knew her, with someone who knew the pain she carried, had overwhelmed her. It had been years since she did not have to pretend. Even with her aunt in *Venezia*, she'd had to conform, had to be someone she was not. Perhaps she should genuinely give Gaston a chance. Explore the possibility of a renewed relationship.

Sophia chose a lavish day gown, a luscious jewel-toned purple, draped low in the back and the front. Cara wound her hair in a simple knot at the base of her neck, and Sophia finished the look with amethyst earrings and a matching necklace. She pinched her cheeks and pushed from the dressing table, feeling as though she was back in her own skin, Sophia Tessaro's skin. Sophia Tessaro was curious about this man Gaston Durand, and she was ready to see where things might go with him.

"Cara, see we are served in the morning room instead of the breakfast room."

If it was to be a fresh start with Gaston, the morning room was the perfect setting. It was bright, like the sun shining on a new day. Swathed in yellow with perpetual fresh-cut flowers and looking onto the small garden, it was a cheerful room, a room in which to get lost in daydreams. Maybe a room where such dreams might now come true.

The door to the library was not fully closed, and she pushed it open quietly, expecting to see Gaston languishing with the morning paper. Instead, he was at the large table. He jumped to his feet when she entered.

"Sophie," he said, coming around the table with his hands held out. "You are as beautiful in the morning as you are at night."

She allowed him to take her hands and kiss each cheek.

"*Ma chérie*, I trust you slept well."

His kiss tickled her ear, and a hint of coffee followed it, making her smile. It was so natural, so comfortable. "*Oui*, it was a dreamless night."

His eyes narrowed with concern, and he cupped her cheek.

"You still dream?"

She pulled away. She did not want to talk of her nightmares. They did not come as often as they'd used to. Well, they hadn't until Gaston had arrived. But she would tame them once again. There was no point dwelling on what could not be undone. Her focus would continue to be on what could be done. Including with Gaston.

"What were you doing?" she asked to change the subject and was surprised with Gaston's unexpected blush.

"Nothing," he said and strolled quickly to the table. He folded a piece of paper and slipped it in the tail of his jacket. "I dabble in sketching when I'm bored," he said, returning to her side.

"Oh, do show it to me," she said, playfully grabbing at his jacket.

"I'll show you something, but it will not be my poorly drawn flowers." He leaned down and brushed a kiss across her lips.

Sophia was entirely agreeable to it, pulling him closer and holding him there until he had thoroughly devoured her. He leaned his forehead against hers. "Sophie" was all he said, but she heard the recollection of their youth, the pain of the years apart, and the thrill of renewed desire. She recognized it because she felt it all too. She took a step back. It would not do to go too fast. She must sort through her feelings for the man he'd used to be before fully investing in the man he was now.

"Let us go have breakfast," she said, scooping his arm. "It is the most important meal of the day, no? Of course, so is dinner. Oh, and buffets. I adore buffets after dancing."

Gaston laughed, and Sophia smiled, pleased with herself. Yes, Sophia Tessaro was back. In full control. She wondered if Gaston was man enough to handle her.

THEY LINGERED OVER breakfast, reminiscing about their childhood, stopping shy of discussing anything beyond it. Sophia was determined to enjoy the day, and that meant leaving the shadows of the past in the corners. For now. Eventually, they must discuss it all, but not today.

"I would like a ride in the park," she announced when the last of their dishes was cleared. "You will join me, no?"

"Although I regret it, I cannot." Gaston stood. "I have some business to attend to. I am free this evening."

"Well, I am not."

"Sophie," he said, his voice a warning. "We are not back to that game, are we?"

Admittedly, Sophia was somewhat miffed by his rebuff, but she truly was not available. Lord Stratton wanted to speak with her alone and had arranged to join her this evening for dinner. It would not be a conversation Gaston could be privy to.

"I play no game. I have plans, and you are not a part of them." She flapped her hand as he tried to interrupt. "I have held to my end of the deal. We have seen each other. Spent time together. And"—she softened her voice—"I have enjoyed it very much."

The stiffness seeped from Gaston's stance, and he smiled, the appeasement she'd hoped for attained.

"I did too." He held out his hand, and she took it, allowing him to pull her to her feet. "Tomorrow?"

"Entirely yours."

They walked through the house, back to the main entrance. He took his hat from Harris and leaned in, brushing each of her cheeks with a kiss before donning it. "*À demain*, Sophie."

"Until tomorrow," she echoed.

Sophia strolled into the library and watched Gaston through the window. He paused on the street as though deciding which way to go. It had not crossed her mind to offer him her carriage, although it might be just as well. She did not much care about gossip, but for now, she did not wish to invite it either. She would like to know where she stood with Gaston before the tongues began to wag. Although, after last night, they'd probably already begun.

Gaston must have sensed her presence. He looked up and smiled. She smiled and gave a small wave. He tipped his hat and turned to the right. She watched until he was out of sight. The room seemed oddly empty. Sophia walked to the table and traced its edge until she was standing by the chair Gaston had been sitting in.

The other half of a sheet of foolscap rested on the table, a pencil beside it. Gaston sketching flowers. She didn't remember him being interested in such things when they were young. He'd been more rough and tumble, more likely to climb a tree than draw one. She ran a finger over the paper, detecting a slight line. His piece of paper must have sat on this one. She was curious to see if he had any talent.

She sat on the chair and lightly brushed the graphite back and forth across the page. There was more than one line. Sophia frowned as she continued. There was nothing flowerlike about the lines. When she was finished, she brought the picture to the window to better see it. While it was difficult to fully discern many details, it was clear it was a map.

Sophia retrieved her glasses from the wooden box on the desk, returned to the table, and penciled across the areas she was certain were words. If they were words, they were obscured, even with her glasses on. However, there was no mistaking an *X*. She grabbed the quill and traced the lines with ink to better see the map. Rivers, hillsides, roads. But where? And why? Why would Gaston sit in her library and draw a map?

She studied it but could make no sense of it. It could be anywhere. Sophia should simply ask Gaston, but something was off. Why would he say he was sketching flowers? Why not tell her he was working on a map? Was Gaston up to something? Was that why he'd reunited with her? Did he know she helped the English?

Mon Dieu! Sophia stiffened as a possibility dawned. Could Gaston be a spy too? And if it were true, the bigger question would be, Whose side was he on?

CHAPTER TWENTY-THREE

Believe nothing you hear, and only one-half that you see.

—Edgar Allan Poe,
"The System of Dr. Tarr and Prof. Fether"

"**N**OW SHE'S A sleek beauty, don't you think?" Bentley asked, his eyes continuing to follow the filly as it walked by them.

"Another year and she'll be a fine specimen," Gaston said agreeably, although he had little interest in racing horses. He did, however, have a great interest in the patrons at Tattersall's. He'd returned to his rooms after a long conversation with Liverpool, enhancing the simple map he'd brought as Liverpool took notes, to find Bentley on his way out. His invitation to join him to look at horseflesh seemed the perfect opportunity to continue in his search for Liverpool's traitor.

"You may be right. I'd enjoy watching her through her paces," Bentley said, turning to Gaston and grinning, "but I find I am exceedingly parched. Join me in the subscription room for a drink, Durand?"

Gaston could not have planned it more purposefully. They pushed through the crowd of men and into the building. The large room, although alive and boisterous, was not as crushing as outside. The room would fill when the demonstrations of horses for auction were finished. The men would all pour in and talk about fortunes won and lost and money yet to be played. Gaston and Bentley settled near the corner with a port each.

"Bloody good timing, you coming back as I was going out." Bentley took a sip of his porter.

"And why do you say that?"

Gaston did not warm to men easily, and Bentley was almost too perfect to warm to at all. He was dressed impeccably with a cache of blond curls dancing on the edge of his too-high collar. Although tall and broad-shouldered, he seemed more porcelain doll than man. But he was amiable and an easy connection to the world Gaston needed to infiltrate.

"Why? Because I'm bursting to know how you managed to leave the Bennets' ball last night…with Countess Tessaro."

"How would you know that?" Gaston was genuinely surprised the news had traveled so quickly, for surely Bentley was only recently out of his bed.

"I was there," Bentley said. "Later, of course. Missed all the excitement, if the buzzing bees in the room were any indication. Matrons flitting one to the other, frenetically waving their fans in front of their faces as though the rest of the room could not tell they were gossiping. And the duke." Bentley guffawed. "A more rankled man I've never seen."

"I don't know the man," Gaston said with a shrug, sidestepping the question about leaving with Sophie. "I would doubt he would find a lowly man like me a threat."

"I beg to differ. He cornered me and drilled me as though I was a criminal. Or a spy."

Gaston searched Bentley's face for innuendo, but the man's eyes twinkled, and his face was guileless. "The countess was distressed after an argument with the duke. I was nearby. I wish it were more complicated than that, for she is a beautiful woman."

"Whatever did they argue about?" Bentley asked, waving for a server and ordering two more drinks despite the fact Gaston had yet to lift his glass to his mouth.

"I have no idea. And I don't know her well enough to have asked."

"But well enough to not have returned to your rooms last night." Bentley looked absurd, raising his eyebrows up and down.

Gaston was taken aback by the man's keen interest but did not show it. "Why would you assume such a thing?"

Bentley casually scanned Gaston head to toe and back up again. Gaston had chosen trousers for the ball last night, so other than a change of jacket before leaving again with Bentley, he was now dressed as he'd been last night. Heat warmed his cheeks as he scrambled for an explanation that did not include spending the night with Sophie.

"I enjoyed watching the countess play faro. I had a yearning to play myself. So I went gaming."

The footman interrupted and set two glasses down, taking Bentley's empty one and eyeing Gaston's full one. Still disconcerted by Bentley's astute observation, Gaston obligingly tossed back the contents and handed the empty glass to the footman.

"Oh, how disappointing. And here I thought someone had finally made inroads with the countess. I was living vicariously, you see." He grinned. "Still, I wish I had known. The ball was deadly dull. I would have joined you. Where did you go?"

"Saint James Square. The name escapes me at the moment. Blocked it out, I'm sure. I didn't fare well."

Bentley chuckled appreciatively, and Gaston was relieved he didn't probe any further. Gaston could name the gaming hells—it was his business to know these things—but his presence or lack thereof could be easily verified if, on the off chance, he was reading Bentley's interest wrong. Which he didn't think he was. He was confident it was idle curiosity. There wasn't an iota of seriousness in that golden-locked head of his.

"Here comes the devil now," Bentley said, looking toward the doors. "And looking as bearish as he did last night."

Gaston glanced over his shoulder. The duke was in conversation with another man and oblivious to the tide of men who parted as he marched through the room. He did not look Gaston's way as he passed and took a seat at the next table. Gaston discreetly shifted in his seat so his back was facing the duke. No need to cause a scene...again.

"Back to the filly. I'm considering buying her. I've never had a horse in a race." Bentley droned on, and Gaston smiled at what he hoped were appropriate moments. In reality, his ear was attuned to the duke and his companion. He wanted to know more about this man who had cornered Sophie's attention, both good and bad.

"I am hesitant to put forth another bet. You lost the first of the season in Newmarket. You have not settled your accounts," the duke's companion said.

"I will," the duke bit out. "I've not had a moment."

"They adhere to jockey club rules and will not bend easily."

"Place my wager for Chester under a different name."

"So it would be great fun, don't you think?" Bentley sat back in his chair, clearly awaiting an answer.

"It would," Gaston replied, trying to refocus on the duke and his companion, but they'd dropped their voices, and he could no longer make out what they were saying.

"Splendid," Bentley said. "I will speak with Walford. The ladies are as thick as thieves, so if one agrees, they will all agree."

"*Très bien*," Gaston said, although he had no idea what he was approving. But if it included Sophie, he wasn't going to argue. After those grueling years apart, there could never be enough time with Sophie.

CHAPTER TWENTY-FOUR

The truth may run fine but will not break, and always rises above falsehood, as oil above water.

—Miguel de Cervantes, *The History of Don Quixote*

"I CANNOT EAT another bite."

Stratton pushed his plate away and patted his midriff as though he had a large belly rather than the trim waist he sported. Sophia had always found him attractive. Like a fine port, he was aging well, with only a touch of gray in his auburn hair, his laugh lines as appealing as the man himself. Despite all his charms, she'd never been interested in him. Nor he in her.

"But I have some delicious desserts planned," Sophia said, pouting playfully.

"I'd much prefer some of the fine cognac you hide in your cellars."

His moss eyes looked more the color of a deep forest in the light from the candles. Catherine had gotten those eyes. Sophia loved them both, father and daughter, but even Stratton did not know her whole story. It was a pain she'd borne alone. Or thought she had until Gaston's return.

"Harris, could you find some for Lord Stratton?"

"Indeed, my lady," he said and quickly left the room.

"While we wait, shall we discuss the purpose of your visit?

For surely you have not simply come for my cognac."

Stratton glanced at the footman and back at Sophia with a slight shake of his head.

Sophia pushed from her chair. "Why don't we withdraw to the library? Stephens, see our cognac brought there." The footman dipped his chin in acknowledgment. "Oh, and the desserts. Don't forget the desserts," she said, hooking her hand in Stratton's proffered elbow.

"But you are sweet enough, my dear Sophia," Stratton said, guiding her out of the dining room and into the room next door.

"And you are an incorrigible flatterer," she said, laughing. "Tell me more."

Stratton waxed on about her beauty as Stephens poked the fire and lit a few more lanterns and candles. Harris arrived with the cognac, while another footman came in with a three-tiered plate of sweets. "Leave them on the table between us. The cognac too." She waited until the doors were firmly closed before turning her full attention to Stratton. "Well?"

"You are a master of subtlety," he said, chuckling, then growing serious. "Laurence has left for the continent."

It was not what she'd expected to hear. Laurence worked covertly for the Home Office on the home front. He'd never been sent directly into war. "Whyever would he have gone there?"

"It seems Wellesley is short two trusted intelligence officers."

"Two?"

"Yes, Leith-Hay is missing. No one's heard from Grant. On the heels of losing Somers-Cocks, it's a blow to operations."

Sophia contemplated the implications. If what she'd overheard at the Bennets' ball was true, the allies were on the cusp of turning this endless war into a win. More than ever, it was imperative to have reliable sources of information.

"Why Laurence?" Sophia asked, taking a deep sip of brandy, the desserts no longer appealing.

Stratton shrugged casually, but she could see the concern in his eyes. Sophia leaned forward and touched his hand. "I am sorry, my friend. It is not easy to see your child head into danger."

He covered her hand with his own. "Thank you, my dear Sophia. It is not. He was keen to go, so I take comfort in his enthusiasm. It would be far worse had he been reticent. But he was reticent about one thing and asked me to keep an eye on you. It's what has brought me here tonight. Your new friend, Gaston Durand."

Sophia pulled away and sat back, staring at the fire, debating how much to share with Stratton. Had it not been for the map this morning, she would be less hesitant in exposing her and Gaston's long-standing relationship. But she was now filled with dubiety. It was likely an innocent sketch, and if she mentioned it, she would unnecessarily be planting a seed of suspicion about him. Even worse, if it was not benign, if he was indeed here to ferret information for the French, she would need to act upon it. And that was a task she would do alone. While Stratton's son was one of the best, Stratton himself had only ever been a liaison. He was no intelligence officer, no soldier. He was a man passionate about politics, his country, and his family.

She was certain Stratton would not be pleased she was entertaining a man whose occupation was entirely questionable. For all she knew, she was fraternizing with the enemy. Stratton had always been protective of Catherine, but the new baby had brought his fatherly instincts to a whole new level. It made his response unpredictable. When the war was over, she would share everything about her life, and hope her chosen family stood by her. But until that time came to pass, she would not risk losing her place in society.

"Sophia?"

"I am chasing memories," she said truthfully, turning to look at Stratton. "Gaston is from my childhood. He is nothing to worry about."

"Why was he skulking around your estate?"

It was no surprise Stratton was direct, but today she wished he'd stuck to pleasantries. Her mind was too full, and she needed time to sort through everything. Still, she could not avoid answering. "He'd seen me one day in London but was not convinced it was me. We had not seen each other since—" She took a sip of her brandy, eyeing Stratton over her glass. "Since we were children. People change. As did my name with marriage. He did not want to approach until he was sure. So he was watching."

Stratton frowned, unconvinced. "What harm could it do to walk to your door and ask?"

Sophia forced a light laugh. "Have you met Raimondo?"

Stratton smiled, and tension eased from his face. "You do have a point."

"In truth, he was unsure about Laurence. He'd seen him come and go freely from the property. He surmised he might be my lover or some such thing."

"Laurence? Indeed," he said and chuckled again.

"You will see for yourself Gaston is no threat to me. But enough about him. Tell me what it is like to be a grandpapa. You are in love with the *piccolo bambino*, no?"

Stratton's face shone with happiness as he talked about little Daniel, surely exaggerating the achievements of a child barely a month old. He was fully distracted from any thoughts of Gaston, so Sophia could relax and enjoy his tales.

Long after he left, she sat and stared at the embers in the grate. Stratton had a point about Gaston. Gaston's wariness of Laurence being the reason he'd hesitated to contact her had sounded exactly like what it was, an excuse. She was sure Gaston was strategizing. But why? Was it for her attention? Or was there a larger game at play? She hoped it was the first, but even if she did not like what she might find, she was determined to find out. For, despite her longing for him, her loyalty was to her country and the memory of her parents. She would ferret out the truth before she let her heart proceed any further. She was strong. She could do it. She was, after all, a master of charades.

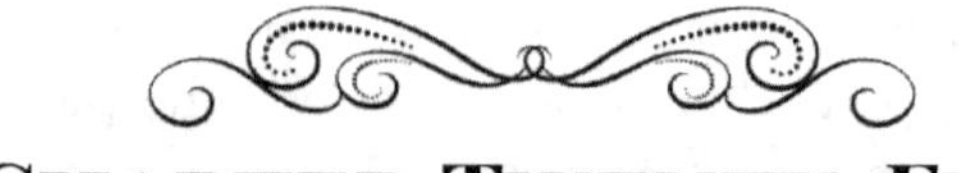

CHAPTER TWENTY-FIVE

So little pains do the vulgar take in the investigation of truth,
accepting readily the first story that comes to hand.

—Thucydides, *History of the Peloponnesian War*

"You have made the papers…again," Elizabeth said. "All of them." She twirled her parasol and looked at Sophia expectantly.

"Oh, do tell," Catherine said. "I've been far too busy with Daniel to keep up with the gossips."

The three of them had not been together since Catherine's soiree, and Sophia was thoroughly enjoying their reliable companionship. No intrigues, no underlying meanings in their words, no hidden pasts. "What have I done now?" she asked, smiling pleasantly at the group of women who passed them on the right. It was a beautiful afternoon for a stroll in the park.

"She has publicly rebuffed Lord S."

"No!" Catherine stopped and turned to Sophia. "You did?"

Sophia pursed her lips contemplatively but did not successfully suppress a smile. "It is true."

Catherine clapped her hands happily, and Sophia laughed. She knew neither Catherine nor Elizabeth was fond of the duke, but their unrestrained elation was unexpected.

"What happened?" Catherine scooped Sophia's arm and

leaned in playfully as they started to stroll again. "You can tell me."

"According to the papers, she has exchanged him for a younger man, a…gasp…Frenchman."

"Oh, that's wonderful!" Catherine hugged Sophia's arm tight and let her go.

"I am sorry to disappoint you, *mie amiche*, but that part of the story is not true." Sophia did not like her friends' crestfallen faces. "But I do not think I will renew my acquaintance with the duke." They both cheered instantly. "You dislike him so much?"

Catherine and Elizabeth looked at each other, then nodded at Sophia.

"I don't know whether to slap you both or kiss you. Should you not have been cheering me on? I would be a duchess, no?"

Elizabeth shuddered dramatically, while Catherine made a face.

Sophia laughed. "At least I know you are not interested in me for my influence in society," she said. Elizabeth held equal ranking to Sophia, and Catherine would one day also be a countess, but a duchess held more sway than all three of them together.

"You would make a splendid duchess," Elizabeth said. "Maybe we could find you another duke?"

"No, we won't." Catherine tapped Elizabeth's hand. "She has a Frenchman."

"Oh, that's right. However could I have forgotten?" Elizabeth grinned at Sophia, and Sophia slowly shook her head.

"I do not *have* a Frenchman." Sophia adjusted her bonnet, eyeing them from underneath its brim.

"But he did conveniently happen to be there when you rebuked the duke? At a private ball no less?"

"It was simple coincidence." Sophia waved her hand dismissively, although she, too, wondered how he'd managed to secure an invitation. The fact he had such connections added weight to her suspicions.

"Then there's your dancing with the *not-your* French-man...and I quote...'like a butterfly newly freed.'" Elizabeth raised an eyebrow, and Catherine laughed, clearly enjoying the teasing.

"Well, Gaston was masterful on the dance floor," Sophia said, laughing at the foolish gossip and her friends' amusement. Although, in truth, she had felt free in his arms. Unlike the duke, Gaston had not chastised her or frowned upon her joy.

"Gaston now, is it?" Elizabeth teased.

"Evil. Both of you. Let us go look at the swans." Sophia steered them off the path toward the water, grateful neither had noticed the duke and his ensemble approaching from the opposite direction. She'd no desire for a scene on this lovely afternoon. Both Elizabeth and Catherine dropped the subject of Gaston, and they enjoyed another hour of fresh air and new gossip before tiring and returning to their separate homes.

When she arrived at the town house, she found the entrance filled with a virtual garden of flowers, and Harris fretting about where she would like them to go. Excitement raced through her until she read the card. It was not Gaston. It was the duke expressing his sincerest apologies. While it was a surprising gesture, she doubted its veracity. Still, she was no fool. A duke as a friend was a far greater thing than a duke as an enemy. She would do well to tread carefully with Salinger.

Chapter Twenty-Six

*If our condition were truly happy, we would not need diversion
from thinking of it.*

—Blaise Pascal, *Pascal's Pensées*

Securing attendance for the Philharmonic Society's performance had been Elizabeth's doing. While they all had their subscriptions to the Argyll Rooms, they did not have one for the orchestra, as it was only newly formed and none of them had intended on being in London for the remainder of the season. Sophia had regretted not seeing their first sessions, so it was something she'd hoped to attend while back in London. It would be delightful to listen to a full orchestra. She'd heard only praise for their performances.

Getting tickets to the event was no easy feat, especially on such short notice. However, Elizabeth was great friends with the principal first violinist, and he managed to secure them four seats. Catherine had declined the opportunity, claiming their walk in the park had taken all her energy, but Sophia suspected she was simply plotting with Elizabeth to put Sophia and Gaston together. Little did they know, Sophia would have been spending the evening with him regardless.

Sophia had sent word to Gaston's rooms and had been pleased when he'd appeared promptly at the appointed time. She, of course, had delayed greeting him, giving him enough time in the library to not only see all the flowers but to find the duke's card. She'd been greatly disappointed when he hadn't said a word about them, yet she was sure he'd read Salinger's apology. Gaston had been thoroughly pleasant during the ride, and she debated whether he was a superior actor or whether he simply did not care. Sophia wasn't sure which scenario bothered her more.

They found the Thornwoods within minutes. Elizabeth looked stunning in royal blue, her hair almost white under the bright gas lamp above her head. Thornwood was his dashing self, dressed in a black jacket and trousers with a waistcoat matching Elizabeth's dress. They were a lovely couple, and Sophia told them so as she kissed each on the cheek. Elizabeth flushed becomingly.

"Nice to see you again, Durand." Thornwood shook Gaston's hand. "Shall we go up?"

"Your Frenchman is looking considerably dapper this evening," Elizabeth whispered as they preceded the men up the stairs. "You make an exotic pair."

"*Bella*," Sophia said, although she agreed they were a handsome pairing. "You are making far too much fuss about Durand. He is a passing acquaintance who I am obligated to entertain while in London. In a month, he will be on his way, as will I."

"If you say so." Elizabeth sounded unconvinced.

They paused on the landing, waiting for the men to catch up. Thornwood placed his arm around Elizabeth's waist to guide her, leaving Sophia and Gaston to follow. She hesitated, thinking Gaston might boldly try to be equally intimate, but he remained the perfect gentleman, presenting his arm instead. Sophia placed her gloved hand on it and smiled. The corner of his lip twitched, before he focused ahead, following the Thornwoods to a box overlooking the grand saloon.

Elizabeth patted the chair beside her, and Sophia happily took a seat. With her friend to her left, she could ignore Gaston to her right should she choose to. He was entirely too self-assured this evening, while she was busy chasing thoughts of him through her mind. Why had he drawn a map? Had he read the card from the duke? What was his purpose in seeking her out? Why was he unperturbed by the flowers?

"You haven't heard a word I said." Elizabeth tapped Sophia's leg with her program.

"*Le mie scuse*, my mind is elsewhere." It was the truth, for her mind had now drifted to where Gaston's leg pressed against hers.

"Preoccupied?" Elizabeth grinned and leaned forward, holding out her program to Gaston. "Perhaps you would care to see tonight's schedule?"

"*Merci*," he said, taking the program. "I appreciate your kindness in including me this evening."

"Not at all." Elizabeth leaned back in her chair and pressed her ear to Sophia's. "How can you resist him? He is utterly charming. And gorgeous."

Elizabeth pretended to fan herself, and Sophia resisted a rolling of the eyes, although she did not disagree with her friend's observation. Gaston was more handsome than any man she'd ever met. She attributed it to his lack of perfection. Flawlessness was far overrated. Gaston's sensual lips were marred by a slight scar on the left bow, the result of a piece of a broken jug bouncing off the floor and hitting him when he was young. He had a row of perfect teeth, but the bottom front one was chipped, and he'd lost a back one in a fist fight. He had always been quick in temper. His long dark eyelashes would be considered feminine were they not balanced by the constant evidence of facial hair trying to emerge, an ever-present scruff on his chin and cheeks. And his skin. Oh, how she loved his dark skin. The English looked ill beside him.

"Careful, I see some drool," Elizabeth said in Sophia's ear and giggled.

Gaston's nose flared, and he pressed his lips together, but Sophia could see the corners twitching as he fought a smile. Heat rose in her cheeks, as she knew he'd overheard Elizabeth. Sophia was to be the one torturing him, not the other way around. Why was it she turned into an incompetent girl around him? Anger bubbled, directed at herself, and perhaps a little at him, since ultimately, it was his fault for returning.

She shifted, putting space between his thigh and hers and scanned the room. She fluttered her fan, both to cool herself and to appear the epitome of nonchalance, as she took note of who was there. The orchestra was assembling, and she watched as they took their instruments and prepared themselves. The violinist turned to the audience and bowed, and everyone clapped. A commotion at the entrance to the boxes on the other side drew everyone's attention. The duke entered as though he had not interrupted the beginning of the program. His entourage tittered and followed him, unmindful to the fact they were delaying the beginning of the performance. Of course, Sophia knew they were not truly oblivious. They simply did not care.

The violinist cleared his throat, drawing attention back to the stage. "I'd like to welcome everyone. Our overture this evening is *Numa Pomilius*."

Two violins opened the set, joined by two violas and a violoncello. Sophia glanced at Gaston. He was not watching the stage. His eyes were on the box where the duke sat unbothered by the disruption he'd caused. The humor that had danced upon Gaston's lips was gone, a grim line in its place. Perhaps he was not as immune to the duke's advances as he pretended? That boded well. She'd far prefer he be a jealous suitor than a nefarious infiltrator.

Sophia caught the duke's glance and saw his face darken when he registered Gaston by her side. She set her hand discreetly on Gaston's lap. He looked at her questioningly but took it in his own hand and ran his thumb across her palm. A thrill ran through Sophia, and she beamed a smile at him, dismissing her plan to placate the duke. After his rudeness, it was far more fun to poke him. Judging by the look on his face, she was succeeding. She'd known the philharmonic was going to be enjoyable, but the night had just gotten superbly delicious.

CHAPTER TWENTY-SEVEN

A subtle, sudden flame,
By veering passion fann'd,
About thee breaks and dances
When I would kiss thy hand.

—Alfred Lord Tennyson, "Madeline"

GASTON WAS FULLY aware Sophie was playing a game. She was clearly baiting the duke. What did he care? From what he'd seen of the man so far, he deserved to be dangled and dallied with. He was a self-centered boar, barreling in late with no sense of courtesy for the audience or the musicians. Not to mention how he'd spoken to Sophie the other night at the Bennets' ball. For that alone, Gaston would as soon punch the man as look at him.

Of course, he did neither. Instead, he returned Sophie's smile and turned his attention to the orchestra. His ears tuned in to the harmonic melodies, but his mind was fixated on holding Sophie's willing hand, tracing circles, her slight tremble passing on to him. She had always responded to his touch. The violins surged toward the crescendo. He closed his eyes, letting the power in the strings strum through him. Memories of their one night together, images of Sophie's beautiful body, open and giving, crashed through his mind with the final notes.

"Your smile leaves me wondering," Sophie said as applause broke the moment.

"Does it?" Gaston shifted, inadvertently drawing Sophie's attention to the uncomfortable rise in his trousers. "And your smile leaves me with no questions whatsoever," he said at her triumphant grin. "I find music stirs my blood," he added, but he knew he wasn't fooling her. She understood well her power.

"And mine," she said huskily as the next set launched with a cello concerto.

Gaston relaxed back in his chair, getting lost, once again, in the music and his reminiscence. When the orchestra began a piece from Cherubini's *Lodoïska*, Sophie gripped his hand tightly. The summer she'd turned eleven, Gaston's father had treated Sophie and her family to a performance of the opera at the Théâtre Feydeau in Paris. He remembered well her joy in it, her tension when the castle wall had exploded onstage, and her happy tears when the young lovers Floreski and Lodoïska had been reunited at the end. Sophie had always been a romantic.

He squeezed her hand to let her know he, too, recalled the performance. He watched her face while the soprano sang as Lodoïska had from the tower, and he did not miss the tear clinging to Sophie's bottom lashes as the last notes hung in the air. The audience erupted in applause, but Sophie sat, staring at the stage, as stiff and still as a mannequin sheathed at a dress shop. Her beauty and her agony made his chest ache. He wanted to pull her into his arms and soothe away her pain.

Lady Thornwood said something to her, and it pulled Sophie from her reverie. A smile lit her expression, and she whispered to her friend, waving her fan in front of her face, her response too muffled for Gaston to understand. But her melancholy had lifted, so his worry lightened along with it. Sophie was not as shallow or vacuous as she wanted this world to believe. She felt the full spectrum of her emotions deeply. Not for the first time, he pondered her pretense. Did she think it her only way to land a duke?

He glanced toward the Duke of Salinger only to find the man staring at Sophie. Gaston's good mood diminished instantly. The duke was far more shallow and vacuous than Sophie's appearance as such, yet he offered her an enviable position in society. What did Gaston have to offer? Gaston Armand, the Marquis de Lyon, existed no more. His family had been stripped of the title when his father had refused to return to the new court. It was a decision Gaston supported, but it had left him adrift. Only Sophie had anchored him. For years, she had been all that mattered. And now?

Sophie cast her smile on him, and he knew the answer. It was embedded in his soul. The darkness that had driven him since she'd married the count no longer thrived in Gaston. His heart had come full circle. She was his reason for being. Now if only he could once again be hers.

"This evening has created a craving in me for more entertainment. More…" Sophie twirled her hand in the air, looking for a word. "*Vita*," she said, snatching at the air as though she'd caught the word.

Life. It was the essence of Sophie's appeal, had been since she'd pulled him along the streets of Paris that fateful day. She delighted in all things.

Gaston smiled in return. "And what would you suggest, Sophie?"

"Sophia," she corrected but continued, unbothered. "Richard has offered to secure tickets for the theater tomorrow evening. There we will find our joie de vivre, even if it is only upon the stage."

"I would be honored to escort you," he said slowly, not entirely sure she was not informing him that her plans did not include him.

"Of course, my dear Gaston," she said, briefly touching his cheek.

Gaston would have been bursting with renewed hope were it not for her surreptitious glance toward the duke and her smirk indicating she had accomplished exactly what she wanted—her triumph lay with inciting the duke, not inviting the commoner. Well, he would not be so easily deterred. May the better man win and, *mon Dieu*, let him be the better man in Sophie's heart.

CHAPTER TWENTY-EIGHT

And I meant to make you jealous. Are you jealous of me now?
—Alfred Lord Tennyson, "Happy"

SOPHIA KNEW SHE should not have done it, but she could not seem to help herself. The duke had treated her like a possession, and she wanted to make it clear no one owned her. Besides, it was fun to prick the air out of his inflated sense of self—stampeding in with not so much as a glance of contrition to the orchestra or the audience. It had irritated her.

She'd also needed a distraction. The soprano's song had shifted something inside her as memories of her first opera had rushed in. It had been at the special invitation of the Marquis de Lyon and had been issued at the insistence of Gaston. Her mother had been thrilled, as it had been years since she'd sat in a private box at an opera. They'd attended with great excitement.

The theater had been newly built and had been remarkable to an eleven-year-old, as had the performance itself. Gaston had held her hand as the wall had unexpectedly exploded onstage, revealing soldiers fighting. It had caught her off guard and been far too real a reminder of what was happening in the streets and around the country. The royal family had been arrested and only recently returned to Paris, and the unrest had been growing, not ebbing.

It wasn't until much later she learned the theater had been used by counterrevolutionaries, including Gaston's father and, eventually, her own. If her father had maintained his neutrality, perhaps he would be with her now. But after her mother had been dragged away by a mob of revolutionaries, he was decided. As was she. She understood the plight of the underprivileged, but the cause did not justify the ways and the means. Her mother had been an innocent, a woman who had chosen a mundane life with a scholar over the glamour and excitement of the Italian court. She'd been no threat to their cause. But, eventually, Sophia had become a threat. For her mother. For her father. And for Gaston.

She glanced at him sitting quietly across from her in the carriage, looking out the window into the darkness. If only a miracle could return the other two to her too. She sighed. She must be grateful for the one. For surely his appearance was a return for her and not for any reprehensible reasons. He had lived what she'd lived and more. Or so he said. Why was he in England, and why had he not come to her sooner?

"You are lost in your thoughts, Gaston," she said.

He turned to look at her. "As are you."

"Perhaps a little. Did you enjoy this evening's performance?"

"Which one? The one on the stage or the one in our box?"

Sophia was surprised by his astute observation. She had not thought he'd noticed, and had been unsure about whether he'd care even if he had. "Either," she said, watching his face, trying to read his expression in the dim carriage.

"The one on the stage was *extraordinaire*. The one in the box? Unexpectedly disappointing. More pedantic and predictable." He looked back out the window.

Sophia's temper sparked. "You are calling me unimaginative? Or dull?"

"No, Sophie," he said without breaking his stare out the window. "You are neither of those things. But your game was. Or is." He locked his gaze with hers in the reflection. "Are you done toying with the duke? Or is it me you toy with?"

He was jealous. It was a good sign, was it not? For if he cared not at all, there would be no bitterness in his voice, no tension between them. Her fire went out.

"I am not toying with you, Gaston. I am upholding my side of our bargain. It was what you asked of me, no?" She did not say she was trying to figure out his motivation, that she was afraid to release her heart to him only to find it crushed beneath his plans. "Why did you not come to me sooner, Gaston?"

He studied her for a moment before speaking. "I did not know you were here, until recently."

She waited for him to say more, to explain how he could be in England and yet not have surfaced until now. How he could not have known about her presence until now. But he said nothing further.

"And how did you make the grand discovery?" she asked, once again irritated at having to pull each item of information from him as though extracting horsehairs from her riding dress.

"It was, as I've told you, entirely by accident. I saw you pass in a carriage with your friends. It was a quick glimpse, but I'd know you anywhere. I followed the carriage to the Thornwoods' town house, then on to your own house."

"You saw me in London yet did not approach me until I was on my estate?" While it was possible it had been a serendipitous coincidence, the delay to connect with her made no sense to Sophia.

"*Oui*," Gaston said, "it is the truth. You are frowning. You still do not believe me."

"Why wait?"

"You were a busy woman, with many suitors. Including the duke. You attended many events with him."

"And with others." She sighed. It was her own fault he was focused on the duke.

"And with others," he repeated. "I had been rejected once. I did not wish to be so again."

"I have never refused you."

He raised an eyebrow but said nothing.

"You cannot call my marriage a rejection of you, Gaston. I thought you were dead." Emotions rolled through her, too many to name, too many to continue this conversation. "Enough of this dance. It leads us nowhere. What is done is done. The question is, Where to now?"

"Your townhome," Gaston said smoothly, being deliberately obtuse. "And tomorrow, the theater."

The carriage came to a halt, rocking as Raimondo hopped off. He opened the door, and Gaston slid out quickly, reaching back in and offering his hand. She took it, and stepped out, the air cool on her flushed face.

"I'm going to return to my rooms," Gaston said, leaning in and whisking a kiss across each of her cheeks. "Good night."

Sophia watched as he walked away without so much as a glance back. She was at sea, tossed around by a tumult of memories and visceral reactions, and he remained passively ashore, calmly detached. Every moment with Gaston was one step forward and two steps backward. She did not know if they were destined to be together or destined to say goodbye. But she knew she had to know one way or the other.

She watched him turn the corner. Regardless of his half-truths, unlike him, she would not walk away now.

CHAPTER TWENTY-NINE

Words are easy, like the wind;
Faithful friends are hard to find.

—Shakespeare, "The Passionate Pilgrim"

"SIGNOR ARMAND IS downstairs," Cara said, entering Sophia's room with a freshly ironed gown over her arm.

"Durand," Sophia corrected, not surprised Cara knew his real name. There were few secrets among her three loyal servants, and Raimondo and Stefano certainly knew Gaston was an Armand. Although Gaston's use of Durand remained puzzling and only fed her suspicions about his motive, he was right. It did work in her favor. No one could connect a Monsieur Durand to her, and therefore her years in France remained unknown.

"*Le mie scuse, signora mia.* Durand." Cara continued in rapid-fire Italian, lamenting the good old days when people were who they were and insisting she was getting too old to keep up. Cara was well aware of Sophia's history with Gaston. She had patiently listened to Sophia's endless stories of her lost love when she'd first moved in with the count. Sophia knew the woman was not bothered by his sudden appearance. No, Cara frowned on Sophia's more covert exploits, and she was seizing the opportunity to lecture her.

"*Basta,*" Sophia said, tiring of Cara's not-so-discreet chastisement. "The war must soon end, and there will be no more need for subterfuge."

The end of the war would be a blessing, but she worried constantly about her friends and how they would react when they learned the grand Italian countess was an illusion created with half-truths. That she was a woman stripped of her home and country, who'd married out of necessity and used her flamboyant widowhood as a ruse. They were family to her, but what of she to them? Would they have let her into their world had they known she was French? Would they feel used? Could they forgive her for not being forthcoming, or would the life she'd built crumble?

She found hope in their husbands, who seemed to have accepted her involvement in the capture of a criminal last month. Thornwood and Walford probably considered it one more of her long list of idiosyncrasies, a minor adventure for the thrill of it. They could not possibly know her dealings with the Home Office were ongoing. Would they stand with her if she told Elizabeth and Catherine about her involvement in war operations, in spying in the drawing rooms of London? Or would they see Sophia as sullied and want their wives far away from her influence? Such thoughts weighed heavily. She sighed and slipped her arms into the dress Cara held up.

"You do the right thing," Cara said quietly in Italian. "The count would be proud."

"Would he?" Sophia asked, wiggling until the skirt fell and tugging at it until it snugged her breasts.

Cara bit back a smile. "No, he is rolling in his grave."

Sophia laughed at her maid's honesty. Cara had been maid for the count's first wife and knew the Tessaros far better than Sophia.

Cara grabbed the sash and wrapped it under Sophia's breasts. "Only because he loved you, *signora mia*, very much, and would be worried for your safety. But he would admire your cause…and your courage."

Sophia turned and kissed the older woman's cheeks. "*Grazie, Cara.*"

She appreciated Cara's sentiment, but while the count had been a kind and generous man, Sophia suspected he'd loved the memory of her mother more than he'd loved Sophia for herself. Maria Amalia Donati, Sophia's mother, had been promised to Carmine Tessaro when she'd run off with Julien Auclair. Sophia's aunt had never forgiven her sister for rejecting a future count and accepting a lowly scholar. But Carmine had.

He'd married another and claimed to have been happy with her. Years later, he'd continued to mourn her death and that of his child, both lost during childbirth. It had been his greatest hope Sophia would produce an heir, but it had not come to pass. Their intimate moments had been few and far between, and while the count had been a considerate lover, he had struggled to do his duty. It had been a great frustration for him but a relief for her. She had been fond of him and appreciated everything he'd done, but her heart had been stolen when she was eight years old, and it had never been returned.

"The rubies, Cara." The oval-shaped pendant, framed with a crust of diamonds, rested comfortably on the rise of Sophia's breasts. Carmine had always had exquisite taste in jewelry. The jeweled buttons on her gloves matched the necklace, as did the embroidery on her sash and slippers.

"Magnificent," Cara said, handing Sophia her reticule. "I have put your spectacles—"

"*Sì, sì,*" Sophia said, waving Cara away. She despised her glasses. They made her feel old. She refused to be seen in them, but she'd missed several opportunities to read what may have been important information. So now she carried them with her in case the need should arise again. She would not let her pride stand in the way of her work. "I have kept Monsieur waiting long enough, no?"

Cara laughed along with Sophia and opened the door. Sophia strolled through her private sitting room, the drawing room, and out into the hall. Below, Gaston paced the front hall, Raimondo standing nearby with arms crossed, watching him. She might have guffawed at the scene, but Gaston spotted her and abruptly stopped his impatient patrol. The look on his face sent a shiver through her, and her body sparked fire, heat pooling in areas she usually disregarded.

She raised her chin and slowly descended the stairs, knowing the effect it would have on Gaston but also to be cautious, as she might trip—such was the distractedness of her physical reaction to his gaze. When she reached the landing, Gaston took her hand and bowed elegantly over it.

He looked at her through those thick, long lashes. "I am not worthy of your beauty," he said gruffly.

Worthy? Her beauty was irrelevant. And, despite her body's response, a question remained to be answered. Was Gaston worthy of her heart?

CHAPTER THIRTY

*Venus in her shell was never so lovely, and Diana in the forest
never so graceful as my Lady.*

—Edmond Rostand, *Cyrano de Bergerac*

GASTON WAS UNCOMFORTABLE. *Bordel de merde!* Sophie stirred his loins like no one else. His body had risen to the occasion when she'd floated slowly down the stairs, a goddess in red. A voluptuous Venus. He could have taken her right there if she'd been willing. And perhaps if Raimondo weren't standing there like a centurion guarding his empress.

Sophie chattered gaily while Gaston shifted on the seat, trying to readjust. Yes, he had risen at the sight of her and remained hard as they slowed in front of the Thornwoods. He should alight and assist Lady Thornwood, but he could not without drawing attention to himself, so he shifted to the far side.

"*Bella!*" Sophie turned and rose a little off her seat, kissing Lady Thornwood's cheeks. Her delicious derriere was on display for Gaston before she pivoted and sat gracefully beside him, her thigh pressed along his. She looked at him coyly.

"*Ma petite belette,*" he said under his breath. She knew exactly what she was doing to him.

"I do hope you mean minx, not weasel," Sophie said, her musical laughter filling the carriage.

"And what is so funny?" Lady Thornwood asked.

"I was correcting Gaston's choice of words. Language is so…" She hesitated, glancing slyly at him before finishing. "…hard."

Lady Thornwood pressed her lips together, fighting a smile, and Lord Thornwood glanced at him. Gaston sensed commiseration in his look. Sophie, of course, laughed again, entirely too pleased with herself. The heat rose from Gaston's crotch to his face. At least the physical strain was lessening.

The moment passed, and they talked pleasantries until the carriage once again stopped.

"Walford. Catherine." Lord Thornwood greeted each of them, assisting them into the carriage. They all snugged together, saying their hellos to one another and falling into easy conversation as the carriage careened through the streets.

Wedged against the far side of the carriage, with the ladies sitting between him and the men, Gaston had little to contribute. They talked of the Walfords' new baby and of nurseries, planning a shopping expedition for the following week. He studied Sophie. She was not simply animated; she was happy. Her ease with these people was not faked. She genuinely enjoyed their company. Why did she hide her roots? His role in her life?

The carriage jolted to a stop. The seductress now gone, Sophie clapped like the small girl he'd once known. "We're here."

It made Gaston smile to see her so full of light and joy. The doors on both sides of the carriage were opened, and he slid off his seat and exited, then assisted Sophie. She looked around the busy street before grinning at him. "Joie de vivre, no?"

It was hard to argue. It was early evening, when day greeted night, and the mix was intoxicating. Bow Street was alive with carriages and vendors. Orange sellers and Punch and Judy toy makers called out their wares while well-dressed crowds buzzed as they gathered beneath the portico and lined up along the building, waiting for entrance.

Gaston had lived in the shadows for too many years, neither part of one place nor another. He had spent most of his time in the ports of France, smuggling information in and out, and had become more comfortable on a ship than in a carriage. But his early years came back at the scene before him, and Sophie's joy for this life rushed through his veins.

"*Oui, c'est magnifique*," he said. Sophie laughed and hooked her arm in his, leading him forward, the others already strolling toward the large, pillared entrance.

"I adore the theater," she said as they mounted the steps and waited with the crowd.

"You always have enjoyed a good performance."

Sophie scowled at him, and he raised a hand. He had not meant anything by his words, yet she took offense.

"Sophie, that is not what I—"

"Sophia," she said and turned her attention forward as the crowd moved.

"Sophia," he said, not wanting to lose the amiable mood they had been sharing. "I meant only as a child, you'd enjoyed such things tremendously."

"*Sì*," she said, returning her attention to him. "I did. You did too, no?"

"Very much," he agreed, relieved she had returned to her earlier disposition.

They climbed the grand staircase, and Lady Walford paused and turned around.

"If we have more events like these, my body will soon forget it had a child. Who would have thought I'd get more exercise in the city than in the country?"

"And when your body forgets you had a child, in will sneak another one," Sophie said jokingly, and Lady Walford turned around and beamed at her husband.

Lord Thornwood had secured their tickets that morning. He handed them over to a money taker, and they proceeded through a saloon to their private box. The Theatre Royal was a newer building, the previous one having burned to the ground a few years before, and no coin had been spared in its design. At a quick glance around the space, Gaston estimated it would accommodate a few thousand, and if the crowds pushing through onto the floor below were any indication, he was going to find out if his estimate was close.

"And what are we seeing this evening?" Lady Walford asked, shrugging apologetically at Lady Woodfield's surprised look. "I'm so busy with Daniel I've not read the papers."

"Of course," Lady Woodfield said. "I sometimes forget what life with a newborn is like."

"Your pack of wild boys has erased the memory," Sophie said, and the ladies all laughed.

As they discussed the evening program, Gaston, again, could not help but notice the familiar ease among Sophie's friends. He both envied their camaraderie and was grateful she had built a life here. He was weary of being a nomad. Could he find a life here too? With Sophie?

"It is a comedy. *Education.* Five acts," Sophie said, settling back against her seat as a few stray notes floated from the orchestra pit.

Gaston relaxed back too. He casually set his hand within reach and was rewarded with the warmth of hers in it. A comedy. Good. For they'd both had enough tragedy to last a lifetime.

CHAPTER THIRTY-ONE

I hear rushing of muskets, and bright'ning of swords; and visages, redd'ning with war.

—William Blake, "The French Revolution"

SOPHIA HAD DIFFICULTY concentrating on the play. She was entirely aware she had ignited Gaston's desire. Unfortunately, she'd also managed to light her own, and his thumb gently circling the palm of her hand was doing nothing to dampen it. Memories of holding hands, of kissing, of making love swirled in her mind, and it was difficult to concentrate.

She tried to focus on the actors. It distracted her during the sillier moments, but the moralist, Damper, demonstrated such disdain for the intelligence of women it got under her skin. Whenever he spoke at length, she looked around the theater at the huge chandeliers, the ornate sconces, the heavy drapery, anything dull enough to quell the passion burning for the man beside her.

By act III, Sophia had gathered her wits. It helped she and Gaston were no longer physically connected. When the actor, Mr. Young, walked onstage and revealed himself as a Frenchman, the other actor posited he might be a spy. Sophia smiled. At last, the play was getting interesting.

Oh, my beloved country! Degraded as thou art, still art thou mine, and with my latest breath will I assert thee! Sir, I was shipwrecked on your coast, and the small remains of a princely fortune, which I had preserved from revolutionary destruction, was buried in the waters.

Sophia would cheer for the Frenchman's speech, for everything she did, she did for the country she'd used to know. But the revolution and lost fortunes struck a little too close to home. When the man declared he was there to seek a lost daughter, her heart rate picked up. The scene shifted, and the dialogue numbed her once again. But when the Frenchman was revealed to be Count Villars, she once again became more alert, waiting for the reveal to the daughter, who must be Miss Bolton, the actress playing Rosine.

The sounds of a harp drifted softly in the background, and Rosine entered the stage. While the audience tittered when Rosine was asked about the doleful ditty she was twanging, Sophia shifted forward on her seat, waiting to hear what the lost daughter had to say.

A plaintive native melody—'twas written by my father; and while I sing it memory recalls those happy hours when my beloved parents listened to the strain, and fills my heart with so sweet a melancholy that joy itself might envy.

Sophia found herself on the verge of tears. Not only had Sophia's mother had a beautiful voice, she'd also played the harp, and the magical sound of the one in the play swept Sophia with melancholy. Gaston clasped her hand and gave it a squeeze. She could not look at him for fear she would see her memories in his eyes, but she gratefully held on.

The play returned to more frivolous dialogue, but she could not relax. She wanted to yell at them to move quickly to the reuniting of the father and daughter, for if it was a comedy, surely there was a happy ending?

Finally, in act V, a scene opened with Count Villars alone onstage. It was barren except for a chair and a bench. Sophia's tension mounted, certain this was the moment. When the harp sounded again and, offstage, Rosine sang a wistful song, she gripped Gaston's hand tightly.

Count Villars heard Rosine, his face pained with longing before he began shouting.

Those words, that voice—it is—it is my child! Rosine, thy father calls!

Rosine shrieked in response, and Sophia bit her lip to stop from screaming too. Tears burned her eyes as Rosine flew onto the stage and rushed into her father's arms.

My child!

My father!

Stand off, and let me gaze on thee, image of thy mother!

Sophia could take no more. She, who rarely cried, was about to make a fool of herself and weep like a small child. "Gaston," she whispered and knew by the look on his face he understood. He assisted her to her feet, and she heard the low mumble of his voice as she strode through the box and into the anteroom. She waved away a footman as Gaston stepped beside her, and signaled the footman to return, giving him direction to get her carriage.

She began to shake, and Gaston put his arm around her waist and guided her to a set of nearby stairs. She was glad not to have to use the grand staircase, where too many people could be lingering. Gaston rubbed her arm as they waited, but her trembling did not subside. She wanted to weep. She wanted to run screaming through the streets. She wanted to strike Gaston for exhuming the past, and she wanted him to hold her and make it all go away.

Was there to be no escape from her memories anymore?

CHAPTER THIRTY-TWO

Alas! I do not know anymore how to flee like before;
I feel my soul is joined to yours.

—Marceline Desbordes-Valmore, "Evening"

GASTON KNEW EXACTLY where Sophie's mind had gone, but he was shocked at how severe her reaction had been. Sophie was always larger than life in everything she did, and he was well aware her emotions were no different. But he'd not seen her lose control except once. A day etched in their lives, never to be erased.

Raimondo jumped from the carriage. While he scowled at Gaston, he was pure solicitousness with Sophie. He grumbled quietly in her ear as he assisted her into the carriage. While Gaston could not hear their words, he did not miss the squeeze she gave Raimondo's arm. It seemed she was able to calm the animal, as Raimondo looked to Gaston with more concern than anger.

Gaston crawled onto the seat beside her, and Raimondo closed the door. "Sophie?" He was uncertain what to say, how to comfort her.

"Not now." She laid her head against his arm, and he readjusted so her cheek pressed against his chest and his arm now held her firmly in place as the carriage careered its way through the streets. With no stops along the way, it was not long before they were back at her townhome.

Raimondo opened the door and assisted Sophie out, still holding her arm as Gaston alighted.

"I told your friends the carriage would return for them," Gaston said, directing that information at Raimondo as well as Sophie.

Sophie's eyes glazed, and she nodded, holding out her hand. Gaston did not hesitate. He took it in his and wrapped his free arm around her waist, guiding her up the stairs without a glance at Raimondo. He was confident the man would inform her coachman.

A footman opened the door, and Harris came hurriedly from belowstairs. Their arrival was unexpectedly early. Harris quickly assessed the mood and stepped aside, nodding his good evening instead of speaking. Gaston held Sophie, and they climbed together to the first level. She paused and took a deep breath, freed her hand, and pushed his arm from her waist.

"*Viens*," she said and walked away from him.

Gaston was a mess of emotions himself, not the least of which was the desire that, at all times, burned beneath the surface of his skin and his every thought. He was not about to decline an invitation to follow her, even if it might not be appropriate considering her state of mind. He assumed she'd pause in the drawing room in which they had spent the night, but she did not. She moved through a smaller sitting room and into her boudoir.

Her maid was dozing by the empty grate. Sophie walked to her and gently shook her shoulder.

"Cara, *parti…per favore*."

The elderly woman jumped to her feet, ready to obey. She hesitated and glanced at Gaston before returning her gaze back to Sophie. "*Stai bene?*"

Sophie's nose twitched, and she clamped her mouth closed, the tension clear in her jaw. Gaston knew she was anything but okay, and her maid did not believe Sophie's assurances any more than he did. The woman had the audacity to look at him with warning as she exited. He should have been angry, but he lauded her loyalty to Sophie.

"Gaston," Sophie said on a whisper, stepping closer and cupping his cheeks before pulling his face down to hers.

Although he knew he should, he did not resist the invitation. He kissed her soft lips gently, but she was having none of that. She opened his mouth with her tongue and slowly, methodically tasted him as he relished the flavor of her. In moments, the tender exploration turned into full-on warfare, and Sophie took siege of his mouth until they both took a step back, panting and staring at each other. Her eyes were still glazed, but he could see the need in them. The desire.

"Gaston," she said again and yanked at her sash, undoing its fastening. He watched, mesmerized, as she pulled her dress over her head, tossing it to the side. Her stays accentuated her shape, and her delicate chemise barely hid her voluptuous body. He shifted uncomfortably but did not take his eyes off her. One at a time, she pulled the pins from her hair, and his *membre* rose higher as each lock fell. She set the pins on the pool of scarlet cloth on the floor and held out her hand.

"Sophie?" His body screamed for her, but he was unsure. Did she truly want this?

She turned and walked away, her derriere sashaying enticingly. Her chemise left little to the imagination, and he grew impossibly hard. He growled, part frustration, part confusion, and stalked her to the bed after she stretched out upon it invitingly.

He stopped and stared, drinking in her beauty, her sensuality, her Sophie-ness. "*Mon Dieu*, you make me ache."

She ran her hand slowly down her neck, between her breasts, and along her stomach, pausing shy of where he'd like to be. "Come, *mon amour*, let me ease your ache."

Gaston need not be asked twice. He tossed his overcoat aside and fell upon her, her soft flesh the sweetest bed he'd known in years. This time, it was he who laid siege, taking her tongue into his mouth, exploring the dark corners of deliciousness that was Sophie. She moaned, and he abandoned her mouth, smelling her sweet scent as he kissed his way toward her breasts.

He pulled back and tugged at the ribbons on her stays. She watched him, her sensuality and vulnerability clear in her eyes. He was awed by her trust in him, by this gift she was offering. He yanked the ribbon free, and the garment fell to the sides, her breasts falling free. He groaned, rubbing himself against her as he leaned in for a taste.

His hands caressed her as his mouth suckled. He was mad with desire, his years of dreaming coming to life beneath his hands. She arched against him, and he knew he could wait no longer. He rose to disrobe and froze. Her dark eyes were watery pools, and the pain in them impossible to ignore. Tears stung his own eyes as he lowered himself and pressed his forehead against hers.

But Sophie was not deterred. She rolled her head side to side and ripped at his jacket. "Gaston, please. *S'il te plaît.*"

His heart broke at her plaintive appeal, but in her plea he found his truth. He could not satisfy his body this night at her expense. For she was not giving it freely. She was using hers to run from the pain.

"*Non. Pas ce soir.*" It could not be this night, but he would continue to hold hope for the future.

Gaston eased off Sophie and lay on his back, his labored breathing slowly abating and, with it, the sound of her quiet crying becoming more apparent. He edged onto his side, watching her. Tears streamed down her cheeks as she stared at the ceiling.

"*Mon petit chou,*" he said, stroking her cheek. She rolled into him, and he held her as her quiet tears turned into a torrent of sobbing.

He was aware of her soft breasts against his chest, of the curves of her hips, of the scent of her hair, but they did not distract him from recognizing the rightness of having sought her out. If Sophie did not need him—if, in the end, she turned from him—he had this moment. A purge. Perhaps an acceptance of all that had happened. For sure, a cleansing. She had run from her past for too long. If his only role was to help her face it and find peace, he would die a happy man.

Chapter Thirty-Three

And ask ye why these sad tears stream?
Why these wan eyes are dim with weeping?
I had a dream—a lovely dream,
Of her that in the grave is sleeping.

—Alfred Lord Tennyson,
"And Ask Ye Why These Sad Tears Stream?"

Sophia had woven her life into a seamless shape, no beginnings, no endings, simply the present. Now it was coming unraveled. She was coming unraveled. She could make no sense of these intense emotions brewing constantly beneath the surface, bubbling and exploding at the mere suggestion of the past.

She curled into Gaston, his gentle strokes and steady heartbeat eventually calming the storm inside her. She felt no shame in her behavior, but she did not understand it. Despite what she'd led society to suspect, she'd not lain with anyone since Carmine. And she would have given her all to Gaston, although now that sanity was returning, she was glad he'd stopped her. It was not how she wanted to entice Gaston back into her bed.

"Do you want to talk?" Gaston pulled a strand of hair from her face and lifted his head slightly so he could see her better. "Sophie? *Est-ce que tu vas bien?*"

Was she all right? She wasn't sure. A numbness was stealing

in and taking the place of all emotion. She shrugged a shoulder, and Gaston rubbed it, sighing.

"You must talk about it." He kissed the top of her head. "You have suffered great loss, *ma chérie*. You thought to escape it, but it has followed you, *non?*"

Was that what she'd been doing? Running from her past? But no, she was seeking revenge in the only way open to her. In passing on information, she was facing it, was she not? It wasn't a question she could ask Gaston.

"It was the Frenchman…the daughter…her mother forever lost to both of them." Her eyes burned, but she did not have the urge to cry. She was certain she had no tears left.

"*Oui.* I know," he said, running a soothing hand over her head.

Gaston had been there. Had he not, Sophia would likely not have survived. He had refused to run with his father, to leave France, had refused to leave Sophia. So he'd moved in with her family in their modest home in Paris. He was sixteen, and she was thirteen. He'd been with them for close to a year when… Her heart beat fiercely, but she forced herself to follow the trail of thought. She couldn't remember where he'd gone that day, nor why she and her mother had been in the streets, but the memory of what had happened had not dulled with time.

She and her mother had been almost safely back home when the noise had grown and a large group of people had come around the corner. They'd been a motley crew. Loud—pitchforks, knives, and sticks raised high—they'd dragged along well-dressed women, one shrieking, her fear piercing the shouting. Sophia's mother had pushed her into the side lane leading to the back of their home, but it had been too late. They'd been spotted.

Her mother had yelled at her to run, but she could not. She'd stood rooted to the spot. The mob had descended like ants on an apple. The rest was a blur of images. An arm raised. Her sweet *maman*'s terrified expression as she disappeared beneath them. A man spotting Sophia. His limping gait as he walked slowly toward her, grinning, his front teeth missing. She'd closed her eyes as he'd grabbed the front of her dress, the rending unheard in the deafening noise from the street. The man curled in a ball on the ground, holding his stomach, blood oozing through his fingers. Gaston pulling her through the alley.

"I still dream of her," Sophia whispered. "Of her beauty. Her kindness. Of the warmth of her hug."

"I am sorry, *mon amour*. If I'd been minutes earlier…"

"No," she said, lifting her head. His dark eyes were pools of sorrow. She'd not considered his pain, his guilt. "No, Gaston. If you had tried to intervene…" She paused, pushing her overwhelming emotions back into the corner. "I would not have you either. Nothing could have been done."

She rested her head back on his chest and closed her eyes, but the scenes played out behind her lids, and she could not bear it. She opened them again, staring across the room at the empty grate. "I have always dreamed Papa would suddenly appear like the Frenchman on the stage. That he would one day be returned to me. It hurt to see it play out." She blinked, trying to relieve the stinging in her eyes. "It is a foolish dream."

"Dreams are not foolish, Sophie. Without them, we have nothing." He stroked her hair. "Dreams of you kept me going in the early years."

Sophia did not miss the implication. She shifted and sat up, turning to look him in the eyes. "And in the later years?"

Gaston held her gaze for a moment before answering. "Dreams and anger, I suppose. I wanted to hurt you, as you'd hurt me."

"Wanted?"

Gaston caressed the side of her face. "Wanted to, yes. Now all I want is you. Back in my arms. Back in my life." He hesitated, and she pressed her cheek into the warmth of his palm. "Perhaps I dream too big?"

Sophia did not answer him, for she did not know herself. She turned her face into his hand and kissed it before pulling back. "Stay with me tonight?" She ran a finger down his chest. "We can make love and forget everything."

He did not appear surprised by her request and seemed to consider it but shook his head.

"You do not want me."

"Oh, Sophie, I have never wanted you more." He leaned in and kissed her nose, then rested his forehead on hers. "But not like this. When we make love, it will be to remember who we were. We will let those two young lovers share the moment with us. It will not be to forget."

Sophia sucked in her lips, fighting a resurgence of emotions. She did not want to be alone, but she would not beg him to stay.

Gaston shifted off the bed and removed his jacket, walked over to a chair, and hung it carefully over it. He tugged at his cravat, loosening it before unbuttoning his waistcoat. She watched him undress until he was wearing only his drawers, the remainder of his clothing neatly piled over the back of the chair.

He walked toward her, and his desire was evident.

"No need to look at me like that. I have not changed my mind, Sophie, despite what my body wants." He perched on the end of the bed and ran his hand over his face before swinging his legs onto the mattress and rolling onto his side. "Come, *mon amour*, curl in. Let me hold you while you dream new dreams."

She did as commanded, and his heat enveloped her. The steady rise and fall of his chest against her back and his arm draped lightly over her waist were not titillating. Instead, they were calming. The weight of fatigue overwhelmed her, and she began to fade into the gloaming between wake and sleep.

"*Je t'aime.*"

Sophia didn't know if Gaston had truly said he loved her or if she was already dreaming new dreams. "My Gaston," she said on a sigh before letting go and drifting off to sleep.

CHAPTER THIRTY-FOUR

Give sorrow words: the grief that does not speak
Whispers the o'er-wrought heart and bids it break.

—William Shakespeare, *Macbeth*

"I T IS MY day of rest, Monsieur Armand," said Liverpool from his horse.

"A few minutes of your time, *s'il vous plaît,*" Gaston said.

Liverpool dismissed his riding mate and dismounted. "Walk with me into the grove. It would not help your mission to be seen with me."

There was nobody else around; otherwise, Gaston would never have considered approaching the prime minister. He'd untangled himself from the sheets carefully and slipped out, leaving Sophie fast asleep. He knew well the prime minister's routines and had been certain he would find him in the park.

"Have you come with news of the traitor?" Liverpool asked without glancing at Gaston.

"Not yet, but I will." Gaston said it with a confidence he did not feel. He'd been far more distracted by Sophie than he should have allowed himself to be.

"If you've no news, why are you here waylaying me on my morning ride?"

"I wish to ask a small favor." Gaston knew he was pushing his luck with Liverpool, but never venture, never gain. And it was for Sophie. He'd do whatever was in his power to help her find peace.

Liverpool paused and turned to Gaston, the lead of his horse in one hand. He ran the other hand over his face. "It is far too early in the morning for games. Speak bluntly of what you want."

"I need to find out the fate of a man named Julien Auclair. He was a scholar in Paris. When the directory annulled the elections in ninety-seven, he was banished to Guiana."

"That was sixteen years ago, Monsieur Armand," Liverpool said irritably. "Whyever is it of interest to you now?"

This was the piece he'd hoped to avoid. The prime minister already knew he had designs on Sophie so would not be entirely surprised. Still, he knew Sophie would not be pleased he had revealed a piece of her past, but he could see no way around it. Liverpool was too astute to attempt to mislead him.

"The Countess Tessaro does not know what happened to her father. It haunts her."

Liverpool raised an eyebrow. "Her father? The countess is French?"

"Her mother was Italian," Gaston said, shrugging, as though that undid her French origins.

Liverpool was quiet, studying him for a moment.

Gaston feared he would not agree, and he could not let Sophie down. "I will find your spy, and I will continue working for you afterward, if you find out Auclair's fate."

Liverpool tilted his head slightly, a slight smile breaking his grim facade. "Indeed?"

"On my word," Gaston said.

"I will see what I can do. But sixteen years, Armand. It is a long time."

"*Merci*, Prime Minister. I will owe you a great debt if you can manage it." Gaston put out his hand, and Liverpool shook it.

"Find me the traitor," he said and walked back in the direction from which they'd come.

Gaston stood watching until even the sounds of the horse had faded. He turned and looked at the lake shimmering beyond the tree line. After last night, he knew he must do something to help Sophie put her ghosts to rest. But he'd not meant to sell his soul again. He took off his hat and ran his hand through his hair, tugging at the ends in frustration. He would honor his pledge to Liverpool, even if it was the last thing he wanted to do. If it meant his dreams of returning to a normal life must be put on hold, so be it. Sophie was worth it.

SOPHIA WAS DISAPPOINTED to find Gaston gone from her bed. She bathed and dressed, grateful Cara kept her opinion on his presence to herself. The woman did not always, but perhaps today, she sensed Sophia had enough of her own thinking to sort through.

She'd been convinced Gaston's return had unburied the past, but the problem might come more from her than him. Maybe she had never fully accepted her losses. Never fully grieved. Her father had insisted her mother had died imprisoned, yet she'd been convinced he was sheltering her from the truth of the guillotine. So she'd turned her anger on him, accused him of lying, when instead she should have been weeping for her mother's death.

Gaston had informed her of her father's exile, and Carmine had explained few lived and nobody returned from Guiana. She'd heard nothing from, or about, her dear papa since. Yet, like in the play, she'd held on to the foolish belief he would someday show up. She must accept he was gone. Gaston was right. She'd been running. Well, last night she'd stopped.

Sophia informed Cara she would take coffee in the morning room. She coasted through her rooms and descended the stairs. A cough from the library drew her attention, and she smiled to herself as she approached, her eyes on the dark head leaning back against the chair by the fireplace. "Gaston," she said, unable to suppress the happiness in her voice.

She was rewarded when he jumped to his feet and turned with a smile. He held out his hands, and she walked to him, setting hers in them. He kissed her cheeks before pulling back.

"You look well rested, *ma chérie*."

"I am, thanks to you."

He tugged her close again and this time kissed her lips so softly, so sensually, that her toes curled in her slippers. It was minutes before he pulled away, and she sighed contentedly.

"I thought you'd left," she said, taking his hand and leading him from the library.

"I would not miss seeing your beautiful face," he said, pausing in the doorway and brushing her nose with a quick kiss. "A Madonna of the morning…although"—he ran his tongue along his lips—"perhaps not as chaste as one."

Sophia laughed, joy filling her soul. She did not need to say goodbye to all things from the past. She was decided. She was going to allow Gaston back into her life. More importantly, she was going to let him into her heart.

Later, after they'd enjoyed a *petit déjeuner*, he excused himself to return to his rooms. She sat quietly, soaking in the last rays of morning sunshine and inhaling the perfume of the early-blooming roses. She could not remember the last time she'd been so content.

Harris arrived with a fresh pot of coffee, and she decided to indulge in another cup as well as a biscuit. He poured, set the pot within arm's reach, and gathered the few remaining dishes.

"*Grazie*," Sophia said, taking a sip of the coffee. "*Delizioso*."

"Monsieur Durand left his overcoat in the library. Will he be returning, or shall I have it brought to him?"

They had agreed to see each other tomorrow, after her shopping excursion with Elizabeth and Catherine. He might need it before then. While the weather was lovely, even for May, the late evenings and early mornings could be chilly. "Have someone run it to him."

She gave him the direction, and Harris nodded, seemingly unperturbed that Gaston had spent the night again or that she knew where to send the coat. She idly wondered if he was truly as uncaring as he seemed or if the starchy British uprightness made his collar tighter when she did such things.

Of course, he'd been an equally blank slate when she'd come home a mess last night and Gaston had led her immediately upstairs to her room. Sophia paused for a brief second, picturing it. "Harris?"

Her butler turned at the door. "Yes, my lady?"

"Where did Monsieur leave his coat?"

"In the library, my lady."

She frowned. She knew for certain he'd not removed it before they'd gone upstairs. "The library?"

"He returned through the servants' quarters this morning, and I did not have the opportunity to take it."

The slight blush on Harris's cheeks, as though he'd been accused of neglecting his duties, would have been laughable if it weren't for the fact Gaston had lied. No, he had not lied. But he had omitted the truth. And, as a master of such avoidance herself, she knew it meant he'd been up to something. But what?

She dismissed Harris and grabbed a biscuit. She bit into it, chewing viciously, taking out her frustration on the pastry instead of her servant. Why was it every time she'd decided Gaston belonged back in her life, something happened to belie her faith in him? Could she truly have fallen back in love with a man she could not trust?

CHAPTER THIRTY-FIVE

But all pretences soon fall to the ground like fragile flowers, and nothing counterfeit can be lasting.

—Marcus Tullius Cicero, *De Officiis*

SOPHIA'S FOYER WAS full of flowers. She'd foolishly thought, this time, they must be from Gaston trying to outdo the duke. They were not. The duke had once again sent them and, according to his note, wished to meet with her at her earliest convenience to make amends. Sophia stared at the letter before tossing it to the table. She would not grant the duke his request. How could she? To toy with a man when there was a possibility of a relationship was one thing. To mislead him entirely was another.

Alone in her bed last night, longing for Gaston's arms around her, she'd recognized it was too late to change course. Gaston owned her heart. He always had. Because of the life she lived, she assumed the worst of too many people, saw spies in every corner. And she was doing it with Gaston. The man could have gone for an early-morning walk. Nothing nefarious in it at all. She would simply ask him this evening, and that would be the end of her concerns.

She'd also been ruminating about England. She no longer had any desire to return to France or to Italy when the war ended.

She had made a life here, found a family in her friends. But she had misled them. Would it matter? Could they forgive her omissions, her half-truths? Should she tell them now and take away Gaston's power over her? Except Gaston was not exerting such power, and she no longer believed there was any possibility he would.

The carriage pulled in front of the Walfords' townhome, and Raimondo helped her out. She'd been restless and was earlier than her appointed time. Catherine's butler let her in and helped her from her cape before escorting her up the stairs to the drawing room.

"I will let Lady Walford know you are waiting."

The door clicked behind the man, and Sophia walked around the room. The house was a rental and did not reflect Catherine at all. It was masculine, dark and austere, whereas Catherine was no such thing. Even during the darkest of days, Catherine had held on to love and hope. Sophia admired her friend's indomitable spirit.

"Sophia." Stratton's deep baritone boomed from the doorway, and Sophia smiled as she turned around. The sight of his cheerful face always lifted her spirits. She adored the father as much as she adored his daughter.

"Stratton." Sophia walked to him and presented her cheeks. "I had forgotten you were still in town."

"More like in the nursery," he said, grinning. "Catherine and Nic are much more comfortable going out if I am around." He leaned in close. "Between you and me, I am determined Daniel's first word will be 'grandpapa,'" he whispered conspiratorially.

Sophia laughed. "*Il mio amico*, even I know that is some time away."

"You can't start too soon. Sit. Catherine will be down shortly. In the meantime, share a drink with me."

Lord Stratton poured them each a cognac and sat beside her on the settee. "You are the only woman I know who has as fine a taste in cognac as I. Have a sip. Nic's partner, Randall, brought a case of it."

Sophia swirled the golden amber in the glass and passed it under her nose. "Oranges? Do I smell oranges?"

"You do indeed. Sip."

The cognac was smooth, and the hint of orange continued to tickle her nose. "I'm not sure I am tasting oranges or if my nose is trying to trick me?"

Stratton laughed. "Me either. But I am enjoying it nonetheless."

"*Sì*, it is *delizioso*."

"Have you heard from my lake houseguest?" she asked, debating talking with Stratton about what weighed so heavily on her mind. He would be discreet, if for no other reason than as a thank-you for keeping his son's secrets.

"Nothing," he said, shifting so he could see her more easily. "But I did not expect to." He tilted his head, looking her in the eyes. "You are not yourself."

"*Non. Oui. Sì*," she said, correcting herself, then sighing heavily. "See, I am not myself, for I do not know who myself is anymore."

Stratton took a sip, his brow furrowing in concern. He said nothing, but his eyes were warm, his stance was relaxed, and he exuded patience. He was no predator waiting to pounce, only a good friend inviting her confidence.

Once Sophia began, she could not stop. She told him almost everything. How her parents had run away together, how much they'd loved each other, how Gaston had become a part of their happy little family. She shared with him the taking of her mother, the frightening trek across France, her father leaving her in *Venezia* with an aunt who detested her. About her mother's death, her father's exile, Gaston's disappearance. She explained why she'd married the count despite loving another. Sophia stopped shy of telling him of her worries about Gaston's current activities. She would address that with Gaston and be done with it. She also did not speak of how she'd come to be in England, as that part had long been shared truthfully. She sat back and blew out a long breath.

"Sophia, I have always known there was more to your story than you'd shared with us. What I don't fully understand is why you have not been candid? Although, I suspect, maybe I do?"

"*Sì*, your suspicions are correct. I am not, as you are, simply a liaison for the Home Office. I work for the war effort. I do not know what is right for my country anymore, but I know it is not a self-appointed man." Her father had supported some of the ideas of the revolutionists, but he'd remained a loyalist. After what had happened to her mother, Sophie despised the revolutionists and could not support their cause or, later, the little emperor bent on destruction.

"No one would begrudge you such thoughts," Stratton said, touching her hand.

"But if it were known I was French, it would not be so easy to gather information. No one would speak openly in the drawing rooms of London to a Frenchwoman. I am more obscure in my politics as I am. And less threatening."

"I see. It makes a certain kind of sense. But no one in this house would question your loyalty."

"I know it now, but I have lied to them for years." Guilt churned uncomfortably in her stomach. "Friendships are destroyed by less things than fraud."

"I think you are not giving them enough credit," Stratton said.

"But I cannot tell them of my work for the Home Office. Not yet. Probably not until the war is over."

"It is my opinion they would support you, regardless of what you do." Stratton squeezed her hand. "But you are right, I suppose. The spying is rather awkward."

"Don't you two look cozy. Sharing deep, dark secrets, are you?"

Sophia and Stratton turned simultaneously.

"What? You two look positively guilty," Catherine said, sailing into the room.

Sophia got to her feet and kissed Catherine's cheeks. "Only your father is guilty," she said. "He is trying to get the baby to call his name out first," she said in a pseudowhisper.

Catherine laughed delightfully and proceeded to regale Sophia with stories of Daniel's exploits. Although Sophia could not comprehend how an infant could be so endlessly fascinating, she was happy for her friend's joy. And for the distraction.

Stratton hugged them both before they left, and all worry slipped from her shoulders. Her secrets were safe with him. She stepped out into the sunlight, feeling lighter than she had in years. Stratton accepted her and was sure the others would too. Gaston was by her side. She was beginning to accept there was light at the end of this long, dark tunnel.

There was work to be done before the war ended, and she would do what she could to see it through. She smiled at Catherine as she climbed into the carriage. But the war effort would wait for another day. Today she was shopping.

CHAPTER THIRTY-SIX

The distinguishing characteristic of the dandy's beauty consists above all in an air of coldness which comes from an unshakeable determination not to be moved.

—Charles Baudelaire, *The Painter of Modern Life*

"I NEVER AGREED to go to Newmarket," Gaston said as they watched the filly go through its paces. He'd nothing better to do until Sophie was available so had agreed to join Bentley again at Tattersall's. Bentley seemed keen to buy a horse, although Gaston wasn't sure why he needed someone by his side to do so. But Bentley was an amiable man, if somewhat frivolous, and he was a friend of Sophie's friends. It could only help to have an ally in her circle.

"You most certainly did. When we were last here."

He mentally reviewed their previous visit to Tattersall's and, unfortunately, did recall Bentley chattering on about something while Gaston was trying to listen to the Duke of Salinger's conversation.

"The others were exceedingly excited and have secured rooms for us all. The Walfords will head back to their estate afterward. Apparently, Lady Walford is running out of enthusiasm for the season. Surprising she was here at all considering how new to motherhood she is. Of course, Walford is more than happy to head back to the country. He was never big on town life. What?" Bentley said, looking at Gaston. "Don't shake your head. It's all set. One week from today."

"I did not… I cannot…" Gaston was not averse to some fun, and he enjoyed a good horse race, but he must focus on his mission for Liverpool.

"Oh, but you must," Bentley said, swiping casually at his cuffs and raising an eyebrow. "Or I will have to tell everyone how you came back to your room a second time in the clothes you had worn the day before."

Anger rose. Quick and fierce, it warred with the wisdom of hitting a lord in the face at such a public venue.

Bentley broke into laughter, and Gaston lost his mental footing.

"I wish you could see your face, Durand." Bentley clapped him on the shoulder. "I tease. I would never. Your business is your business." He turned back to face the horse. "She is a beauty, don't you agree?" He glanced sideways at Gaston. "The horse, not Countess Tessaro. She is beyond beauty. And she will be joining us, I'm sure. She never misses a good party."

Gaston was not used to this strange camaraderie. He'd spent too many years on his own, pretending to be anyone but himself. To be invited into Sophie's private world was equal parts disconcerting and cheering. It seemed a good place to start if he and Sophie were to build a new life together.

"It would seem I have no choice in the matter," Gaston said, and Bentley smiled triumphantly.

"Right. Everyone who is everyone will be there." Bentley turned his attention back to the horses.

Gaston considered the number of people in attendance at such an event. Perhaps Newmarket would prove to be more fertile for information than London. He glanced around at the other spectators, wondering how many were actually interested in horseflesh and how many were there to see and be seen.

He spotted the duke over by the small temple in the middle

of the courtyard. He was in conversation with the same man as last week, and it appeared to be a heated one. The other man shook his head, and the duke's face fired red. Gaston truly could not see what appeal the duke had held for Sophie other than his title. But Sophie was much like her parents in her disregard for such things, so he could not credit the idea that she'd been considering marriage simply to become a duchess. Of course, they had both changed over the years, so he could be wrong.

Bentley turned and followed Gaston's gaze. "It would seem His Grace is not a happy man this day."

"It would seem. I wonder what the countess saw in him?" Gaston voiced his question out loud.

"Saw?" Bentley said and clapped Gaston on the back. "I knew it. Impressive. Well done, Durand."

Gaston felt heat rise in his cheeks. It was not how he meant it, but he did hope his use of the past tense was true.

The duke left his companion and stormed in their direction.

"Your Grace?" Bentley said, stepping into his path.

The duke was plainly in a foul mood, and Gaston was surprised Bentley was foolish enough to block his way. The duke scowled at him, then glared at Gaston, scanning him from head to toe before saying, *"You."* The simple word contained a world of disdain, and Gaston bristled.

"Are you heading to Newmarket for the race next Monday?" Bentley continued, oblivious to the interplay between Gaston and the duke. "We are off, are we not, Monsieur Durand? With Lords Walford and Thornwood."

The duke turned his glare on Bentley.

"And Countess Tessaro, of course," Bentley added.

Gaston watched as the Duke of Salinger tempered his ire and schooled his face before he spoke. "Did the countess inquire if I was attending?"

"I'm certain she would be pleased to see you there," Bentley said smoothly, and Gaston once again had the urge to punch the man.

"I will be going," the duke said and walked away without another glance at Gaston.

Bentley brushed at his cuffs absently. "A bit of a hothead, don't you think?"

"Why would you mention the countess?" Gaston still wanted to hit him.

"A little competition to keep you on your toes." Bentley glanced at him and grinned. "Besides, wagers are being placed at White's on who is going to win her hand at the races. Bets are off if all three of you aren't there."

Gaston was displeased they were in the betting books. Such foolishness to occupy idle minds. His anger slipped away. Bentley was not malicious, simply a man with too much money and time on his hands. A thought struck him. "Who did you bet on?"

"A silly question. You forget I have seen what the others have not." He scanned Gaston from head to toe much more appreciatively than the duke had done. "Two rumpled morning returns. Since the countess has already secured her position in society and has no need of coin, my money's on you."

CHAPTER THIRTY-SEVEN

Good cousin, give me audience for a while.

—Shakespeare, *Henry IV*

"YOU DID NOT!" Elizabeth and Catherine exclaimed in unison, but neither of them looked remotely appalled as they clapped their hands gleefully.

"*Sì, le mie belle*, I did." Sophia could not help but laugh at her friends' reaction.

"And what did he say?" Elizabeth asked.

Sophia shrugged both shoulders. She had sent a note to the duke informing him no amount of flowers could woo her back, as she had her own garden to enjoy and had no need of his. "I do not know. I sent it before I joined you. But it does not matter what he responds. I will not be treated like property by any man."

"And perhaps you now have a different gardener to tend to your flowers?" Elizabeth raised an eyebrow.

"Perhaps," Sophia said, and both Catherine and Elizabeth squealed. A ripple of genuine excitement flowed through Sophia. Sharing with her friends made her tentative decision about Gaston seem less tenuous.

"I never understood what you saw in the duke anyway." Catherine sat back as the carriage rocked. "I mean, if he was a royal duke, there might be some fun in it. But even then, he is excessively condescending."

"And dull," added Elizabeth.

"Well, he does have a big…" Sophia deliberately paused and raised both eyebrows, and her friends' eyes grew round. "…estate," she finished. They laughed so much they were wiping at their eyes when Raimondo opened the carriage door.

They spent a good hour in the small shop, picking out ribbons, feathers, and small odds and sods to embellish bonnets and outfits. Catherine was returning to the countryside soon and wanted to update some of her items as well as have something to do while the baby slept.

"I'm so happy you will join us in Newmarket before we return to Woodfield," Catherine said as they stepped back outside.

"How could I deny you anything?" Sophia watched Raimondo put the packages on the carriage.

"I'm sure your easy acquiescence had nothing to do with the fact Monsieur Durand has already agreed to join us all." Elizabeth bumped her hip against Sophia playfully.

"You are devilish conspirators," Sophia said and smiled.

"Oh, we are near Madame Moreau's. Can we stop by and see if she has a minute to spare? I seem to need a few gowns with a bit more room here." Catherine splayed a hand across her bosom.

"Of course," Sophia said, but her mind scattered. How could she have forgotten about Jocelyne? "Raimondo, we are to the modiste."

She knew he would inform Charles and follow discreetly behind. Raimondo always insisted on being around, even when there was no need. A simple footman could be an escort, but Raimondo would have none of it. It was both irritatingly overprotective and comforting. Elizabeth and Catherine chatted happily as they strolled the block and a half to Jocelyne's shop, and Sophia debated how she was going to tell Jocelyne about Gaston's surprising resurrection.

The bell tinkled when they entered. They were greeted by a young maid and seated in the small salon. Jocelyne, tall and elegant, looking more like Gaston's sister than his cousin, joined them a few minutes later.

"*C'est un plaisir*, my ladies." She smiled at Catherine and Elizabeth and shot a quick questioning glance at Sophia. "But I am afraid I am in the middle of a fitting…"

"Oh, I'm sorry," Catherine said, getting to her feet. "It is my fault we arrived unannounced."

"Sit, *bella*." Sophia turned to Jocelyne. "It is a simple request." Her tone left no room for argument. It was not like Jocelyne to turn her away, and today it would not do at all. She needed to find a moment to talk with Jocelyne privately.

The quick flare of Jocelyne's nostrils was the only sign she was not pleased with the interruption or the command. She smiled at Catherine. "*Non, non*, I am happy you have come once again. What is it you need?"

"We are leaving London soon, and since the baby, I am finding my dresses a little snug, here." Catherine drew a line across her breasts with a finger. "I would like one or two new ones."

"Ah, I see. I will send Grace in to measure, and you will tell Lucia what fabric you like, *oui*?"

"Wonderful," Catherine said. "I truly appreciate it."

"*Pas de problème*," Jocelyne said, then turned and left the room without another glance at Sophia.

"It is lovely of Madame Moreau to take this on unexpectedly," Catherine said.

While Elizabeth agreed with Catherine, Sophia was not so impressed. Jocelyne owed her shop and standing in society to Sophia, and Sophia asked for little in return. She should have been quickly accommodating. Sophia smiled at her friends, hiding her irritation. Grace entered and began her measurements, while Elizabeth shuffled through fashion plates. Sophia took the opportunity to slip out.

She tapped lightly on the door of the other salon. Jocelyne opened it a fraction and frowned at Sophia.

"*Pas maintenant*," Jocelyne whispered.

"*Oui*, now."

"I am working." Jocelyne glanced over her shoulder. Sophia could hear a woman's voice followed by another woman's laugh but could not see who they were. "*Je travaille*," Jocelyne repeated slowly and emphatically in French, and Sophia stepped back as she registered Jocelyne's meaning.

"What time do you finish?" Sophia asked, all annoyance instantly dissipating. Like Sophia, Jocelyne was a good listener. She passed on any information that might help their cause on the continent. It was surprising how much women knew and how freely they talked as they sipped sherry and chose gowns.

"Today I can close at six o'clock."

"I will return. We must talk." Sophia did not wait for Jocelyne's answer. She turned and strolled back into the small salon. Her friends looked at her questioningly.

"I tried to find some fabric for a new dress, but there is too much in the back room, and I am too tired." She sighed melodramatically and sat on the settee beside Elizabeth. "Some lemonade, please," she said to Grace as she finished scratching down measurements.

Sophia looked forward to the evening. An unexpected reunion and, with a little luck, some much-needed information. She had been lax lately, and it would be rewarding to have a contribution for the effort. She looked at her friends, so at ease and without worry, without the knowledge she had misled them. She longed to end her facade. The sooner this war ended, the better for everyone. Including her.

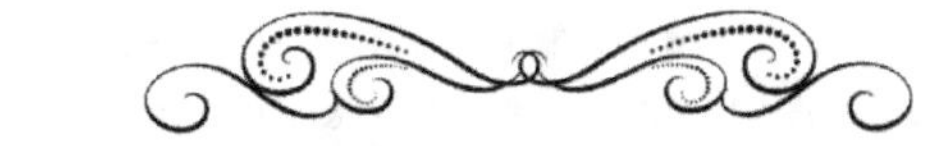

CHAPTER THIRTY-EIGHT

Is she kind as she is fair?
For beauty lives with kindness.

—Shakespeare, *The Two Gentlemen of Verona*

"I DO NOT understand your secrecy, but I sense your excitement. And it is titillating." Gaston sat on the opposite bench and watched Sophia from under his lashes, a smile dancing at the corner of his lips. He had arrived promptly at six, and Sophia had been waiting for him in the entrance. With him resplendent in a navy-blue jacket with an intricately embroidered waistcoat, buff breeches, and a crisp cravat highlighting his rich skin, she could have devoured him on the spot. She still could.

"You look ravishing, by the way," Gaston added. "Although I suspect you are more than aware of it and have heard many wax eloquently about your beauty over the years."

Sophia waved his comment away. "Flattery easily falls from the lips of people who want something." She tilted her head, contemplating him. "What is it you want, Gaston?"

He didn't answer her right away. The clopping of the horses, the rumble of the wheels, and the myriad of muffled sounds from the street filled the carriage as he studied her. Her skin prickled in response as his gaze softened and grew appreciative.

"You, Sophie. I want you."

Sophia could not hold back her smile. It was what she wanted to hear.

"And you, Sophie. What is it you want?"

The carriage rattled to a stop, saving her from answering. She did not question what she wanted, but she was unsure as to whether to hand him the power such knowledge would bring. Raimondo swung open the door, and Gaston leaped out, preempting Raimondo from assisting her from the carriage. Sophia laughed at the two of them, at Gaston's triumphant expression and Raimondo's disgruntled one.

Gaston stared at the sign. "Madame Moreau's. A modiste?"

"*Oui*," she said, renewed excitement percolating through her veins.

"Do I get the pleasure of watching a fitting?" He wiggled his eyebrows lasciviously, and Sophia laughed.

"I promise the evening will be filled with unexpected delights," she said and tapped on the locked door.

Grace opened it and smiled apologetically. "Madame Moreau remains with her last client. She begs your patience and asks if you'll wait in the small salon."

"*Non*," Sophia said. "We will wait in her private rooms."

The girl nodded, her expression unchanging, then turned and led them to the back warehouse, past bolts of fabric to where two seamstresses continued to work side by side, an oil lantern lighting the small corner. Both women looked up, then jumped to their feet.

"My lady," they said in unison.

"Sit, sit," Sophia said, and the women obediently dropped back onto their chairs. "Let me see." She held out her hand and took the dress, tracing the delicate pearls being sewn into the lace edging. "Your work is exquisite, Lucia, but it is hard in this light, no?"

Lucia thanked Sophia for the praise but did not comment on the lighting.

"Grace, two more lanterns here." Sophia turned her attention back to the women. "If it is not enough, get more. I will have some delivered tomorrow if need be. Do not strain your eyes. They are your windows to the world, no?"

Sophia walked past them, toward the stairs. Sensing Gaston was not behind her, she turned around. He was standing where she'd left him, watching her. "*Allez*," she said, and mounted the steps without turning to see if he'd obeyed her command to come.

Like many shopkeepers, Jocelyne lived in her building. Her rooms were not spacious, but they were well appointed. Sophia had insisted she have any luxury she required, and Jocelyne had taken full advantage of it. Sophia entered the door to the left and untied her cape, dropping it over a chair before taking a seat. Gaston remained in the doorway.

"*Quoi?*"

"What?" Gaston repeated. "Who was that person I saw downstairs, concerned about workers' lighting in a stranger's shop?"

"Do you think I do not care for others?" she asked, vexed he thought so little of her.

"Sophie did," he said quietly. "I was not sure about Sophia. She seemed a little more demanding. Definitely more commanding." He took a step into the room and paused, a slow smile spreading on his face. "I am happy to see the bighearted Sophie, who once led a young boy away from the rabble, is still there."

Sophia had forgotten what it was like to have someone in her life who truly knew her. All of her. But she could not let the emotions rolling through her overwhelm her. Not now. She wanted to enjoy her surprise fully. She gave a dismissive shrug. "I am merely sensitive to people's sight. My eyes are growing old before their time."

Gaston's smile dropped, his eyes dark with concern as he grabbed her shoulders gently. "Sophie, you are going blind?"

"What? *Non.*" Her heart opened even more at his worry. "But I need to wear glasses to read. Wretched things. I'd not wish them on anyone."

Gaston burst into laughter and pulled her close, kissing the top of her head. "Oh, Sophie, how I've missed you."

"Gaston?"

They both swung around at the sound of his name.

Jocelyne stood in the doorway, the color washed from her face. "Gaston," she repeated blankly. "Is it you?"

CHAPTER THIRTY-NINE

Old faces glimmer'd thro' the doors,
Old footsteps trod the upper floors,
Old voices call'd her from without.

—Alfred Lord Tennyson, "Mariana"

GASTON WAS SURELY looking at a ghost. Jocelyne's home had been set on fire, and all within it had perished. He had verified the information himself, visited the shell that remained, sifting through the ashes for some memento of a family he'd loved. He'd been wild with fury. The mob had robbed them of their lives even though they'd been supporters of the revolution. No one had been safe in those dark days.

"Jocelyne," he whispered, the whooshing in his head settling as her eyes grew bigger and color returned to her face. "*Viens ici, cousine.*" She seemed rooted to the spot, so he held out his arms to reinforce his invitation. "*Viens,*" he repeated.

Jocelyne walked slowly toward him, glancing quickly past his shoulder at Sophie, then back at him. He stayed still as she touched his arm, his hair, his cheek, a mix of fear and wonder in her eyes.

"It *is* you," she said gruffly in French.

"*Oui, Jocelyne. C'est moi.*"

He pulled her close and hugged her, memories of yesteryear

chasing through his mind. They were the same age, the only children of sisters, and had their fathers agreed on politics, they might have been as inseparable as he and Sophie had been. But the men had been stubborn in their ways and had refused to come together, even for the sake of family. Still, their mothers had managed to secretly see each other when they could, and they had been as close as could be under the circumstances.

She sobbed quietly in his arms, and he continued to hold her. Sophie stepped from behind him into his sight line. Her smile was tentative, as though she was not sure the surprise had been a good one. It had been a shocking one, but to know Jocelyne lived was an incredible discovery. He mouthed, *"Merci,"* and her smile grew.

When Jocelyne calmed, she stepped back, wiping at her eyes. "How?" she asked, looking from him to Sophie and back again. "How can this possibly be?"

"Let us sit," Sophie said, taking the lead and settling on a chair, leaving the small sofa for Gaston and Jocelyne.

"I thought you were lost to me," Jocelyne said, her eyes watering with fresh tears.

Gaston took her hand in his. "And I thought the same of you, cousin. Tell me how you have come to be a modiste in London."

"Non, you first. I would know how you have come to be sitting in my drawing room." Jocelyne looked at Sophie. "How long have you known?"

There was fire in her eyes, and Gaston did not want to see it ignite into unnecessary words, so he interrupted and told her his tale, leaving out the same parts he'd left out for Sophie. He glanced at Sophie. He didn't know where she stood anymore. Her father had been in some agreement with the revolutionists' ideas, but look where it had gotten his wife. It must surely have tainted Sophie's view of them. And she knew Gaston had joined *les Bourbons.* But it was so many years ago. Where did her loyalty lie now? Or had she washed her hands of it all? Regardless, he had learned the hard way the fewer people who knew his true business, the better.

He turned his attention back to Jocelyne. "And you, cousin. What happened? I saw your home."

"I was not there." Her eyes misted, and she shook her head slowly back and forth. "I had snuck out to see Henri. You know *Maman* had forbidden me to see him."

Gaston remembered Henri as an overbearing donkey, braying about his achievements at every opportunity, but he also remembered Jocelyne was quite taken with him.

"They must have come shortly after I left, for I was only gone for a few hours and the fire was well advanced along the row of houses."

Gaston touched her hand, knowing how horrific the moment of discovery must have been. "I saw it when I returned," he said quietly. "There was nothing left."

"*Oui.* Nothing. I fled back to Henri, but he wanted nothing to do with it. Said it was Papa's own fault, that he'd fed the dog that bit him. I did not know what to do. I could not find you. I was lost. I had nobody." She pressed her lips together, and he squeezed her hand.

"*Je suis désolé.* So truly sorry. I was helping Sophie and her father to the outskirts of Paris. I assumed you would be safe, since your father was—"

"A supporter. I know," Jocelyne said, finishing for him. "I did not know you returned to Paris, *mon cousin.* I wish I had. Until Sophie told me of your visit to *Venise*, I assumed you, too, had been taken by the rioters. I was filled with rage. I still do not understand why they killed *Maman* and Papa."

"Sometimes there are no answers, no explanations. An angry mob does not act with a single rational mind. The good get swept up with the bad. It is unpredictable."

"*Oui*," Jocelyne said. "It's true. But it is why I now—"

Sophie cleared her throat, and Gaston did not miss the look the two women exchanged.

"Why you now live in London, no?" Sophie said, finishing

Jocelyne's sentence for her.

Gaston heard the warning in Sophie's voice, and he wondered what he was missing. "How did you come to reconnect with Sophie?" he asked.

"It was by chance," Sophie said again, interjecting before Jocelyne could answer. "I had gone to a new seamstress when I was visiting Bath. Jocelyne walked into the room with a tray of tea. I could not believe my eyes."

"Nor could I. It was a miracle. And now I have a second one." Jocelyne leaned over and touched his cheek. "Although, perhaps you are my third, since I, too, should have died in the fire. I used to wish I had," she said quietly, dropping her hand.

"And now?" Gaston watched her closely, looking for the truth in her eyes. She'd had a position and standing in Paris. The loss of those things must be difficult too.

"I am content. I have a good life. And…" She glanced at Sophie before continuing. "I have purpose."

"And what purpose is that?" Gaston could see the shifting landscape of thought on Jocelyne's face, but after another look at Sophie, she clearly decided not to be forthcoming.

"My purpose? To get us all a drink to celebrate the return of Gaston Armand, Marquis de Lyon."

Before he could point out he was marquis of nothing now, she jumped to her feet, smiled at him, and disappeared out the door.

"Excuse me," Sophie said. "I shall check on her. This has been a shock, no?" She did not wait for his response before quickly following Jocelyne.

Something odd was going on, but Gaston could not fathom what it was. He walked to the door and stepped into the hall. The second door on the opposite side was slightly ajar, and a light shone through, flickering against the wall like an erratic dancer. He stepped closer, and it became clear someone was pacing. Their rapid French made him smile, a smile he quickly lost when their words became audible.

"I forbid you to tell him," Sophie snapped.

"Forbid? You *forbid* me?"

"A poor choice of words. But you cannot, Jocelyne. We are too close to a win to take any chances now."

"But it is Gaston, Sophie."

The pacing stopped, and the tension between the two women was palpable.

"Who has a lot of years to account for, and he has not."

A long sigh followed Sophie's pronouncement on his absence, but Gaston was not sure who did it.

"You are right, of course. It is the shock. I am not thinking. It is just… I do it in honor of him, *non?*"

The light extinguished momentarily, blocked by what he imagined was the two women embracing. Gaston's mind raced, corralling the words he'd overheard, trying to make sense of them.

The light flickered again, and Sophie spoke. "Were you successful today?"

"I was. There is something afoot, although I do not know what. Apparently, their men are meeting at a rout the day after tomorrow. They became more interested in their dresses than their gossip, but I did manage to find out where."

There was the unmistakable sound of paper, and Sophie thanked Jocelyne. "Soon, my friend, we will be free of all this. I am certain."

Gaston slipped back into the drawing room. Who was the *him* Jocelyne referenced? Were they being blackmailed? It did not sound it, but it was a possibility. Unquestionably, Sophie and Jocelyne were in league together, but against or for what? *"Who has a lot of years to account for, and he has not."* Sophie dared doubt his integrity! His honesty! Well, by the end of this night, he would test hers.

CHAPTER FORTY

*She was more than human to me. She was a Fairy, a Sylph, I
don't know what she was—anything that no one ever saw, and
everything that everybody ever wanted. I was swallowed up in
an abyss of love in an instant. There was no pausing on the
brink; no looking down, or looking back; I was gone, headlong,
before I had sense to say a word to her.*

—Charles Dickens, *David Copperfield*

IT HAD BROUGHT Sophia great pleasure to watch the two
cousins together. Once they'd moved past the sharing of their
journeys, they'd reminisced. Sophia remembered some of it, but
much was from a time she had not known Gaston, the time
before the husbands had tried to keep the sisters apart. It had
been a foolish attempt. The women had been French, and family
was everything. Their mothers had not obeyed. Instead, they'd
met covertly. Sophia was convinced it was how Jocelyne had
learned her wiliness and discretion.

Gaston had grown quiet in the carriage, and she had not
probed. She knew what it was like to see someone you'd long
thought gone, so she'd left him to his reflections. She'd assumed
he would want to go home, but when they'd arrived at her town
house, he'd hopped out and escorted her to the door. It was not
merely to antagonize Raimondo either, for he'd come all the way

in without invitation, promptly shed his coat, and handed it to Stephens.

She'd not been averse to him staying, so she'd turned and walked upstairs and on toward her private sitting room. She'd invited him to help himself to a drink and left him there and was now staring at herself as she contemplated the meaning of his presence. She'd removed her jewelry and slipped into a simple, more comfortable gown. Her head ached a little, so she'd had Cara take her hair down and was now enjoying the brush dragging slowly over her scalp. Cara always tried to be gentle, and Sophia had never appreciated her magic touch more.

Gaston's reflection appeared in the glass.

"May I?" he asked, holding his hand out for the brush.

Cara looked at Sophia in the mirror, and Sophia nodded. Cara did not need to be asked to leave the room. The door clicked quietly behind her.

Gaston did not look at her, his focus entirely on his task. He pulled the brush slowly through her locks, his fingers caressing the strands as he did so. The sight was comfortingly domestic and entirely sensual. Sophia's body stirred, but her mind warned it to still. She sensed something more was going on.

"Your hair is my first memory of you," he said, pausing in his task and rolling a lock between his thumb and forefinger. He cleared his throat. "You were small, a pixie, but your hair was thick and full and far too big for your waiflike body. I wanted to touch it. Even though I was petrified by everything going on around me, I wanted to know what your hair felt like."

Sophia watched the play of emotions on his face but said nothing. She was not surprised his head was full of memories. She now knew firsthand that that was what happened when one saw a ghost come to life. The past enveloped you like an early-morning fog rolling across the fields. One looked for landmarks to anchor one in place.

"It did not take long for me to recognize your hair was the essence of you. Big and bold, too much, and yet just right."

He leaned in and kissed the top of her head, and her stomach fluttered in response. Still, she remained silent.

"You asked me earlier what it was I wanted. I told the truth, Sophie. I want you and only you. But I would like to amend it, if I may?"

"Of course," she said calmly, although now her heart had joined her fluttering stomach and not in a good way.

"I want your truth. Your honesty. I want you to hold no secrets from me."

Gaston's eyes bored into hers. She squirmed uncomfortably, her brain momentarily clogged. She swallowed, and her thoughts began to swirl again. Could he know? But how? Her conversation with Jocelyne? Even if he'd overheard them, it would make no sense to him unless...

She pivoted on her stool, and he stepped back in surprise. "In the carriage, you turned my question back on me and asked me what it was I wanted from you. I did not have time to answer, but I want what you want. Us together. Wrapped in honesty, comforted by truth."

Gaston broke eye contact and ran a hand over his face, walking away from her but quickly returning. "I overheard you and Jocelyne. I would know what you were talking about."

Sophia crossed her arms and eyed him. "And you went out Sunday morning and made no mention of it. I would like to know where you went."

"I went for a walk, Sophia," he said smoothly.

"And the flowers you sketched? Why did you not show them to me?"

He quickly covered his surprise. "I am not an artist. They were not worthy of sharing."

"So honesty is not attainable." Sophia got to her feet and marched past him into the sitting room.

"Apparently not," Gaston said, fast on her heels. He grabbed her arm and spun her around. "What did you forbid Jocelyne to tell me?"

Sophia's heart pounded fiercely in her chest. He had definitely overheard them. It was now or never. She either had to tell him or walk away from him.

"That we spy," she said, pulling her arm from his and stomping over to the decanter. Hands shaking, she pulled the stopper and poured a brandy. Gaston stepped behind her, and his hand prevented her from raising the glass to her mouth.

"For whom?" His voice was so quiet she'd think she'd imagined it, was imagining the entire scene, were it not for the heat of his body pressed against hers and the firm grip on her hand.

"Who do you think, Gaston?" she said, suddenly exasperated. Did he believe she'd spy for the revolutionists who'd taken her mother? For the man who'd used those revolutionists to declare himself emperor? The man who'd taken both Gaston and her father from her? She pulled from his grasp and spun around.

"And you, Gaston, who do you work for?"

SHE KNEW. HE was certain she was not fishing. She had knowledge of his activities. What she knew, how she'd acquired the knowledge, was all irrelevant right now. *She knew.* The band around his chest loosened. For better or for worse, there would be no pretense between them. But he needed clarity first.

"Tell me, Sophie," he said as steadily as possible considering he longed for her to say the right words. For if he had misread her meaning, they would not only be on opposite sides of this war but of life. He did not lightly take on the role as traitor to France. It was not a case of revenge, although there often was a satisfying element of vengeance. His father had been a royalist at heart, born and bred. Gaston was somewhere in between. The short-lived constitutional monarchy had been, to him, the ideal. One thing he was sure of was that one didn't overthrow a monarchy to have a man appoint himself as ruler. He despised the little emperor.

He could see the moment the fight left her and she decided to tell him. His breath stalled as he waited for her answer.

"I help England."

Her eyes were dark. He could only imagine the myriad of worries dancing behind them. He cupped her cheek.

"As do I, Sophie. As do I."

He pulled her close and held her as tight as possible without crushing her. He wondered if she could feel the hammering of his heart, sense the happiness flowing through his veins. For the first time in sixteen years, he considered joy as one of life's possibilities.

CHAPTER FORTY-ONE

*For a few seconds they gazed silently into one another's eyes—
and what had seemed impossible and remote suddenly became
possible, inevitable, and very near.*

—Leo Tolstoy, *War and Peace*

"And the masquerade, where you knocked me to the ground. It was an important night, and my idea." Sophia was enjoying regaling Gaston with some of her escapades. She took a sip of brandy and eyed Gaston over it.

"Your presence was not one of coincidence? You were a part of capturing the traitor?" Gaston asked.

"I was." Sophia sat straighter. "How do you know him?"

It was Gaston's turn to smile. "I am the one who fed him the information, to trap him."

"*Non! Incroyable!*"

Gaston's face grew grim. "He was a dangerous man. You have put yourself at much risk, *non?*"

Sophia raised her eyebrows at him but said nothing. She had never felt in jeopardy. And Raimondo had followed her like a hound to scent.

"You must stop," Gaston said, brushing a stray hair from Sophia's face. "I will take it from here."

Sophia laughed at the suggestion. Gaston had always been

overprotective.

"I mean it, Sophie. I will not have you in harm's way."

"You'll not have me in harm's way?" Her hackles rose. "I have lived my life quite fine without your protection. And I will continue to live it as I please."

She did not get the expected spark from Gaston. Instead, he pressed his forehead against hers and sighed heavily.

"It is only that having found you, Sophie, I don't want to lose you." He pulled back and tucked a finger under her chin, lifting her head until she was looking directly in his eyes. "I love you, Sophie Auclair."

Could it be in disclosing what she'd worked so hard to hide that they had come full circle and could have a fresh start? She wanted it to be true, but despite knowing her love was irrefutable, she hesitated. To repeat his words would give him power over her. Power she'd never given anyone but him. Power she was suddenly afraid to give him once again.

He leaned in and kissed her lips gently, whispering words of love as he whisked back and forth over her lips. When he was through, he smiled sadly at her. "It is not easy for me to accept you have no need of me."

"That is not true," she said, and he placed a finger on her lips before she could say more.

"We will work together, you and I. I shall attend the rout too. *D'accord?*"

Sophia nodded. "Agreed."

"In the meantime, I will see if I can make you love me once again." A smile played at the corner of his lips. "For tonight, though, I will leave you with your thoughts and me with mine. There is much to think about."

"You don't have to leave." Sophia did not hide the need in her voice. For while she could not yet say the words to him, her body certainly knew where it stood.

"*Oui,* I do." Gaston stood. "Tomorrow, we will do something special. *Non,* don't get up." He kissed her cheek. "*Je t'aime beaucoup*," he whispered in her ear and left the room.

Later, as she lay unable to sleep, the wind rattled the windows. She imagined she was the girl from long ago who'd padded across the room to let in her young lover. He'd whispered those words, and she had held them to her heart as she'd gifted herself to him. She had never regretted giving herself fully, nor saying those words in return. Tomorrow she would be brave enough to let go and tell him.

She rolled onto her side and stared at the window. She was determined there would be more nights for them. A lifetime of them.

"I love you, Gaston," she whispered, liking how they sounded. Eventually, the weight of fatigue settled, and she drifted to sleep.

CHAPTER FORTY-TWO

*I shall do one thing in this life—one thing certain—that is, love
you, and long for you, and* keep wanting you *till I die.*

—Thomas Hardy, *Far from the Madding Crowd*

"WHERE ARE WE going?"

Gaston tsk-tsked. "It would not be much of a surprise if I told you, would it?"

Sophia laughed. It had been years since she'd allowed someone to take control of her day. Even when she was not seeking information, she kept strict charge of her schedule. She was a meticulous planner and was the one who led the way. Her friends always enjoyed her outings and events. But today was Gaston's. She had agreed to do whatever he wanted.

The weather was gloriously warm for May, yet Gaston had insisted she bring her cape. He'd also encouraged her to carry a parasol. So whatever he had planned, it must involve being outdoors. The carriage jolted to a stop. Raimondo opened the door, and they both got out.

They were at Westminster Bridge. She peeked over the edge. Boats flowed beneath the many arches, reminding her of her days in *Venezia*. Gaston offered his arm and guided her slowly down an adjacent set of stairs where a long boat bounced lightly, its captain bowing when he spotted them.

"Is there a water party today?" Sophia asked, looking across the water where two other boats were moored on the Lambeth side.

"*Oui*," Gaston said. "A party for two."

Sophia loved when his grin was large enough for her to see his chipped tooth. She could see the boy in him, although it was the man in him now that she wanted. She leaned in and kissed his cheek. "It is a delightful surprise. An adventure, no?"

The captain stepped onto the boat and held out his hand, assisting Gaston first. She took both their hands and stepped lightly into the boat. It rocked slightly, and she stumbled, bracing her hands against Gaston's chest. "Oh," she said, looking up at him.

"Oh, indeed," he said and kissed her nose.

She turned in his arms, and he held her securely against his chest. Raimondo handed the captain her cape and parasol.

"*Non!*" Gaston's bark was sharp as Raimondo stepped into the boat. "Not today. She has no need of you today."

An ugly storm washed across Raimondo's face, but Sophia had to credit him with solid self-control, for he did not tear her from Gaston and proceed to pummel him.

"I am fine," Sophia said soothingly.

"Countess," Raimondo growled. "I do not—"

"Enjoy a day off." She waved a hand at him, softening her dismissal with a smile.

Raimondo held her gaze for a moment before grunting unhappily and disembarking, further rocking the boat. He was well and truly angry, for he stomped up the steps without a glance at her. She would have laughed out loud were it not for Gaston nuzzling her hair. She turned in his arms, and he smiled before giving her a breath-stealing kiss, broken only because the captain cleared his throat.

Gaston kept his arm around her waist, and they ducked under the wood-framed awning. Lush blankets and feather pillows covered the seats, and a large picnic basket sat in the middle.

"I will not need my parasol. This ship is perfect."

Gaston chuckled. "Not a ship, *ma chérie*. A shallop."

"A ship. A boat. A shallop. They are all the same to me. They float on the water, no?" She sat down, pleased by the comfort of the cushioned seats. "Those men. They will not work too hard?"

Four solemn men sat facing them, dressed rather raggedly, oars in hand. She had seen drawings of the slave ships to America and had found them disturbing. While she knew these were no slaves, the parallel image bothered her. She said so to Gaston. "I fight an emperor who has stolen a throne, not the people who honestly wanted to better themselves. I do not like to keep people down, to…" She searched for the word, but Gaston sat beside her, wrapped his arm around her shoulder, and pulled her snug to his side, and the word became irretrievable.

"You are truly Sophie returned to me," he said, pressing a kiss to her temple. "They are no different from the gondoliers who ferried you about in *Venise*. And, I assure you, I have paid them a small fortune to accommodate us this day. Each of them personally. And the coxswain." He looked at the captain, then back at her, and rolled his eyes.

She laughed and clapped her hands. Not simply because this day was going to be enjoyable but because Gaston still understood when one was blessed in life, one must share their bounty. It had been a tacit agreement between them since the day she'd pulled him away from the rabid crowd.

The boat rocked lightly, and Sophia looked back. The captain had stepped onto the landing. He tugged at the loop, threw the rope onto the decking, and stepped in after it. He sat on the wooden bench in the rear and shouted. Water splashed as the oars dipped, and she turned to face forward, watching the men as they rowed from the edge, further out onto the Thames. They cast their eyes down, not looking at her, but they looked hale and healthy and at ease in their work. Sophia relaxed.

Gaston watched her, and she grew uncomfortable under his gaze.

"Why is it you stare?" she asked.

Gaston hesitated before speaking, and Sophia shifted, trying not to squirm. She could predict most people but not Gaston.

"I think you have grown more beautiful," he said and tapped his chest. "*Ici*. Inside."

She should have been offended by his apparent amazement. But Gaston did not know the years in between. He didn't know that she supported Elizabeth's orphanage project as well as many other worthy endeavors. That Jocelyne was not the only person she'd helped find a new life. That she did not have to bring Raimondo, Stefano, or Cara with her but could not leave them to find their way on their own in a land full of turmoil. Her mother had married a scholar because she'd considered him her equal. She'd loved him, had faith in all he'd done, including his humble role in society. She had been, at all times, a generous and giving woman. Now Sophia used her position to honor her memory. These were things Gaston could not know, so she would forgive him his assumptions.

"There is much about me you do not know." She would tell him one day. But not today.

"That is becoming clear with every moment I am with you. I would happily spend the rest of my life discovering all there is to know."

Gaston raised her hand to his lips and brushed a kiss across her gloved hand. Her body trilled in response. He eyed her from under his lashes and opened his mouth to speak, but the captain shouted directions. The moment broken, she smiled ruefully at him. They both relaxed back on the bench and looked out at the water.

A boat sailing briskly in the wind whisked by on the left side, startling her as spray splattered her face. The captain was on his feet, fist raised, shouting at the passerby. Gaston took out his handkerchief and wiped at her cheek, cursing in French.

"I should fear for what has hit my cheek, no? But the birds survive the water, so maybe me too?" Sophia laughed, feeling more alive than she had in years. She raised her hand and covered Gaston's, holding it close to her cheek. "I have survived worse, *mon amour.*"

Gaston froze, and had he not whispered words of love to her last night, she would have worried she'd overstepped bounds with words of endearment, had misread his intentions. A slow smile crept across his face, and he leaned in. She was anticipating another deep kiss, but he pecked her lips briefly and pulled back. Her need was great, but he refused to return to her, a smile playing at the corners of his lips.

She grabbed a pillow and threw it at him. "You are a tease. You have always been so."

He laughed and looked to the side. "Behold the great river, Sophie. Behold London." He swept his hand toward the passing banks. "Behold our home."

Her heart stalled for seconds and then accelerated, thumping madly in her chest. *Our home?*

Gaston slid from the bench and onto his knees in front of her. "I would give anything to turn back time and live as we once dreamed. And I would give anything to ask for your hand and celebrate our joining with your friends. I would give anything to show this world that even as I claim you, you own me."

Gaston's eyes glistened, and her sight blurred as her eyes watered in response. She bit her bottom lip and waited.

"I want you, Sophie. I have always wanted you. Only you. Yet I cannot give you my name, for my name does not exist."

Sophia put a finger to his lips. "I am a widow. I'm not chained to propriety."

Gaston kissed her finger before grabbing it and pressing her hand to his chest. "But I am, Sophie. I want both a wife and a lover."

Sophia's joy dropped from her heart and landed, leaden, in her stomach. She'd thought this day was about beginnings, but it would seem it was about endings.

He lifted her chin and stared into her eyes, his as glazed as hers must be. "One day, I will formally stand before all and declare...*non*, shout...you are Sophie Armand, wife of the Marquis de Lyon. But I cannot wait until that day to be with you."

Sophia let her joy float freely again. "I need no formality," she whispered.

"But I do." Gaston pushed from his knees back onto the bench, turning so he was facing her. "During the time I spent in Scotland with *mon père* and the Count d'Artois, I learned some things." He raised one finger. "First, I learned the Scots are incredibly difficult to understand."

She gave Gaston the laugh he was seeking, but it did not lessen the excited tension stretching her nerves.

"Second," he said, raising another finger, "they are friends to the French, much more than the British, who seem to be enamored of our fashions more than our people."

Sophia could not argue. Jocelyne's numerous patrons inevitably wanted to be styled after the French court despite their countries being at war.

"Third, they know how to seal a deal."

Sophia was confused. What deal was he referring to?

Gaston rubbed a little circle on her forehead with his fingertip. "Unfurl, *ma chérie*. You are thinking so hard *my* brain hurts. Ah, a smile from my Madonna." He kissed her gently and pulled back. "In Scotland, you need only say you are married to make it so."

Sophia laughed with joyous delight. He was talking marriage. "Did we not already do so the night you snuck through my window?" Sophia immediately regretted her words, for she could see the years in between crushing Gaston's enthusiasm. She touched his hand, and he smiled, but it was weighted with sadness.

"*Oui*, we did, but..."

She was grateful he did not mention Carmine, for the count had no place on the boat today. The count had no place at all except in the recesses of her memories.

"It is called a handfast. We're not in Scotland, so it will not be legal. But it will be binding in my heart. I promise you, after the war ends, we will stand before the clergy, and we will celebrate our joining with whomever you would like. As for me, I need only you. Here. Now. Saying you will spend the rest of your life with me."

Sophia could not speak. Her eyes burned, and she bit her bottom lip to prevent herself from bawling like *un petit bébé*. For it would not do to be a bride with puffy, red-ringed eyes.

"Sophie?"

She loved the doubt in his eyes, his blatant vulnerability. She nodded, and a smile lit his face. He turned toward the back of the boat. "Monsieur."

It was all he said, yet the man shouted a command, and the rowers stopped. One got up and shuffled toward them, joining the captain in their small space.

"Sit, *mes hommes honorables*," Gaston said casually, and the two dropped onto the bench facing her and Gaston.

"This day, I have asked Sophia Tessaro to marry me, and she has agreed." He took her right hand in his. "Is that correct, *ma chérie?*"

"*Oui*," she whispered as his thumb traced a path up and down hers.

"You will both stand witness, *non?*"

"Aye, indeed we weel." The captain grinned and clapped his man on the shoulder. Then he produced a strip of tartan cloth and held it out like an offering.

Sophia tugged her hand free of Gaston's and clapped in sheer appreciation. A thick Scottish accent and a Scottish tradition. However Gaston had managed it, she did not know, but it was an impressive feat. She stretched her right hand back out, and Gaston put his beside hers. The captain wrapped the cloth around their wrists, tying it in a bow before sitting back on his bench.

"Sophie Auclair, I have loved you since the day I met you and will never stop. Will you be my wife?"

Sophia could not believe after all the dark years, she was sitting on the River Thames with Gaston declaring his undying love. If she was dreaming, she did not wish to wake up. She would embrace it. Would throw herself fully into it as she did with everything. As she had done with Gaston since she'd first seen him on the street.

"Gaston Armand, I have never forgotten what we shared, nor stopped wanting to have you for myself again," she said, speaking in French as he had done. "If you will be my husband, it would be my honor to be your wife."

Gaston's eyes were dark and glassy, and Sophia wanted to weep at the love she saw in them. He leaned in and kissed her lightly, his gaze lingering on her before he turned to the captain, who was eyeing them with uncertainty.

"We have said our vows," Gaston explained, and the captain grinned. Gaston produced a paper, and both the captain and the rower made their marks, congratulated them, and stood. "Wait," Gaston said, rooting around in the picnic basket. "You must toast with us," he said, pulling out a decanter of Madeira.

Sophia loved that he had not four but seven glasses in the basket. He poured three, handing them to the two men and Sophia, then poured three more and carefully moved from under the awning to the rowers. When he returned, he poured one for himself. He raised his glass, and everyone followed suit.

"To the luckiest man in the world," Gaston said to the men in English and turned to her. "And to the woman who has made him so. May he prove worthy of her love."

The men cheered, and they all took a drink.

"If I may," the captain said, raising his glass again. "May the best ye've ever seen, be the worst ye'll ever see."

All the years flashed quickly through Sophia's mind as she raised her glass. Today, and from this day forward, his toast seemed like a possibility.

"I'll drink to that," Gaston said, clinking his glass against hers.

"Me too," Sophia said quietly. "Me too."

CHAPTER FORTY-THREE

We must laugh and we must sing,
We are blest by everything,

—William Butler Yeats, "A Dialogue of Self and Soul"

THE MEN RETURNED to their positions, and Gaston had Sophie all to himself. He sensed her eyes on him as he untied each roll of material on the awning. The sheer fabric fell easily, covering the sides. Fluttering lightly in the breeze, it was the perfect balance between light and air and some privacy.

"It is like a harem's den," Sophie said, her dark eyes radiant as she took another sip of Madeira and eyed him over her glass.

"And what would you know of harems?" he asked, teasing her. He was pleased at her excitement. He'd returned to Jocelyne yesterday, and they had talked late into the night. When he'd told her of his intention for this day, it had been her suggestion, and she'd sent the bolt of fabric with him.

Gaston leaned in and brushed her cheek with his lips. "It was a gift from Jocelyne."

"Jocelyne knows?"

"*Oui,* and she can be the only one for now, *mon amour.* We cannot risk too many questions." He could see disappointment warring with logic, the latter practicality winning. "I know it is hard not to share with your friends."

Sophie sighed. "It is not the only thing I hide from them."

"Let us not dwell on it today, my wife."

"You are right. Not today, *mon époux*."

My husband. How many years had he dreamed of this moment? Even when he'd been convinced she was lost to him forever, images of it had haunted him. Her friends would survive not knowing. And the world could turn on its own for a while. This day was long awaited, and he was determined to claim it.

He pretended to lean in for a kiss and laughed at the surprised look on Sophie's face as he reached past her and tipped the basket lid back open. "I'm starving," he said, and Sophie swatted him. He pulled out the food and set it on the opposite bench, closed the lid of the basket, and draped a tablecloth over it.

"Bentley directed me to Gunter's for catering." He moved the food off the bench and onto the basket.

"Bentley? He knows about this?" Sophie frowned and waved her hand in a circle in the air.

"He knows only I wanted to provide a picnic." He unwrapped the cheese and the bread. "I suspect he knows who for. He's been curiously attentive to my comings and goings."

Sophie relaxed back against the bench. "That is Bentley. He amuses himself with the trivial to avoid anything serious."

"Yes, he does come across as a bit of a dandy. If he rambles on one more time about that man Brummell, I'm certain I shall hit him."

"You would not."

"Perhaps not." He held out a piece of cheese. "Here, *ma chéric*, try this. Bentley highly recommended it. If you agree with his opinion of it, then I shall refrain from punching him."

Sophie took a bite and, looking thoughtful, chewed slowly. "I am not certain…," she said, then burst into laughter.

"Poor man doesn't know how close he came to a thrashing." Gaston slipped the remainder into his own mouth. It was pungent in flavor and entirely delicious. "Enough about Bentley." He stared at Sophie's lips, and his hunger for food was immediately replaced with his thirst for her.

Sophie's tongue slipped out as though to remove a stray crumb. She held his gaze as she raised her hand and tugged at each finger of her glove. She slowly slid the cloth down and pulled it off, dangling it before dropping it to the bench. She repeated it with her left hand, never wavering in her stare. She ran her bare forefinger over her lips. It could not have been more erotic. His body burned.

"I find myself hungry for more," she said, slowly letting her finger drop and trace the valley of her breasts.

Gaston swallowed the lump of anticipation in his throat, and Sophie smiled slyly as she leaned forward and looked into the basket. The coquette knew what she was doing to him. He looked around at the nearby boats in frustration. He knew what he'd like to do in response to her taunting, but he also knew he must restrain himself. For now.

Sophie pulled out a cake and sat back on the bench, turning slightly to face him. She smiled her satisfied smile and took a bite. "Mmm," she mumbled as she closed her eyes and threw her head back.

Gaston bit back a groan. Yes, she undoubtedly knew the power she held over him. As if hearing his thoughts, she opened her eyes and held out the cake. He leaned in and whispered a kiss along her inner arm, pausing at her wrist, pleased to feel her rapid pulse as he twirled his tongue on her sweet flesh. He watched her as he took a bite and mimicked her humming. She shifted on the bench, and he hoped her need was as great as his.

"I adore gingerbread cakes," she said huskily before taking another bite.

"*Je t'adore, mon amour*," he said, his voice equally gruff.

Shouting broke out, and the boat roughly veered portside. Gaston righted himself and looked starboard in time to catch a glimpse of the occupants of the other leisure boat, surprised to see the Duke of Salinger among the party. Gaston did not imagine his glare.

The coxswain cursed loudly enough to be heard and called out to the oarsmen. Gaston turned to Sophie, who was twisted in her seat, looking astern, a frown replacing her sensual gaze of moments before.

"Your duke seemed none too pleased to see you with me."

"He is not my duke." Her eyes flashed angrily. Whether her anger was directed at him or at the duke, he wasn't sure.

Gaston took her hand in his. "But he still thinks he is, doesn't he?"

"His arrogance does not allow him to easily accept rejection."

"And you did reject him?" Gaston hated the sense of uncertainty creeping in despite her pledge today.

"You have to ask?"

Sophie's haughty look told him all he needed, and he laughed loudly, the joy of the day back.

"It is not amusing that you question me." Sophie was indignant. He loved her passionate responses. It would make for marvelous times and, he knew from experience, many arguments. He'd cherish it all as he'd promised to cherish her. He pulled her close, and she slapped at his arm until he tasted her delicious lips. She moaned and allowed him entrance, and he proved to her he was not filled with doubt. He was overflowing with passion. And love.

CHAPTER FORTY-FOUR

I loved you first when young and fair, but now I love you most.
—Alfred Lord Tennyson, "Happy"

SOPHIA RELISHED THE boat ride, but she was even more excited about the night ahead. When they arrived at Greenwich Pier, both her footman, Stephens, and Raimondo were waiting for them. Stephens assisted the captain in gathering glasses and plates, and together they brought the picnic basket onto shore. Raimondo stood with arms crossed, a surly old bear.

"You were to take the day off," she said with a smile, refusing to allow his displeasure to taint her day. "You do not follow orders well."

He grunted and took over from the captain, helping Stephens carry the basket to where her carriage waited. Charles tipped his hat at them from where he still sat on the box, and Gaston kept his arm around her waist as they watched them secure the basket. It felt so domestic and mundane on a day that had proven to be anything but.

Raimondo opened the door, and Gaston assisted her in.

"And where might we drop you, signore?"

Sophia did not miss the antagonism in Raimondo's voice. He was far too overprotective, and it did not usually bother her, but she was tired of fighting his displeasure with Gaston's presence.

He might as well know what direction the wind was blowing. She leaned out before Gaston responded.

"Raimondo," she snapped, garnering his immediate attention. "We will go directly home. Then you and Stephens will go to Gaston's rooms and gather his things. He will be living with us." She paused, taking a second to digest the reality of her statement. "Permanently," she added at Raimondo's frown.

Gaston hopped into the carriage, a grin splitting his face almost in two as he closed the door on Raimondo. "I can't say I did not enjoy that."

Sophia could not return his enthusiasm. Raimondo meant well. She trusted him and Stefano with the details of her activities. He worried greatly about her involvement. Compounded with a general distrust of the English, it made him a formidable protector. Stefano was not so intense, but Raimondo always insisted he remain at the country estate so nothing untoward could happen there while they were in London. She believed Raimondo's overbearing behavior was not simply in honor of Carmine but because he truly cared for her well-being.

Gaston rubbed her leg. "I jest. I am grateful you have had someone to look out for you."

She set her hand on top of his. "Thank you. It is important you accept him as he is, for he is not going anywhere either." She had been as loyal to Carmine's staff as they had been to her. She'd set them up with pensions, but they chose to continue with her anyway.

The carriage began to roll, and they returned their attention to the day, reminiscing as though it had happened months ago and not simply in the last few hours. When the carriage rattled to a stop, she looked at Gaston. "Welcome home, husband."

His face grew serious, and his eyes misted, and Sophia's heart grew too big for her chest. "At last," he said quietly, raising her hand to his mouth and whisking a kiss across her knuckles. "At last."

Later, after the arrival of Gaston's meager collection of items, they sat across from each other in her small sitting room. She had offered him one of her guest rooms if he preferred it to sharing hers. Carmine had kept his own rooms and rarely entered hers. She understood it was often a preference for couples. Gaston had asked what she wished and had given his chipped-tooth grin when she'd said she wished for him to join her in her bed every night. Her body was strung as tight as the strings on a violin. A bath was being poured, and the anticipation of sharing it with Gaston was both titillating and unnerving.

"You are worried," he said.

"Why would you say such a thing?" she asked, although it was precisely what she was. She was not a young girl of seventeen anymore. She was a mature woman of thirty-three, and her body reflected those years. She knew she was voluptuous and enticing in a gown, but she had not tested it without clothing. It was daunting.

"When you worry, two little perpendicular lines appear between your eyes." Gaston pushed from his chair and strode the short distance between them. He pressed a finger between her eyes. "Right here." He rubbed her skin, his finger slowly circling. Like a dog who loves a good scratch, she wanted to lean into him and let him soothe away her anxiety.

A tap sounded at the door, and when bidden entrance, Cara stuck her head in. "The bath is ready, *signora mia.*"

"Thank you, Cara. That will be all for the night." She waited until the door clicked before returning her gaze to Gaston. "I trust that is fine with you. I may need some help."

Gaston's smile was slow and sensual as he held out his hand. "I am at your service, but I may need some instruction."

Sophia suspected he knew exactly what to do, a notion she'd not wish to dwell upon. Instead, she smiled in return as she put her hand in his and let him pull her to her feet.

They walked into her boudoir, and they both stopped and stared at the bed. Sophia had had many nightmares in that bed recently. The last few nights, the dark memories had been supplanted with visions of young lovers. It would seem those dreams were about to come true. Except for the young part. She turned into Gaston before she dwelled any longer on the years in between.

He tasted of the brandy they'd enjoyed, and she savored him, tracing his tongue with hers before gently sucking it. He groaned and pushed away.

"*Non*. My body is too hot for you and must cool." He turned her around, and his fingers swept across the back of her neck before he settled into the task of undoing the clasp of her necklace.

She took it from his hands and set it on her dressing table. When she straightened, he pulled the pins from her hair methodically, one by one. When he was done, he leaned past her to set them down, his rough chin grazing her shoulder. She ran her fingers across her scalp, loosening the chignon and shaking her head to make her hair fall. Gaston lifted her hair and kissed the back of her neck before letting the weight of her locks settle again.

She debated whether they should undress in her bedroom or in the bathing room. She decided the bed would be far too great a distractor and they would never find the bath, so she took his hand and led him into the adjoining room. She smiled, glad she had. Cara had drawn the drape across the window that lit Sophia's morning bath and had scattered candles around the room. Rose petals floated delicately on top of the water. She swallowed a smile. She assumed the petals came from the duke's flowers. Like Catherine and Elizabeth, Cara had never liked him and had probably had great pleasure at plucking his gift apart.

From behind, Gaston wrapped his arms around her, his hands fisted together just below her breasts. He rested his chin on her shoulder and tilted his head sideways until their temples touched. "It is magical, *mon amour*. *You* are magical." He turned his head and kissed her temple. "I am unsure," he said against her head.

"As am I." After so many years playing the seasoned widow,

she was overwhelmed by the reality of her limited experience.

"Together, we will find solid land beneath our feet."

She turned to him, grateful he understood, oddly pleased he was as unbalanced as she. She stood on tiptoe and kissed him, losing herself in the sensuality of his response. Eventually, she pulled away, anxious to move on to the next level of intimacy. "It is a simple sash," she said, turning and presenting her back.

Gaston undid her sash, and she turned back to face him.

"The dress slides easily over my shoulders."

She held his gaze as he slid the dress off her shoulders, leaving a fiery path in the wake of his fingers. The garment pooled at her feet, and she stepped from it, kicking it to the side. She watched him as her fingers fumbled with the lace on her short stays. He placed a steadying hand over hers and kissed her cheek.

"It is too much, *non?*" he said, his face looking concerned.

"*Oui,*" she said, tugging the ribbon and letting her stay fall to the floor. "And not yet enough." She watched his face as she scooped the bottom of her chemise and raised it over her head. Except for her stockings, she was naked and more vulnerable than she'd ever been in her life.

"*Mon Dieu,*" he whispered reverently and fell to his knees.

He untied her ribbon, his lips following the trail of silk as he slipped her stocking down her calf, gently lifting her leg and removing her slipper before discarding the silk to the side. He repeated it with her other leg. A chill ran through her. She stood, immobile, both unsure and excited.

Gaston shifted, grabbed her calves, and slightly spread her legs. His tongue ascended slowly. He teased the backs of her knees before continuing upward, alternating between feathery kisses and gentle sweeps of his tongue. When his breath warmed her womanhood, she thought she would swoon, but his hands shifted and held her buttocks securely.

He looked at her and grinned, his eyes dark with sensuality, not humor. Then he nestled between her legs.

"Gaston, *non!*"

Sophia squirmed as his tongue licked a path, but he held her firmly. When he found her bud, she buried her fingers in his hair. He swirled and sucked, and she wanted to scream. She had never felt such sensation. Pressure built to a crescendo, but rather than shriek, she instead moaned, the lament filling the air more akin to pain than pleasure. It was a surprising sound, for she had never experienced anything so freeing.

Without Gaston's hands holding her, she might have collapsed. Instead, she stood there, squirming in deliciousness and grabbing at his hair. When the pulsating waves subsided, she looked down and caught the self-satisfied, incredibly smug look on his face. Yet she could feel no anger at his arrogance. She had little experience by which to judge him, but if her rubbery legs were any indication, his lovemaking skills were superb. She tried not to think of how he'd learned such things, for in all fairness, she had taken another man to her bed. Not often, and certainly not like this, but she suspected neither the frequency nor the experience itself lessened the sense of betrayal.

Gaston pursued a slow path of butterfly kisses up her body until he was standing. "Come, my lady, a bath awaits. As does your servant."

He bowed and urged her toward the large tub, holding her hand as she stepped into it, the warm water soothing as her womanly parts continued to twitch from Gaston's administrations. He pulled over a stool and rolled up his sleeves before snagging a cake of soap from the small table beside the tub. He dipped it in the water and rubbed it with his hands, lathering it as he watched her. She squirmed beneath his stare, and he smiled. He was extremely confident in the power he wielded, and she should rebel. But he did not hold it like an anvil ready to strike.

Gaston moved out of sight and sat behind her. He kissed the top of her head, rested his chin there, and ran his slick hands along her arms. He swept the lather in a sensual return and, excruciatingly slowly, repeated the process down her chest, around her breasts, and in between them. When each hand veered from the path and meandered to her nipples, pressing and circling, she squirmed with renewed longing. She tilted her head back and was rewarded with a lingering kiss.

When they finally pulled apart, her nipples and nether regions were aching with need. She spun around as gracefully as she could in the tub. Both breathing heavily, they stared at each other.

He shifted on the stool, and her eyes were drawn to the evidence of his desire. He needed her as much as she needed him.

She shifted in the tub so her back was against the other side, and she could fully watch him. "It is your turn, *époux*."

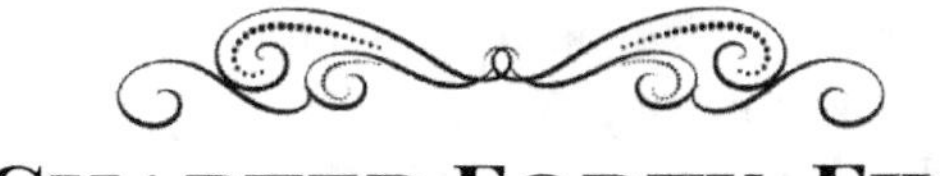

CHAPTER FORTY-FIVE

For nothing this wide universe I call,
Save thou, my rose; in it thou art my all.

—Shakespeare, "Sonnet 109"

HUSBAND. GASTON WOULD not tire of hearing her call him that. Nor would he argue with Sophie's invitation to disrobe. His body was on fire with unspent passion. Had been burning with it for sixteen years. He tugged at his cravat and slowly unwound it, tossing it onto Sophie's clothing. He unbuttoned his waistcoat and discarded it too. He undid a couple of buttons, then was pulling his shirt over his head.

Sophie squirmed, and his body responded. He slipped out of his shoes and impatiently tugged at his stockings. He watched her from under his eyelashes as he undid the front fall of his trousers, letting it drop so she could see the growing evidence of his desire before he took them off. His drawers quickly followed. Sophie gasped.

Her eyes were drawn to his crotch, but it was clear by the look of horror on her face it was not his manhood she was staring at.

"It is nothing," he said, tracing the welted scar running along the inside of his leg. He'd feared he'd been emasculated the night he'd been lanced by a sword. Sadly, the man had been an ally to the cause but had mistaken Gaston for the enemy. "A souvenir from a fellow Frenchman."

The candles flickered, and her glazed eyes looked like glass. He walked to the side of the tub, fell to one knee, and cupped her cheek with his hand. "We both have our wounds. The visible ones are the easiest to manage."

She rewarded him with a sad smile, but it was not enough. He did not want to make love in the shadow of the past. "Everything that has happened has brought us here. Let us honor all that has gone before but set it aside for tonight. Remain in the moment. Can you do that, *mon amour?*"

Sophie nodded, and he let his hand flow along her jaw before tracing her full lips. He leaned in and kissed her gently, cupping the back of her head and tugging her closer. Their kiss deepened as did his need. When she moaned, he could not stop a smile against her mouth. She pulled back.

"You are far too smug, no?"

"*Non.*" He stood and stroked himself, watching her watch him. "I am far too anxious," he said, letting go of his member before it could burst prematurely. "May I join you?"

"*Mais oui,*" she said, inching forward so he could slip in behind her.

They both laughed like the young lovers they once were as he awkwardly climbed into the tub, almost falling backward before he managed to settle. He wrapped his arms around her waist and tugged her close, her soft flesh warm against his length, which twitched merrily in response.

"I had forgotten it did that," Sophie said, giggling.

"*Ma* coquette." He kissed the top of her head. They had only made love once, but they had tentatively explored each other's bodies long before that night. The memories of those innocent times made him smile. He let his fingers creep across her stomach and tease the top of her mound.

"*Non,*" she said, grabbing his hand and setting it on the side of the tub. "I have had my turn. It is yours."

Sophie shimmied along the large tub and turned onto her knees. Water ran off her breasts. He wanted to lick those drops before they fell, but when he went to move, Sophie arched an eyebrow in warning. He chuckled and sat back against the tub, resisting the urge to reach into the water and once again pull at himself.

"Put your foot on the edge of the tub," she instructed as she lathered the small cake of soap.

She started with his toes, her touch gentle and methodical, as she kneaded each one and the arch of his foot. A slight smile played at the corner of her lips, but she was focused and did not look his way. He relaxed as her thumb massaged the muscles of his calf. His erection became less demanding, so he closed his eyes and got lost in the simple sensations. Until her hand swept his inner thigh. Then it went back on full alert.

Sophie got tantalizingly closer with each sweep. Her fingers, finally, lightly brushed his sacs. After several repeats of the movement, he squirmed and tried to pull her close, but she sat back on her heels, out of reach.

"Tsk. I did not interfere with you." Her chastisement was contradicted by her knowing smirk.

She set his leg back in the water, lifted the other one, and repeated her administrations. When she gently cupped his sacs, they grew so tight he was sure they would burst. He groaned as she ran a finger along his length, and her smile grew. She grabbed him firmly and pumped several times. He sat up abruptly, and she splashed backward, startled and unsure.

Gaston grabbed Sophie's hand and kissed it. "I have not waited sixteen years to spend myself in the tub, *mon amour*."

He stood carefully and swung one leg out onto solid ground. Once he was out, he helped her from the tub. Gaston loved how Sophie stood unabashed as he dried her before quickly drying himself. He tossed the linen on the floor and held out his hand.

"Come," he said softly. "Let us finalize our wedding vows. Let the love from my heart flow through my body and into yours."

CHAPTER FORTY-SIX

Here is the golden close of love,
All my wooing is done.

—Alfred Lord Tennyson, "Marriage Morning"

SOPHIA CONSIDERED PINCHING herself, for surely she was dreaming. Mere weeks ago, she'd thought Gaston was lost to her forever. Now he was leading her to her bed, as her husband. For, legal or not, she had meant her vow. It was *incroyable*.

He paused and turned to kiss her, his full length pressed rigidly against her. It should be awkward, this blatant nakedness between them, but it was not. It was as it should be, as it always should have been. There was nothing standing between them now. She swayed her hips, making sure their contact was as stimulating for him as it was for her, and he groaned into her mouth.

She lightly nipped his lip and let go of his hand. She placed one knee on the bed and pulled herself up. She glanced over her shoulder to ensure she had his attention. It would seem it was undivided, so she crawled slowly across the coverlet to where Cara had turned down the bedding, and repositioned herself so she was kneeling at the edge of the mattress.

"Come, husband. Let me bring you pleasure."

Gaston visibly swallowed but did as commanded.

"Closer," she said, gripping his buttocks and pulling him snug to the bed. She ran her tongue along his length, circling the tip before returning to his base. She repeated her foray, looking up from time to time to see his face. His lips drawn tight, his nostrils flaring, he was watching her administrations. Power flowed through her, and she decided to take him into her mouth as he had her, but he pulled away.

"*Non*, Sophie. It is bed sport for another day."

Gaston lifted her chin, and their gazes met. Heat pooled at the look in his eyes. She sat back on her haunches, eyeing his erection, the evidence of how close he was to spending glistening in the candlelight. She was in perfect accord. She did not want this night to end too quickly, but nor did she want it to end before the pleasure of their joining.

Sophia rolled onto her back and patted the empty space beside her in invitation. Gaston crawled onto the bed, and his gaze swept the length of her body.

"*Mon Dieu*," he whispered. "You are a Titian Venus. *Non*, much more," he said, shaking his head slowly. "He never had a subject such as you. If he had, he would never have painted again. You are perfection."

Tears misted her view of Gaston. It was not that she doubted her looks; it was more she worried they would no longer be enough. For he had seen her in the bloom of youth and might have had illusions she remained unchanged. He kissed her stomach, and butterflies swirled and danced beneath his lips.

He shifted and lay beside her on his side, his hand delicately tracing her breasts, running along her flesh, outlining her hips, and finally lingering where she most wanted it. When he began to play, opening her, teasing her bud, she arched in pleasure. He worked his magic until she was ready to cry out with need. Then he abruptly withdrew his fingers.

"*Mon amour*, I cannot wait," he said.

"Nor can I," Sophia said, clawing at him until he was on top of her. She opened her legs and pressed upward in invitation.

Gaston braced his weight on his elbows, and she mourned the loss of connection. His enlarged pupils made his eyes as dark as midnight.

"I love you. I have never stopped," he said, his voice thick with emotion.

Before she could respond, he plunged into her, and she moaned at the fullness of him. He nested there, watching her. She stared back but said nothing. He rolled his hips, and she moaned again. His smile was slow as he withdrew before returning at an equally leisurely pace. It was delicious for a few minutes, but when he ground himself against her, it became sweet agony. Sophia pounded his back.

"More, Gaston! I want more."

Gaston gave it to her. He was rhythmic and relentless, and just when she was certain she would lose her sanity if she did not release the exquisite pressure, he reached between them and rolled her bud. Her body let go. She let go. No anticipated scream. Instead, a groan, a sigh, followed by tears. Silently they rolled down her cheeks. He trailed their path with kisses and rested against her shoulder.

"*Je t'aime beaucoup*," she whispered into his ear, and she meant it. She, too, had never stopped loving him.

Gaston rose onto his elbows and renewed his assault. It did not take long for him to culminate, his pulsating release a triumphant satisfaction. His chest still heaving from exertion, he rested his forehead against hers. A tear splashed on her cheek, and she pushed at him so she could see his face.

"You are crying," she said softly, swiping her thumb across his cheek.

"*Oui*," he said, holding her gaze. "I cry tears of happiness. For I am finally home."

She pulled him close, and he nuzzled her neck. They lay joined for a while. Sophia thought Gaston had fallen asleep, but he suddenly rolled onto his back, pulling her with him and adjusting beneath her until she was settled comfortably on his chest. His heartbeat was slow and strong beneath her cheek.

She trailed her finger along the path of the rigid scar on his inner thigh. "Tell me about it," she said quietly.

Gaston harrumphed. "There is not much to tell. I think of it as a gift from a friend."

"What?" She tried to raise her head, but he held her gently against his chest.

"In times of war, it is sometimes difficult to discern who is your enemy. I had an urgent missive for Wellesley. I was riding alone and was overtaken by three Frenchmen. They did not ask questions first."

Gaston chuckled at the memory, but Sophia could see no humor in it and told him so.

"I can laugh because we were on the same side. The man became my friend and is one of my best contacts on the peninsula. I can also laugh," he said, taking her hand and setting it on his growing length, "because I am still intact."

Sophia was not one to waste an opportunity, especially one as delicious as Gaston was offering. He could not bear her stroking for long, and she squealed playfully when he quickly rolled with her, desperately seeking entrance. Later, after their shared pleasure made them both cry out, she lay curled against him, listening to his steady breathing. She relived every moment, every touch, every word. *I am finally home.* She stared at the darkened ceiling and smiled. She had found family in her friends. But for the first time since fleeing Paris, she, too, was finally home.

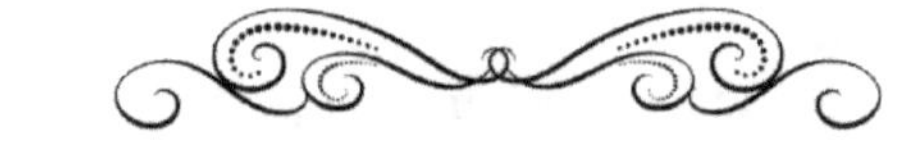

CHAPTER FORTY-SEVEN

And therefore if any two men desire the same thing, which nevertheless they cannot both enjoy, they become enemies.

—Thomas Hobbes, *Leviathan*

"THERE WILL BE gossip." Gaston swung his legs over the side of the bed, letting them dangle there as he stretched. "The entirety of London probably already knows."

"I do not agree. My staff is discreet. They have Raimondo to answer to."

Raimondo was undeniably formidable below stairs, but Gaston was not convinced even that beast could keep Gaston's presence in the town house under wraps. Besides, he had quickly abandoned his rooms but had not left London. He would be spotted coming and going from her town house. Bentley would likely initiate a new wager at his club. Discretion did not seem to be part of the man's makeup.

"I am simply saying, people will talk. You must prepare your answers."

"As must you."

He flopped back on the bed, trying not to smile. "I have."

"And what will you say?"

He wished she had not slipped on a robe. He'd like to see her breasts, to touch them, to trace those delicious dark orbs—

"Well?"

"Well, I will say I am the luckiest man in the world."

Her smile was one of sheer satisfaction.

"And that I was seduced. That I am exhausted because you are a wicked *femme* who cannot get enough of my body."

Sophie squealed and pressed a pillow against his face. He threw his legs back onto the bed and rolled on top of her, making love to her until they were both replete and genuinely exhausted as he'd said he'd claim. He wasn't sure how long he dozed before registering another voice in the room.

"At this hour? Indecent. Tell him I am not at home."

"*Sì, signora mia.*"

"No, wait. I do not want him to think he has simply missed me. Tell him I am unavailable. I am indisposed."

Gaston lifted his head, frowning in question.

"The duke," Sophie said. "He is not surrendering easily." She shrugged indifferently.

"*Un momento,*" he said to Sophie's maid, who quickly averted her eyes when he threw back the cover and swung his legs off the bed for the second time that morning. "Tell him to wait in the library. I will be there shortly."

Her maid scooted out the door without another glance at him, and Gaston stomped into the bathing room to retrieve his clothes. He grabbed his shirt and his trousers and shook them to no avail. Those wrinkles weren't going anywhere, and he'd no time to have them pressed. He would not face the duke as a rumpled usurper, for he was neither unkempt nor had he appropriated anyone. Sophie had always been his as he had always belonged to her.

He marched back into the bedroom and stopped, hands on hips. Sophie remained unfazed, sipping from a dainty cup, eyeing him over it.

"*Où sont mes vêtements?*"

She pointed to the small hall that led to the bathing room. He did not wait for detailed directions. He spun around, strode past the bathing room, and opened the next door beyond it. Sophie's scent wrapped around him, and he smiled. He looked around. It was appropriate her dresses looked like a collection of rich-colored jewels. For it was what Sophie was—a jewel. *Mon bijou.* And he was not going to let anyone come between him and his jewel.

His clothing was tucked in the far corner, but it was clear her maid had taken the time to ensure everything was stored correctly. All items of clothing were neatly pressed, and he dressed quickly. When he returned to the bedroom, Sophie was in her chemise and her maid was brushing her hair. She was breathtaking.

"I will come with you," she said.

"*Non.*"

Her eyes darkened in anger at his denial. Sophie never liked to be told what to do or not to do. Her maid moved out of the way, and he took her place, resting his hands on Sophie's delicate shoulders. They stared at each other in the mirror, and he gently massaged her, his thumb kneading the stiff muscles behind her blades. "You have tried, *mon amour.* Perhaps he will accept it from me."

Beneath his fingers, the tension slipped from her shoulders. "Perhaps. But he is a man used to getting his own way, Gaston. Tread carefully. We do not need more enemies to conquer."

He kissed the top of her forehead. "You are right, *mon amour.* I will pick him up carefully by his coattails and trousers and gently toss him into the street." Sophie's eyes grew large, and he laughed. "I jest."

He smiled and left her before she could convince him to wait for her. She had told the duke to step aside, and the man had chosen to be insistent. Well, Gaston would make it clear his tenaciousness made him look like a tedious, ratting dog and further overtures would only be viewed as pathetic.

Raimondo watched Gaston as he descended the stairs, but said nothing. He tilted his head in the direction of the library, and

Gaston nodded in acknowledgment. He opened the door, and the duke swung around.

"You," he barked, his face blossoming red.

Gaston stepped into the room and closed the door. "Can I help you?"

The duke's nostrils flared, and Gaston briefly thought the man might charge like an enraged bull. He rather hoped he would. Gaston suspected he could easily best him. But the arrogant fool stood there glaring as if Gaston would cower beneath him and slink away.

"Your Grace?" he asked smoothly, pleased with himself for remaining calm. For he would truly like to show the man who was superior in life.

"I would speak with Countess Tessaro." The duke bit out the words, so stiff he might snap in two should anyone want to try— and Gaston longed to.

"She is…" Gaston deliberately trailed off and stared at the ceiling as though looking for his words, although he had no lack of words right now. His problem was filtering them. The man was, after all, a duke. He could make life miserable for Sophie. "…in dishabille," he said, despite knowing he shouldn't. He was unable to resist making it clear he had come directly from her private rooms.

The duke stomped toward him, and Gaston braced himself. But the duke turned and walked away, his arm jutting out abruptly and knocking a vase of flowers to the floor. The glass remained intact, landing on the thick woolen carpet. The roses lay limply as the water bled around them.

"Not quite the dramatic gesture you intended." Gaston snorted. He'd not meant to, but it escaped him nonetheless and continued into a full-blown guffaw.

The duke swung around, fury making his otherwise acceptable face look much like the dog's his behavior reflected—which only served to give Gaston's laughter momentum. He knew he should stop, but once started, he found he could not. His newfound euphoria mixed with his disdain for this man. The absurdity that after everything he'd been through to get to this point, he was supposed to stand here politely while the duke demonstrated his discontent. It was too much. He wiped at his eyes, spotted the purple tones developing in the duke's cheeks, and doubled over in a fresh bout of laughter.

"I will see you banned from society," the duke said, waving a finger at Gaston.

"And I will ensure everyone knows you chased my skirts for money."

Gaston's laughter abruptly died, and he straightened up. Sophie stood in the doorway, resplendent in an emerald silk. *Mon bijou*. His jewel, yes, but she was rigid, severe—a diamond that could cut glass with her stare.

The duke laughed disdainfully. "Welcome to the real world, Countess. If you believe anyone will be remotely interested in that little tidbit, you are more of a simpleton than I assumed."

Gaston growled, ready to fly at the duke, but Sophie barked his name and held up her palm. She did not take her eyes off the duke. "Think of me what you wish. Your opinion is of no value to me. Nor are you."

"I will see you crawl."

"And I will see you humiliated."

Gaston's head swung between the two. The duke positively apoplectic in color and Sophie calm and regal.

"I know your truths, Your Grace," she said. "I truly considered marrying you, so I had you investigated. Credit so endless even my money might not bail you out." Sophie tsk-tsked at him, and Gaston bit back a renewed laugh. "Using an alias to gamble." She shook her head slowly. "And embezzlement? Whatever will the people who lost money in your little scheme think?"

She tilted her head and arched an eyebrow, and Gaston wanted to run to her and swing her around. He had thought she'd been tempted by the duke, but she had a clearer head than he'd ever had.

"I will see you ruined," the duke said and took a step toward her.

"Try," Sophia said, not looking away.

Gaston stopped the duke in his path. They were of the same height, and they glared into each other's eyes. "And you. I will see you returned to the gutters of Paris," the duke said quietly.

Gaston grabbed the man by his cravat and twisted it so it tightened. His already purple face darkened to a plum as Gaston raised him to his toes. "Try," he said, echoing Sophie's challenge.

"Raimondo!"

Gaston heard the stampede that was Raimondo before the duke was yanked from his grasp. Raimondo held the duke by the scruff of his neck and walked him out of the library. Seconds later, they heard the slamming of the door.

"Was all you said true?" he asked.

"I only recently received a full accounting."

Gaston held open his arms, and Sophie strode to him. He wrapped his arms around her, holding her tight. He was not sure if it was his heart thumping between them or hers. It did not matter. Like their hearts, they were in perfect accord. He held her until her trembling subsided, and she looked at him.

"*Nous sommes un maintenant,*" she whispered.

"*Oui, mon bijou.* We are one."

CHAPTER FORTY-EIGHT

Thy friendship makes us fresh.

—Shakespeare, *Henry VI*

"*Sì*, IT IS true. There will be gossip." Sophia repeated Gaston's earlier words. She had considered canceling Elizabeth and Catherine's visit but decided she would like them to hear about Gaston directly from her.

"So just like that, you decide to offer Monsieur Durand your guest room?" Elizabeth's eyes narrowed. "There must be more for you to risk your reputation."

"My reputation?" Sophia laughed. "*Bella*, you have known me for years. What is this reputation you refer to?"

"But you have always been discreet. Don't you agree, Catherine?"

"The soul of discretion," Catherine said, looking concerned.

Doubt clogged Sophia's throat, and her chest constricted. If her friends could not accept this indiscretion, then perhaps they would never be able to accept the whole truth of her, especially the fact she had not been forthcoming through the years.

Elizabeth sat forward on her chair and touched Sophia's knee. "I apologize. I have upset you. You know, of course, we stand by whatever you do. Nothing will change that."

"*Grazie*." Sophia looked at Catherine.

Catherine nodded solemnly. "Even if you are now a lady-bird," she said and burst into laughter.

Sophia's chest unclenched, and she swatted Catherine before joining in. When the laughter petered out, Sophia told them she was not a kept woman, but perhaps she would decide to keep Gaston. "Would it make him a manbird?"

Another round of laughter ensued, and their conversation moved on to more ordinary things. Sophia had not admitted she and Gaston had a long history together, nor that their futures were now permanently entwined through their pledge to each other. She'd told them he was in need of a place to stay and she owed him a favor. She'd discovered she enjoyed his company, so it made sense for her to make the offer. It was, after all, a big house.

She did not mention the confrontation with the duke. She doubted the man would share this morning's humiliation publicly. Besides, should he try to humble either herself or Gaston, she had the investigative papers as insurance. She had not had time to fully read through them, but she'd read enough to know the duke could not afford such exposure.

Eventually, they discussed their next adventure, the races at Newmarket on Monday. Not only would the change of scenery be welcome, it was an event swarming with people and usually rife with gossip. She was hopeful she would find out something of value. *They* would find something of value. She smiled at her correction. It was the two of them now.

"A pleased little smile if I've ever seen one." Catherine looked at Elizabeth and raised an eyebrow.

"I have secured ample suites in nearby Cambridge," Elizabeth said to Sophia. "Would you have me send a messenger to cancel one?"

"Evil," Sophia said before adding, "Perhaps." She enjoyed their wide-eyed response far more than she probably should. "I tease, *mie amiche*." Although she wished they could share a suite, she was not about to flaunt their impropriety in front of her friends.

"We will be traveling on to Woodfield afterward." Catherine set down her lemonade. "It has been fun, but balancing society and motherhood is taxing. Nicholas is done with what he has needed to do, whatever that is. Making sure boats float, I suppose." She smiled.

Sophia did not fall for Catherine's pretense at vacuousness. Catherine knew exactly what was going on with Walford's shipbuilding company, as did Elizabeth with her husband's dalliance in the shipping industry. Sophia sat up. When the war was over, Gaston would need something to call his own. He said he'd spent much time in ports and on ships these last years. The shipping industry would be a good fit. She would speak to Woodfield about investing in his shipping company and make it a wedding gift for Gaston.

"What do you think?" Elizabeth was looking at Sophia questioningly.

"*Scusami*, I seem unable to hold on to thoughts today."

Elizabeth and Catherine looked at each other and smiled knowingly. She could not chastise them, for their assumptions were correct.

"Richard would like to remain near parliament. Apparently there is movement on the continent, and he would like to be here for debates. I will be sending for the boys if we stay much longer. But I digress. Since we will be returning to London, you and Monsieur Durand can join us in our carriage, if you'd like. We will leave early Saturday morning."

Sophia pictured two days in a carriage, dancing around the truth of their relationship in front of her good friends. Then she envisioned her and Gaston alone in her carriage, and she was quickly decided. Her body tingled in anticipation. "*Grazie, bella,* but I have some business to attend to and must remain flexible."

"Flexible?" Catherine asked, looking at Elizabeth. They broke into fits of giggles.

"You are children," Sophia said, adoring how her friends had already taken Gaston's presence in stride. "Evil, evil children."

CHAPTER FORTY-NINE

The cause of all these evils was the lust for power arising from greed and ambition.

—Thucydides, *History of the Peloponnesian War*

"I THINK RAIMONDO is softening," Gaston said, adjusting his neck cloth and watching Sophie in the mirror. She had offered to hire a valet, but having a stranger in their midst did not seem a wise idea. Besides, he had been dressing himself for years and was adept at it.

"Why do you say that?" Sophie, fully dressed, sat elegantly on the chaise in the corner of the room.

"Those bushy eyebrows narrowed like an eagle's when I came back, but his glare was absent. His eyes weren't warm and inviting, but I got the feeling he didn't have the urge to hit me. It's progress, *non?*"

He got the laugh he was seeking and turned to look at her. "It is a pity we must work tonight, for I would far more enjoy undressing you than dressing me."

"There is always later," she said, her voice husky. "And tomorrow. I have no engagements for tomorrow."

Often one night of work led to another, but he would not ruin the moment by saying so. He loved that she was dreaming of their tomorrows. It was still a little surreal, but he would not pinch himself, for if this was a dream, he had no desire to wake up.

"I wish we were attending together."

"It would not aid our purpose to be the center of attention." He wanted to kiss her pouting lips. "It is best you go with the Thornwoods as planned. Bentley is the perfect cover for me. *Deux hommes élégants* out on the town, prowling for women with low standards."

"You are not much of a dandy, and you'd better not be prowling."

He turned from the mirror and scanned the length of her body. "One does not go fishing for cod when one has caviar at home."

Sophie's eyes narrowed in contemplation. "I am unsure if it is flattering to be compared to fish eggs."

He strode to the chaise and pulled her to her feet. "My apologies," he whispered in her ear. "You are incomparable. A diamond of the first water. *Mon bijou.*" He nipped her earlobe and swept soft kisses across her neck before seeking her mouth. They were both breathing hard when they parted.

The amber in Sophie's dark eyes danced in the lamplight. "You are forgiven." She touched his cheek, then dropped her hand. "You must go. Elizabeth will be here soon and insist you join us. She is valiantly rising to the cause of helping me assure your acceptance in my public life."

It was difficult to leave her, but he had an obligation to fulfill. He hoped tonight would provide some information that would be of help on the continent so he could alleviate his immediate debt. As for his promise to remain under Liverpool's direction after the month was over, it was entirely in the prime minister's hands as to whether he would hold Gaston to it. Never truly knowing the fate of her mother had haunted Sophie. If he could provide answers regarding her father, give her some closure, it would be worth it.

⇛⇚

"THE NIGHT IS young, *bella*. I would like to stay," Sophia said when Elizabeth declared she was ready to end the evening.

Sophia could not blame her. To ensure the evening flowed naturally, and it was not obvious she was seeking out anything or anyone in particular, Sophia had insisted they attend several of the five routs being held. They were at their third one, and it had grown tiresome. But this was the rout Jocelyne had named, so she was not going anywhere.

"Then we shall remain also." Elizabeth looked to her husband. Richard nodded in agreement, although he did not look enthused by the prospect.

"Not for me, *bella*." Sophia touched her arm. "I am a big girl, no?"

"I cannot leave you unattended."

"And she will not be so."

Sophia instantly recognized the deep baritone and turned as Lord Stratton stepped beside her.

"I will happily see the countess home."

Elizabeth smiled, and Sophia could see the worry slip from her eyes. "Perfect," she said. "I didn't know you were coming. You could have attended the other routs with us too."

"Well, Nicholas had accepted several invitations, but neither he nor Catherine wanted to leave the house. And since we will soon be back in the country, I decided I would wander about and see what London looked like through a grandfather's eyes."

The Thornwoods said their good nights, and Stratton offered his elbow. Sophia smiled at him, then glanced around the room. The Marquess of Acherton lived a life of excess. While he was a member of the House of Lords, Lord Acherton seemed to have little interest in politics. He far preferred to eat too much, drink too much, and rumor had it, love women too much. His townhome, larger than most and made all the more spacious by the removal of some furniture and the sliding open of walls between rooms, was decorated with gaudy artifacts from around the world. The collection was proof that money could not buy good taste. The front drawing room in which they stood had proven as uneventful as it was unappealing, so Sophia was happy to stroll and see which rooms drew the men. She could decide where it was best to eavesdrop.

"Catherine is pleased with the new developments in your life," he said quietly, although with the din around them, there was not much need for discretion.

Sophia was glad Stratton knew the truth about her and about Gaston's long-standing role in her life. "I am glad to hear it."

"As you should be, since you were so concerned about her good opinion. If she's your canary in the mine, your friendships will be fine. She could not be happier for you. Come the time you want to tell her your whole story, she won't run. She will only love you all the more. As I do."

"Why, Lord Stratton, are you revealing a hidden passion for me?" Sophia said flirtatiously, trying to dismiss the emotion threatening to rise into her eyes. What had happened to her? Crying had never come so easily.

Stratton chuckled. "A foolish old man may dream of such things, but a wise one knows realistically you would wear him out and send him to an earlier grave."

Sophia laughed, delighting in her relationship with Stratton. They chatted amiably as she paused in several doorways, considering the value of what was happening.

"I presume you are working?"

Sophia quickly glanced at him, surprised by his comment.

"I was watching you in the drawing room. You avoided groups of women and lingered wherever there were men. And now you loiter longest where the men gather."

"I am so obvious?"

"Only to me, Sophia. I've learned much from Laurence about this game you all play. I doubt anyone else will notice. You have always toyed with men in public. No one will give it a second thought."

"I grow weary of the game," she said quietly. Since the return of Gaston, she dreamed of a normal life once again. No flitting about where she'd rather not be. No subterfuge. No lies.

Stratton squeezed her arm in acknowledgment. "Where shall I escort you? Have you decided?"

"The games room would be best." She was glad Stratton had stayed. There were few women in there, and she would have been too obvious had she strolled in unattended. Two gentlemen were putting aside their cues. "I would have you teach me billiards," she said.

"But you know how to play."

"They don't know I do. Teach me. Flirt with me quietly, so no one is drawn to initiate a conversation with us. The men will be convinced you are preoccupied with me."

"A painful job, but I'll do it."

She smiled at Stratton's loud laugh and looked at him adoringly as they strode into the room. She spoke coquettishly to a few of the men nearby before turning her undivided attention to Stratton. At least, she hoped it looked like it was her undivided attention.

Stratton spoke softly about chalk and pockets, and she watched attentively as he bent over and demonstrated. There were four tables within hearing. One discussed the sequence of cards being played and whether it was easy to cheat. Another spoke loudly, each man trying to outdo the other in boasting about accomplishments. The third was focused on their game and said little.

The fourth table held her attention. Two men she did not recognize sat there. Their tones were subdued, but she sensed an underlying tension. They seemed to be playing vingt-et-un but far too slowly, and neither of them looked terribly interested in the game itself.

Lord Acherton's girth filled the doorway, drawing Sophia's

attention. He scanned the room and scowled before entering. He paused at several tables, and in contrast to his expression of seconds ago, he laughed jovially at something someone said. Then he moved on to join the two men, his face once again reflecting displeasure. "He has not yet arrived. I've only a few minutes, gentlemen. Get to your point."

Stratton must have sensed something was afoot, for he stopped talking. He leaned in behind her and took her arm in hand as though teaching her how to hold the cue. His breath lifted strands of her hair, his mouth moving as though he was whispering to her, but he said nothing.

"Overthrow? And how am I to do that?" Lord Acherton asked.

"It should not be all that difficult. A scandal."

Lord Acherton guffawed. "With Prinny at the helm, nothing is scandalous anymore."

"Then an assassination. It wouldn't be the first."

Lord Acherton did not respond.

"We don't care how you accomplish it. Create confusion. End the direct line of communication to Wellesley, and we'll begin a campaign of misinformation."

Sophia strained to hear more, but the man's voice had dropped to an indiscernible level.

"I don't see how—"

"Just do it."

Chairs scraped the floor, and the two men walked by the billiards table without a glance at her. She pushed back against Stratton lightly, and he immediately pulled away. She turned, smiling, risking a glance at Lord Acherton, who remained in his chair. He pulled out a handkerchief and wiped at his brow, seeming to notice her for the first time. He glanced at Stratton and frowned.

She returned her attention to Stratton, laughing as though they were having a grand flirtation. Her mind was busy sifting through what she'd heard, but she could make no sense of it.

Overthrow here or somewhere on the continent? Assassinate who? What confusion? Lord Acherton rose and stepped to the billiard table, a scowl darkening his face.

"Lord Acherton," she said politely. "A lovely rout this evening."

His eyes darted to Stratton before he fixed his gaze back on her. "Where is *your* duke tonight?"

She tilted her head sideways, hoping she looked annoyingly vapid. "*My* duke? I don't believe I own one of those," she said, and Stratton chuckled appreciatively beside her.

Lord Acherton shook his head and walked away, and Sophia laughed. She wouldn't be bothered by his rude departure even if she didn't know he was part of something untoward. Something she needed to find out more about.

"Let us go see where he's off to," Stratton suggested.

He set aside the cue, and she rested her hand in the crook of his arm. She spotted Bentley in conversation with Lord Acherton, who was not looking any more pleased with him than he had been with her. She directed Stratton to stroll to them. Before they reached the two, Lord Acherton spotted her and scooted out of sight around a corner.

Bentley nodded at them as they approached. "Countess." He bowed and whisked an imaginary kiss over her gloved hand. "A sight for sore eyes," he said, straightening up, a smile playing on his lips. "Lord Stratton. An unexpected pleasure to see you both here." He looked from one to the other. "A little subterfuge going on, I assume?"

Sophia's breath stalled. Bentley could not possibly be aware of what she was truly doing there. He burst into laughter, shaking his head.

"You should see your faces." He leaned in and whispered conspiratorially, "I know Monsieur Durand is entirely taken with you. I also know he has abruptly moved from his rooms to an unknown location. Coincidence? I think not. Stratton's a bit like throwing a ball for this pack of wolves to chase. A masterful move."

Heat rose to her face, but relief washed over her body. He assumed she was using Stratton to hide her true relationship. "And you, Bentley? You are busy upsetting the host?"

"I'm what?"

Bentley looked genuinely confused. Sophia wondered if the man ever held a thought for more than a few seconds. She looked pointedly in the direction Lord Acherton had gone.

"Oh, Acherton," he said, frowning. "A small gentleman's quarrel. He owes me on a few bets. I can never pin him down for payment. Seems I'm not going to tonight either."

"You still chasing the horses, then?" Stratton asked.

"When I can outrun the women, sir," Bentley said.

Sophia rolled her eyes, while Stratton chuckled and clapped him on the back. "You never change, son, you never change."

"I have had enough for tonight. Take me home, please." Sophia directed the command at Stratton.

"A certain Frenchman is upstairs." Bentley shrugged when she scowled at him. "I thought you might be interested."

"Perhaps you should not think so much, Bentley," she said and was instantly contrite when his face fell. She was tired and frustrated she had not managed to gather enough information to be of value. It was not Bentley's fault.

"I will see you in Newmarket," she said. "You can advise me what horses to bet on."

"It would be my pleasure," he said, his optimistic expression returned.

"He means well," Stratton said as they made their way to the front of the town house. "He was equally boisterous as a young lad, always putting his foot in his mouth."

"He is much different from Walford and Thornwood, no? They are serious, and he is..." She could not find the word. "Empty," she said, although it was not exactly what she meant. Thinking in three languages made her head ache sometimes.

Stratton contemplated her words before answering. "No, not

empty. Lighthearted, perhaps, but not empty."

They waited in the foyer, making idle conversation with people coming and going. The footman announced the arrival of her carriage, and they stepped outside. The Duke of Salinger had his foot on the first step, one of his lackey friends directly behind him. Sophia lifted her chin and continued down the stairs. The duke glared at her and Stratton.

"Excuse me," Sophia said, smiling benevolently at him.

He scanned her top to bottom. "There is no excuse for you," he said, a sneer twisting his face.

Stratton stiffened, and she squeezed his arm, much like she did with Raimondo when his anger rose.

"If you would move, we could be on our way and you could enjoy this lovely rout..." She spoke slowly and carefully as though she was speaking to a small child. "...with your little friend." She looked past the duke's shoulder at Lord Drake. The man should be flirting with women at balls or playing cards at the club instead of trailing an old man like the duke. She raised a regal eyebrow at him, and he had the decency to become instantly interested in his feet.

Of course, it had the intended effect on the duke, his nostrils flaring, his face growing darker in the dim light.

"A rose by any other name would smell as sweet. And a whore by any other name would still be—"

"Raimondo!" Sophia snapped, and turned quickly to Stratton. "Stratton!" she barked. She would not have either of them assault a duke. Not in public. She looked directly at the duke. "You are not worthy of anyone, Your Grace. Not even a whore."

The duke looked ready to dive at her but hesitated as he registered Raimondo's towering presence. He stepped aside, and Sophia and Stratton walked past him without another glance. It was difficult to comprehend why she had ever considered the man. It would seem Gaston had saved her twice in her lifetime. She would have to thank him properly when he returned home. She could hardly wait.

CHAPTER FIFTY

God the tyrant's hope confound!
To this great cause of Freedom drink, my friends,
And this great name of England round and round.
　　　　—Alfred Lord Tennyson, "Hands All Around"

DAYLIGHT WAS TEASING the horizon when Gaston returned. He'd tried not to awaken Sophie as he slipped into bed, but he'd not been successful. Groggy from sleep, she had roamed her hands over his body, and it had not been long before they were entangled. He'd fallen asleep soon after they'd made love, and now he was waiting for her to return to bed.

He sat up, pulling the coverlet over his lap. The room was opulent and definitively feminine, as rich and luxurious as Sophie was herself. He didn't want to change a thing. He liked being surrounded by the essence of Sophie in every room. Her library was plain should he ever want a more austere, less distracting environment.

"I will take it, Cara." Of course, the biggest distractor in the house was its mistress, who now stood in the doorway, tray in hand, staring at him. *Mon Dieu*, she was *une beauté*. Her hair tied in a simple twist at the base of her neck, her violet dress una-dorned, she was even more magnificent than when she set out to seduce the elite of London.

"I like seeing you in my bed," she said, walking into the room.

"And I like being here," he said, "especially when you're in it too." He patted the mattress.

"I better not." Sophie set the tray on the small table between two chairs. "We have much to discuss, no?"

She was, of course, disappointingly correct. He threw back the covers and stood, stretching languidly, knowing her eyes were upon him. His body responded accordingly, and he briefly considered allowing it to have its way, but Sophie was right. She'd said she'd heard some things of promise last night, but he'd fallen asleep. It was time to focus.

Gaston tugged on his underclothes and trousers and pulled on a shirt. Not bothering to tuck it in, he strolled over and joined Sophie where she sat. She poured him a cup of coffee, and he relaxed back in his chair. "You first."

Sophie relayed the conversation she'd overheard. Gaston grew excited. "It would seem we have found our traitor." It was a tremendous breakthrough, and Liverpool would be well pleased.

"Yes, for certain Lord Acherton is involved in something." She scrunched her nose adorably. "But who do you think they were talking about? There are many possibilities."

Gaston might have thought the same thing had he not overheard several comments from Acherton about Liverpool's ineffectual leadership and about how England had enough of its own problems without fighting somebody else's war. It had struck him as odd, conversation meant more for the clubs than for drawing rooms, but he could now see it for what it was. He was laying the groundwork for discontent so any actions he took might be looked upon more favorably. Gaston explained his conclusion to Sophie.

"But why Liverpool?" she asked.

"Liverpool was appointed, not elected. It has left many unhappy, especially Whigs and Radicals. Perhaps these men are simply disgruntled by it? Perceval was assassinated last year by an aggrieved merchant. It was an extreme reaction to his financial situation, but he'd convinced himself Perceval deserved it. Was so confident in its rightness he shot Perceval in full sight of everyone. Men are not always predictable, nor are their motives."

Some of the Radicals leaned toward revolutionary concepts. Many did not support involvement in the war. Especially now the colonies were fighting too. But Sophie knew all this, so he'd not belittle her by reviewing the obvious.

"But if they eliminate the prime minister, would the regent not simply put in another?" she asked.

"Yes," he said, "but it could be someone more in favor of ending the war."

It was a long bet and seemed unlikely Acherton would wish to jeopardize himself for such a random possibility. *Create confusion. End direct line of communication.* Gaston sat up.

"Unless," he said slowly. "Unless they do not care who becomes prime minister. The chaos another political assassination would create might be enough for the war to lose support. It would ruin relations with allies..."

"And Napoleon is struggling now, no?" Sophie put down her coffee. "So a little distraction may give him an opportunity to regain his edge."

Gaston stood and paced, trying to put his mind on what was bothering him. For certain, he could see the benefit for the French in such a plan, but what was in it for Acherton? Why would he risk everything for such a thing? Gaston put the questions to Sophie, who knew far more about these people than he did.

"Bentley said Lord Acherton owed him on some bets. Perhaps it is for money?"

"Perhaps. But I would hazard a guess it is more than a few bets if he is willing to chance getting caught betraying his country. I will have Liverpool look into it."

"*Si.* You should see him today. These men may not wait long."

Gaston continued to chew on the problem as he washed and got fully dressed. Sophie walked him to the door, and he brushed her cheek with a kiss, whispering words of love before stepping out into the fresh air. He had decided to walk, not simply for discretion's sake, but to clear his mind. It wasn't until he was rounding the corner of the prime minister's rooms that it struck him what was bothering him.

Acherton was not the only traitor. *Who* had the men been waiting for?

CHAPTER FIFTY-ONE

Kind is my love to-day, to-morrow kind,
Still constant in a wondrous excellence.

—Shakespeare, "Sonnet 105"

TWO DAYS LATER, Sophia and Gaston weren't any closer to figuring out who the fourth man could be. Sophia's housekeeper had attempted to secure the invitation list under the pretense Countess Tessaro was planning a soiree and wanted to be sure to include many of the delightful people she'd conversed with at the rout. Lord Acherton's housekeeper had not been forthcoming.

They'd listed as many as they could remember, but the truth was, it could be any one of them, or none of them. They had no way of knowing whether the man Lord Acherton had been waiting for had ever shown up. It was an entirely frustrating exercise.

"No, Cara, the other blue one."

Cara ducked back into Sophia's clothing room to grab the correct parasol. They had decided to continue with their plans to attend the races in Newmarket. Liverpool had been grateful for the warning and was now fully guarded. He would remain so until the other traitor was identified. Lord Acherton remained unaware his intentions were known, so they were optimistic he might lead them to the other man. It had been easy to discover he, too, was going to Newmarket.

The footmen arrived and gathered her trunk, and Cara scurried after them. Sophia trailed them down the stairs.

"I will take care of her." Gaston sounded exasperated, and when she heard Raimondo's rumbling response about Gaston's lack of ability to protect a chicken in a henhouse, she knew why. She stepped into the library, expecting fisticuffs, but Gaston stood by the window, rubbing his forehead, and Raimondo stood nearby with arms crossed.

"Raimondo, you will do as I ask. We are in no danger, and I wish to enjoy the view. We will probably pass you on the road." She had decided to treat her and Gaston to a post chaise. It was a much faster way to travel, and the view was less obstructed. And Sophia had always enjoyed watching the postilions astride the horses. She and Gaston might be working, but there was no reason they could not also have a little fun. Raimondo rattled on in rapid Italian about postilions not being able to protect her. She let him speak until it seemed there would be no end to it. "*Basta!* Enough!" she said, effectively cutting him off. "Besides, you can argue all you want. There is no room for you."

Raimondo grunted and stomped from the room. She looked at Gaston, who was biting back a laugh.

"Keep it inside you, Gaston, for if he hears it, he will storm back in here and take his frustration with me out on you."

He walked over to her and wrapped his arms around her waist, pulling her close. "He's growing on me," he said, kissing the top of her head. "I mean, he cares for you, *ma chérie*. I cannot begrudge that."

"Good," she said, leaning back so she could see his face. "He has been a loyal friend through the years. He will adjust. And hopefully, soon there will be no more of this business for him to worry too much about. He and Stefano will be able to garden until their hearts are content."

They strolled to the window and watched as Raimondo

climbed onto the box beside Charles and her coach left, taking Cara and Stephens along with their luggage.

Sophia presented her lips for a kiss, and Gaston obliged, slowly at first but deepening it until she was bursting with need. "The chaise will not be here for another hour," she said, running her finger down his chest and lingering on the button of his trousers' fall.

Gaston growled and scooped her up, carrying her out of the library. Harris stepped out into the hall, saw them, and stepped back into his room. Sophia laughed. Her poor staff had been treated to many unusual sights these past few weeks. At the top of the stairs, he set her on her feet and took siege of her mouth once again. When he finally surrendered, he looked around. "Eerily quiet without Raimondo banging around," he said and grinned.

"I have given everyone two days off. Except for Harris."

"A nice treat for them," Gaston said, kissing her nose.

"I wish I could also give Harris his time, but I think, maybe, the house should not be empty right now, no? Just in case?"

"Agreed. We will make it up to him when we are through."

"And we will make up for our lost time, a little at a time. Where were we?" She licked her lips, turned, and ran into the drawing room. She managed to make it into her boudoir before Gaston caught her around the waist and lifted her, spinning her around. She squealed, and he laughed, setting her on the bed. She rolled over, and he fell on top of her.

"*Je t'aime*," she said and showed him the truth of that love with her body. She would never get enough of him. Ever.

CHAPTER FIFTY-TWO

From the sublime to the ridiculous is but a step.

—Unknown

"I DO BELIEVE it was our quickest yet," Gaston said, catching his breath, his heart still thumping from their shared release. "I promise tonight we will linger."

Sophie rolled onto her side and smiled. "Quick is good. There is time for some food. A spice cake, maybe? You ring, and I will change my dress. Cara will not be happy with my wrinkles." She laughed and wiggled off the bed.

Gaston watched Sophie disappear into the other room, before getting out of bed and pulling the cord. He was hungry too, but he was always hungry. Perhaps he should get Harris to throw some food in a basket for the ride. Including cakes. Sophie loved her sweets. He slipped back into his drawers and trousers, tucking his shirt back in and buttoning the fall. He brushed at his waistcoat. He didn't look too worse for wear.

He wandered into the small drawing room and stared at the laneway that ran between Sophie's house and the one next door. Nothing. Not even a stray cat. He walked over to the cord and pulled again. Harris was usually prompt. He must be up to something. Gaston pulled out his watch. They would need to leave soon. He glanced in the bedroom. Sophie was still out of sight, presumably dressing, so he decided to go downstairs and find Harris himself.

It was odd to stand at the top of the stairs and see no one scurrying about. There was always someone busy doing something. A noise sounded from the library. *Ah, Harris found.* Gaston went down the steps and opened the door, stopping abruptly, his heart pounding in his ears. The room was upended, with paintings torn off the walls and scattered on the floor. A man's shoed foot stuck out from beyond the desk. Gaston stepped through the threshold, and seconds too late, he registered movement behind him. He spun around.

"You!" he said before crippling pain blurred his vision and he fell to the ground.

SOPHIA HAD TAKEN her time, sponging herself with cold water before strolling into her dressing room to select a new gown. She'd hoped Gaston would come looking for her and find her naked. She knew what she would ask him to do. Heat pooled in her abdomen, and she smiled. It seemed she was hungry for more than spice cake.

She chose a white linen and sash, imagining herself playing the younger version of herself for Gaston when they were safely away from prying eyes. Elizabeth had said she would ensure the suites were side by side. They could recreate that night of long ago. She laughed gaily, picturing Gaston climbing through a window.

Some strands of hair had fallen, but she liked the look so decided to leave them down. A little bit of naughtiness to contrast with her pristine attire. Gaston was not in the bedroom, nor in either of the drawing rooms. She had thought they'd eat in their room, but he must have had other ideas. She drifted down the stairs, trailing a finger along the banister, humming softly. She knew it was off-key, but happiness was bubbling through her, and she had to let it out somehow. Besides, there was no one around to hear her not-so-dulcet tones. Except for Gaston, but he'd love her anyway.

The door to the library was closed, but she could hear muted voices. Knowing Gaston, he'd had their tea set in there to make it easier on Harris. She pushed open the library door and froze, trying to process what she was seeing. Gaston was bound, his hair matted, a river of blood covering the right side of his face. Harris lay beside him, bound and gagged but clearly unconscious. She swallowed a gasp and scanned the room but could see no one. She listened for noise elsewhere but heard none. The thieves must have left.

She ran to Gaston, fell to her knees, and swiped at the blood on his face. He rolled his head back and forth groggily, trying to speak. "Shush, *mon amour*, let me untie you." She leaned over his body and pulled at the rope. It was snug, and she could not loosen it. Gaston squirmed, and she sat back on her knees. "Oh, my darling," she said, leaning forward and wiping again at the blood.

"Well, well, isn't this a pretty tableau?"

Her mind scrambled for a foothold, quickly processing this turn of events. Not thieves. She'd know his derisive voice anywhere. She swung around. The Duke of Salinger stood in the doorway to the anteroom, a look of utter disgust twisting his face. Sophia quickly calculated her chance of success if she charged him, and dismissed it immediately. She must keep her distance so he could not bind her too.

"What do you want?" she stood slowly, trying not to alarm him.

"I wanted *you*, but you have become quite..." He did not disguise his disdain as his eyes swept her from head to toe and back up again. "...distasteful."

"So why bother with this?" Sophia waved her hand around the room, sparing a quick glance at Gaston, who seemed to be rousing, his eyes looking clearer as he watched her. "Why come here if you find it all so distasteful?" But she already knew the answer. It was clear by the barren walls what he was looking for.

"I said I found you distasteful. I find your money incredibly attractive." He took a step into the room, and she took one back toward the foyer door, calculating how close she needed to be to successfully run out onto the street. At this time of day, there should be others about. And surely he would not harm Gaston if others knew he was here?

"Where is your safe, Countess?"

"I do not keep money on the premises. A woman alone would not be so foolish."

"Liar!"

The duke's shout was startling. He took another step toward her, and she backed up one more. His face had reddened, and she could not risk his anger propelling him toward her. It was time to bolt. She spun around, stopping instantly, her battering heart plunging to her stomach. Lord Drake stood in the foyer, the gun in his hand pointed at her head. *Mon Dieu*, what was she to do now? The only thing she knew for certain was she could not let them see her fear, especially for Gaston.

"Lord Drake," she said smoothly, "how lovely to see you again so soon."

The man's expression did not change. She turned her back to him and strode into the library, avoiding looking at Gaston. She could not be Sophie Auclair right now. She must be Countess Sophia Tessaro. "Oh, do tell your lackey to lower his gun, Your Grace. I am hardly worthy of such dramatics."

She didn't wait for an answer. She went to the side table and poured two brandies, proud her hands were not shaking, even when she handed one to the duke and took a seat on the chair. "Come," she said. "Let us talk like civilized human beings."

The duke eyed her suspiciously but did as she said. He did not order Lord Drake to lower his gun, so she had no idea whether the man still had it aimed at her. She refused to show her concern by turning to look.

"Now why would you do something as"—Sophia searched for a less inflammatory word than *cowardly*—"uncharacteristic as this?"

"You were supposed to have left for Newmarket," he said as though that explained it all. The red in his face had receded, and his customary dough-colored flesh glistened with sweat.

Sophia tilted her head, now fully immersed in her role as countess. "And you would steal from me?"

"I would take what I am owed." He took a sip of his brandy, apparently unfazed by the accusation.

"Owed?" She arched an imperial eyebrow.

"Indeed, owed. We had an understanding. I would make you a duchess, and you would make me rich."

"We had made no such agreement; although, I have admitted I did consider it."

"You were more than considering it. It was clear to everyone. It was simply a matter of when."

It was ludicrous that they were sitting, calmly having this conversation, while Gaston and Harris lay bleeding a few feet away. However, there was no choice but to engage him. She needed to buy some time to work out a strategy. Again, she resisted the urge to look in their direction. To see Gaston might undo the countess.

"Perhaps. But I broke no promises, for none had been exchanged. And you would never have gotten the bulk of my money. Thornwood helped me ensure no one could touch it. It's in a trust. He is thoroughly knowledgeable about the laws, you know."

"I would have found a way to break anything you'd put in place. I am a duke, Countess."

The derision had returned to his voice. He thought himself impervious to rules. "But not a *royal* duke. Your position has limitations, no?"

"You dare to goad me?" he asked, the color once again rising in his face.

"And you dare to enter my home and assault my husband!"

"Husband? That gutter rat who scurried from Paris, too afraid to take a stand and fight for his country?"

"You know nothing of him." Sophia bit her bottom lip to stop her rising anger from making her say more. It would do no good to antagonize him further.

"Enough," he said, slamming his glass on the table and standing. "I'd force you into marriage, but I don't want a Frenchman's whore." He spat out the words, spittle glistening in the corner of his lips. "Hand over the information you have gathered on me. And show me your safe."

Sophia stood and dared a glance at Gaston. He shook his head slightly. He was correct, of course. The duke's behavior was erratic and unpredictable. Extreme even for him. To give the man what he wanted would not end well for any of them.

"As I have told you, Thornwood has tied up much of my money. But..." She looked at the desk, pursing her lips as though trying to make a decision. She looked at Gaston and Harris, and she determined a course of action. It was a long shot but worth a try. "I have buried a strong box."

"I don't believe you," he said, quickly moving closer and gripping her arm. "Why would you do that?"

Sophia yanked from his grasp, swiping at where he'd held her. She was in a perfect position to draw her knee up hard, but she could see Lord Drake out of the corner of her eye. She could not possibly overcome them both.

"It is for emergencies. I have never trusted the English." She casually shrugged a shoulder, but she could tell he was still wary. "It is true." She sighed heavily. "The map is in the second drawer."

The duke walked to the desk, opened the drawer, and pulled out the etching she'd done of Gaston's map. He set it on the desktop and studied it. "Why is it penciled over?"

"It is how I made a copy. One here, one on my estate. It was too much work to draw two. I am lazy, no?"

"It makes no sense. Where is this? There are mountains."

"Château Nouveau. My estate. Those are hills. I don't draw well," she said, but he still looked unconvinced. She'd hoped he'd take the bait and leave. She would figure out how to deal with him after she'd taken care of the men. Gaston was watching her from beneath his lashes. Harris remained still. If not for the slight rise and fall of his chest, she would worry they had killed him.

"I will give you direction for the keys to the safe at Château Nouveau. The painting of the hunt in my library, the one you so admired because of the dappled gray beneath the rider,—it is behind it. There you will find some cash as well as the investigation reports on you. And the treasures in the buried box will tide you over until you secure another widow. Go. It's all yours."

He looked at the map and back at her.

"It is my apology for disappointing you," she added, trying to mollify him into acceptance.

"I would not get past your guard dog."

"Raimondo? He is on his way to Newmarket and not expecting me until tomorrow." Sophia could tell he was contemplating it. She had never taken him for a stupid man. He must truly be desperate.

"If you are lying to me..." He didn't finish his threat. He grabbed the map and folded it. "You're coming with me. You will show me where." He gripped her upper arm so tightly she could not break away.

"*Non*, Sophie. Don't leave with him," Gaston whispered hoarsely in French.

Sophia looked over her shoulder to where Gaston struggled against his binds. How could she leave him? How could she not?

The duke paused in front of Lord Drake. "Take care of them."

"No!" Sophia managed to yank free. "You harm them and I will not help you."

The duke hesitated.

"I swear to God you will not find so much as a penny if you

hurt them." Sophia glared at the duke. It would end here if it must. She would rather die with Gaston than live without him again.

"Hold them. I'll send word." The duke yanked her along the hall and on through her morning room before pulling her out the rear door and down the few steps to her garden, damaging newly budding lilies as he dragged her to his coach waiting discreetly in the mews. His coachman did not look at her as the duke tugged open the door. She put a foot on the step, debating the wisdom of going with him, but he roughly pushed her in. She clambered for a grip and pulled herself onto the bench while he shouted directions to his coachman, then joined her.

"You make a scene anywhere along the way, and I will send word to finish your Frenchman."

Sophia stared at him, genuinely perplexed. Why would a man in such a position resort to such treachery? One minute normal, the next unhinged. And she knew which he would be when he discovered there was no buried treasure. She had only bought some time. *Mon Dieu*, how was she going to save Gaston?

CHAPTER FIFTY-THREE

Where one door shuts, another opens.

—Miguel de Cervantes, *The History of Don Quixote*

GASTON STRUGGLED TO sit, but trussed like a sheep for shearing, he could not manage it. Pain split his head, and the dripping blood was congealing, making his eyelashes stick together. He kept blinking them so they would not seal shut. He had to get free. Had to go to Sophie. Her plan was foolhardy. While he'd been unable to see the scrap of paper, he was certain it was a copy of the map he'd drawn for Liverpool. There would be no buried money. The Duke of Salinger would truly lose what was left of his mind when he found out. Gaston needed to get there before he did.

The other man—Lord Drake, Sophie had called him—came into the room and paced back and forth by the front window. Finally, he walked over to the chair, grabbed the duke's glass, and downed the brandy only to return to his pacing. Like a cat on edge. The man was nervous. That could be a good thing or a bad thing.

He stopped suddenly and swore an unintelligible string of epithets. A few minutes later, the knocker sounded at the front door. Gaston debated shouting but decided his voice would not carry from where he lay. But if Drake would go answer the door, there might be a chance.

"You might want to check on that. I assume it's our curricle arrived."

"They will leave," Drake said indifferently, stepping away from the window but jumping as the knocker banged loudly in the empty foyer. It was obvious he was not a man used to doing such things. Gaston pondered how the duke had managed to get him on board for this nasty little escapade.

Disappointingly, Drake was right. After a third attempt, the hallway fell silent. Gaston knew the postilions had left when Drake sighed heavily. Drake walked to the table and poured a large brandy before returning and sitting in a chair where he could watch Gaston.

"What will you do when the staff return? Truss them all up? Or do you think they'll simply go about their business and ignore the fact their mistress is gone, her husband is bound and battered, and their butler is lying unconscious in the library?" Gaston could tell the practicalities of remaining behind had only just registered with Drake. "Whatever he has on you, it's not worth this."

"Shut up," Drake said and took a swig of the brandy.

"If you kill me, you will swing. If you free me, I guarantee I will hunt you and ensure you stand before a magistrate. And if so much as a hair on Sophie's head is harmed, I will skip the magistrate and make a noose myself for you. So you see, whichever way this plays out, you lose, lose, or lose. The duke has put you in this tenuous situation."

"I said, shut up," he barked, finishing the brandy in one long gulp and coughing as he wiped at his lips. He got up, paced again, returned for his glass, and glared at Gaston. "So I might as well kill you and be done with it."

"You haven't got the courage." Gaston wasn't sure he was helping things any, but he couldn't lie passively while his mind reeled with thoughts of what was happening with Sophie.

"Bloody foreigner," Drake said, stomping over to the decanter.

It was not Drake's continuing rant that held Gaston's attention. A shadow had shifted in the foyer; he was sure of it. He glanced at the window. It was impossible for a change of light there to affect the hallway. Again. Barely perceptible but definitely there. His heart ramped up. Someone was in the house. Whichever servant had returned, he hoped they had the good sense to go get help. Hope blossomed in his chest. He needed to stop poking Drake and instead get him talking, keep him preoccupied. He wiggled again, trying to sit, but to no avail. All it did was make his head ache more.

Drake returned and threw himself into the chair again. He raised the gun, pointed it at Gaston, and made the sound of a shot firing. "That's how easy it would be."

Gaston might have given the threat more credence if the man had put his finger on the trigger, and if his hand didn't have a slight tremble. Drake was no killer. Although, now there was hope of someone alerting authorities, he had no desire to test that theory.

"What does he have over you?"

"Over me?" Drake laughed bitterly. "It is not the duke I worry about. No. He is not my problem. In fact, we are bedmates in our troubles."

"I do not comprehend your meaning?"

"We have both lost everything."

"So? You start again. It is not unusual."

Drake shook his head. "Not so easy when you still have debt outstanding to men who are not forgiving. When you've had to do things you would never have done…things that would see you hang."

It was a weighted confession, and Gaston nodded solemnly, trying to keep his eyes from roving to where a man was walking quietly into the room.

"What things?" Gaston asked.

"Yes, do tell, what things?" asked Laurence, the man from Sophie's lake house, as he pressed a gun against the back of Lord Drake's head. And, unlike Drake, his steady finger was on the trigger of a cocked gun. This man knew how to kill.

CHAPTER FIFTY-FOUR

Though this be madness, yet there is method in 't.

—Shakespeare, *Hamlet*

"I AM HUNGRY and tired." Sophia had hoped the duke would doze so she might be able to somehow knock him out, but neither had he slept nor could she see anything heavy enough to do any damage.

"And I grow weary of your complaints." The duke brushed at his jacket dismissively. "But you are in luck. My coachman must rest, so we will be stopping soon."

Anticipation coursed through Sophia's veins. If they were stopped, she might have a chance to escape. She watched the duke. While half his face was hidden in the shadows, his eyes were unmistakably opened as wide as they had been all day.

"Don't even consider it, my dear Countess," he said, finally looking directly at her.

"Consider what?"

"You can feign innocence all you want. I know there is nothing innocent about you." He snorted in amused disgust. "If you try to leave my side, or try to alert anyone, I assure you, your Frenchman will die."

Sophia weighed her options. Gaston was in London. She could get the authorities to her town house if the duke was taken into custody. Lord Drake would not know the duke had been caught and would be waiting for word.

"You don't really believe Drake has remained at your town house?" he said, reading her mind. "If so, you truly are naive. He has moved your Frenchman elsewhere and awaits word from me as to how to proceed. And how we proceed is entirely up to you."

Her stomach churned. He could be lying, but she could not take the chance. She decided it was best she wait until they arrived at her estate. There was only a skeleton staff at Château Nouveau, as many had come to London with her, but Stefano was there. He would take care of the duke. She could send word to London about Gaston. And Harris.

She bit her lip to stop the emotion bubbling at the memory of the two of them lying on the floor. She glanced at the duke, who was now staring blankly at the shuttered window. Hate rose within her. Strong and righteous, it subdued all other emotion. The duke would pay.

The carriage rolled to a stop. The duke grabbed his overcoat from the hook and tossed it at her. "Cover yourself. You're a mess."

She looked at her dress. Gaston's blood stained her left shoulder and breast. She could not remember wiping her hands on herself. Had it been only this morning she'd exchanged her violet dress for this one because she'd rumpled the first when making love? Choosing white because she'd felt like that young girl from long ago? She ran her hand across the dried smears. *Gaston. Oh, mon amour, stay strong.*

"I said, put it on. And remember, not a word. Not an inkling of distress."

The door opened, and the duke quickly ducked out. Sophia slid across the seat and took the coachman's proffered hand. He kept his eyes averted as he assisted her. She would find no help from him. She hadn't truly expected to. The duke would keep servants as loyal to him as hers were to her. She thought of Raimondo and how this would not have happened had he been allowed to stay by her side. He was going to kill her when he found out.

She didn't recognize the small coaching inn, but she did not travel for as long at a time as they had today. They'd stopped only to change horses and, once, to allow her to relieve herself on the side of the road. She would have been indignant had the need not been so great.

The inn smelled of sour ale and horse dung, and she was surprised the duke stooped so low in accommodation. Of course, it might be to avoid anyone they might know, or simply because he could afford nothing more. She had always known he was interested in her money, had known the debts he'd incurred through gambling. The embezzlement discovery had come the morning after she and Gaston and had done the handfast. She'd decided to keep the information to herself, should she need it to ensure the duke did not harass her or Gaston. Never had she imagined he would threaten their very lives.

The grizzly innkeeper fawned over the duke and ignored her. He led them to a room on the second floor, facing away from the courtyard. He left the lamp, promising someone would come with the requested food, sparing her a leering glance before bowing his way out of the room and shutting the door behind him. Sophia dropped the duke's coat to the floor, detesting the scent of him on it, and went to the window. She stared out at the darkness, grateful to be standing and letting the blood flow through her stiff legs.

"You might as well sit, Countess."

She ignored him but watched his dark reflection as he scraped a chair across the floor, bringing it closer to the door. Some time later, there was a tap. A servant came in and quickly lit a fire. He was followed by a maid who set a tray on the table and scurried back out. Still, Sophia kept her back to the duke, her mind too tired to think, her heart too weary for her to look him in the face again. Who was this man who had courted her? She prided herself on her ability to read people. How could she not have seen the beast within?

"I thought you were hungry."

Sophia wasn't any longer, but she knew better than to let her strength ebb from lack of nourishment. She needed to have her wits about her if she was to get out of this situation safely. The duke got up, bolted the door, and pushed the chair against it, effectively blocking a quick exit for her. She had no intention of trying it anyway. She was no longer certain Gaston was at the town house, and she could not risk the duke sending word to Lord Drake. She did not know the way out of this yet, but she would find it. She and Gaston had not come this far to be parted by this man's greed.

She turned from the window and watched the duke saunter to the table. He pulled off the cloth from the platter and grunted before looking at her. "Come, Countess," he said and pulled out a chair. "Sit."

Sophia did as instructed, glimpsing in his gray eyes the return of the man she'd once thought she knew. He put some cold beef and a few wedges of cheese on her plate and pushed it toward her before filling a plate for himself and sitting opposite.

She nibbled the cheese, trying to ignore her rolling stomach as she watched him eat heartily, filling his plate a second time before speaking. "We could have been something special, you and I. We were most certainly compatible enough."

Sophia picked up another small wedge, breaking off a piece and popping it into her mouth. She chewed it slowly, watching him, not saying a word.

"Careful, Countess. You are looking oddly enticing right now." He grinned and tore off a chunk of beef, waving it at her. "I could spread you and breach you. No one would care. You could scream. No one would disturb us. You're merely a duke's whore here."

It was not fear clogging her throat. It was anger. With difficulty, she swallowed the cheese, knowing to show either emotion would only fuel the duke more. She took a sip of the watered ale, and when she had successfully washed it down, she dabbed her lips with the grayed linen before setting it back on her lap.

"Why are you risking everything for money? Surely you are not the first man who has too many debts." She was pleased with how calm her voice sounded.

He chewed his beef slowly, looking as though he was giving her question honest consideration. She waited.

"I have forfeited my holdings, except for Salinger House, which I cannot. I am indebted to men who…" His voice trailed off.

"Who?" she prompted.

"Whom I would prefer to no longer deal with. It is past time I left the country. It was my intention to marry you and politely disappear. But you have ruined my plan." He pinched his forehead and rubbed his eyes, shaking his head. "Enough talk. Go to sleep."

"But I don't understand—"

"You don't have to understand." He took a sip of ale, and his face contorted. "Swill!" he roared and drew his arm back, whipping the tankard at the wall.

A chill ran through her body. She understood men, knew how to manipulate them, steer them where she needed them to go. But the duke was gone, and she did not know what to do with the wide-eyed man now raving mad over bad ale. Realization struck her as though she'd been slammed in the stomach.

Mon Dieu! The duke's actions were not born of need or even desperation. Nor was he simply temporarily not in his right mind. The man was insane.

CHAPTER FIFTY-FIVE

No, I'll not weep:
I have full cause of weeping; but this heart
Shall break into a hundred thousand flaws,
Or ere I'll weep. O fool, I shall go mad!

—Shakespeare, *King Lear*

LAURENCE TOOK CHARGE. He made Drake carry Harris to his bed. The butler had groggily awoken, and a maid had returned only to be sent off immediately to fetch a doctor. Gaston had wanted to head straight out, but Laurence had convinced him to wash and change first, while Laurence interrogated Drake.

Gaston did so quickly, going mad with the scent of Sophie in the room, her jeweled gowns hanging casually as though it was any other day. His head ached. Although it had slowed, the gash still dripped blood. He pressed a folded handkerchief to it and strolled through the bedroom. The rumpled sheets made him want to sit and weep. He stood still for a few minutes, allowing his fear to transform into anger. Anger was an emotion he could handle.

There was satisfaction in seeing Drake bound as Gaston had been. From the red marks and the split lip gracing Drake's swelling face, Laurence was a none-too-gentle interrogator. Gaston's satisfaction grew. He would like to have a go at the man himself, but he was slightly dizzy.

Laurence stood and walked to him. "Let me see."

Gaston pulled back the cotton cloth, and Laurence whistled through his teeth. "You are not going anywhere."

"It is nothing. Let's go." He wobbled slightly but forced his shoulders back, willing himself to stand tall.

Laurence studied him. "I'll not have you traipsing after me and dying somewhere on the road. So you can come as long as you get your head seen to."

"And him?"

"Your maid had a second errand. She should have delivered my message by now. There will be someone here soon to take over."

Gaston did not know why this man had miraculously appeared and was about to ask, when there was a rap on the front door. Laurence disappeared and returned with the doctor. The man looked at Gaston, then glanced at Drake before returning his attention to Gaston.

"Sit," the doctor said calmly as though he saw men tied up and bloodied every day.

Gaston did not need to be asked twice. The doctor worked quietly, the sting of a solvent nothing compared to the pain. It was as though someone had cleaved his head with an ax. The doctor pulled several items out of his case and looked at Laurence. "A bucket, then mix this tonic."

"No laudanum," Gaston said, flinching as the needle pierced his flesh and the doctor tugged the thread through. He'd had laudanum when his leg had been lanced, and his brain had been useless for days.

"Not laudanum. Ground cinchona. It won't erase the pain, but it should dull it."

Laurence appeared with an empty coal bucket and went out of sight again. The doctor was a man of few words and said nothing further as he stitched Gaston's scalp. Gaston closed his eyes, but Sophie danced before him, and he could not bear it, so he opened them again.

The doctor tugged one last time as he knotted the thread. He handed Gaston the bucket. Gaston took it, looking at the man questioningly. Seconds later, his gut swirled, and he retched, vomiting repeatedly until there could be nothing left in his stomach. When he was through, the doctor handed him a dampened linen and removed the bucket.

Gaston wiped his mouth. "You've done this before," he said quietly.

"A few times." The doctor smiled and dropped the bloodied cloth in the bucket at his feet. He wiped his needle and gathered the few things he'd taken out. "Now where is my other patient? I'm assuming it's not him." He jutted his chin in Drake's direction.

"You assume correctly," Laurence said, surprising Gaston with a hearty chuckle. The man was unflappable. "Down the hall and to the right. I'll need you to stay with this one, though, when we leave, until someone arrives." The doctor nodded and left the room, and Laurence turned his attention back to Gaston. "Here."

Gaston took the glass and drank the tonic, heaving a few times, glad there was nothing left to throw up.

"It will take a while to ease. I have laudanum if it becomes unbearable."

"No. No laudanum. We need to go."

"We do. But let's give you a few minutes and wait for the doctor to return to sit with our friend. Close your eyes. It will work faster."

Gaston rested his head back. This time, Sophie danced and smiled at him invitingly. He promised her he was coming. Her colors faded into darkness as he whispered words of love.

CHAPTER FIFTY-SIX

O mistress mine, where are you roaming?
O, stay and hear: your true-love's coming.

—Shakespeare, *Twelfth Night*

EARLY-EVENING SHADOWS WERE creeping in again, and although the carriage windows remained shuttered, Sophia was sure they must be approaching her estate. They had stayed at the inn only a few hours before the duke had dragged her out of bed in the middle of the night and they'd begun their journey again.

She had tried several times to probe the duke for answers but to no avail. He was not antagonistic, more sullen and uninterested in conversation. The day had been endless, with imaginings of Gaston lying bleeding to death making it truly unbearable.

The duke pinched his nose and rubbed his eyes, glazed and ringed in red. She doubted he'd slept at all. She had tried to stay awake but, in the end, had drifted off for a short while. He caught her gaze and tilted his head, and she could see the duke again in his eyes.

"I watched you sleep last night."

Sophia's stomach turned at the idea of him staring at her while she slept, but she did not show her distaste. Perhaps while he seemed to be in his right mind, she could reason with him.

"Your Grace—"

"I have changed my mind," he said, cutting her off and leaning forward. She suppressed a flinch as his hand touched her chin, and he tilted his head one way, then the other. "Yes, a most worthy prize. Despite your betrayal, I will marry you anyway."

"But you cannot. I am already married."

He laughed as though she had said something terribly amusing.

"Oh, but my darling Countess, I have been watching everything you do. You may pretend you are married, but you are not. No banns. No ceremony. Nothing. No, I am decided. I want it all." He sat back in his seat. "Don't worry, I still must leave." He scanned her slowly from head to toe, and a shiver of distaste shimmied across her flesh. "After I claim my reward. Of course, once we lie together, you may want more. I'll consider allowing you to accompany me."

"I will never agree to it." Fear and anger brewed inside her, and she knew better than to antagonize him yet could not seem to help herself.

"I'm convinced you will," he said, brushing at his sleeves as though he was making idle conversation. "Your Frenchman's life is in my hands. I need only send word…"

"Gaston will kill you," she said through gritted teeth.

He laughed uproariously, far too long and dramatically, wiping at his eyes. The carriage slowed, veering to the right. The duke sobered instantly. "Of course, the point is moot if there is no buried box. I could not trust a woman who so misled me. And I could not allow you the opportunity to tell others about our little escapade, now could I?"

Sophia rubbed her arms, chilled despite the stuffy carriage. She hoped Stefano was on full alert, because she could not deal with this madman alone. Unfortunately, Stefano would recognize the carriage and would merely think it slightly odd the duke would come calling while she was in London. She would have only seconds to warn him. It was not long before the carriage pulled to a stop. She held her breath, waiting to hear Stefano's voice, debating how she could assist him, hoping he would make enough of a distraction for her to do something.

The carriage rattled as the coachman disembarked, and Sophia heard muffled voices. "Stefano!" she shouted. The duke flew across the short space, covering her mouth so forcefully her tooth pierced her bottom lip. He flattened her against the bench before she could get out a warning. She did not struggle. It was pointless. She could hear nothing more than his heavy breathing and her own heart beating in her ears. They both turned when the door opened.

"Your Grace," his coachman said as though the sight of the duke splayed on a lady was a common occurrence.

The duke straightened, smiling, offering her his hand. She slapped it away, and he raised an imperial eyebrow before sidling out of the carriage. Sophia sat up, swiping at her lips, wiping away the blood and the taste of his flesh.

"Come, my darling," the duke cooed from outside.

Sophia steeled her back, slid across the bench, and ducked out of the carriage, refusing his assistance. She bit back a gasp as the coachman dragged a facedown Stefano to the far side of the carriage, out of sight of the house. She moved toward them, but the duke grabbed her arm, his grip painful.

"There is still enough light left to locate this box," he said smoothly. "Spencer, grab the lanterns from the carriage and find a shovel."

The coachman avoided direct eye contact with Sophia. He had proven he would stand by the duke, so she was well and truly on her own. If she went into the woods with them, she was certain she would never come back. In the house, there were still several footmen. It was her only chance.

The duke released his grip to pull out and unfold the map. "So, my darling Countess, which direction?"

"It is around the back and through the gardens," she said, hoping to lure him closer to the mansion.

"Where is that on the map?" he asked, his suspicion obvious.

"I do not know," she said.

He growled angrily, and she shrugged. "I cannot see without my spectacles. And since I do not have my reticule with me, I do not have my spectacles."

"And it is now you tell me this?" The duke lost his pretense of civility, grabbing both her arms and rattling her.

Sophia resisted the urge to scream in his face. Instead, she smiled slowly, pacifyingly. "I keep others here, Your Grace. I cannot read without them, so they are everywhere."

He frowned. "Why have I never seen you with them?"

"I am vain, no?"

The duke scowled, studying her for a minute, then yanked her forward toward the manse. "If you think you are going to trick me, you will be sadly disappointed. Spencer, stay with the carriage. And you, not a word of warning to your servants. If Drake doesn't hear from me soon, he knows what to do."

They walked across the expansive courtyard and up the sweeping stairs. No one opened the doors, so the duke insisted she do so and step into the foyer. There were sounds of footsteps on the stairs, and young Patterson's head appeared.

"My lady," he said breathlessly, "we weren't expecting you." He moved swiftly toward them but stopped abruptly, staring at her chest. "You are hurt."

"A small accident," the duke said, squeezing her arm. "I will see to it."

"Yes, Your Grace," Patterson said, bowing. He glanced questioningly at Sophia, and the duke's grip tightened.

"You can let the others know we've arrived. We are famished." Sophia said it calmly but tried to flash warning in her eyes.

"Do not interrupt us until we call for you," the duke barked.

Poor Patterson seemed confused as he scurried away. She didn't know what help he would be. She wanted to scream, bring her small staff to her aid, but the duke still had his weapon, and someone might get hurt. Besides, the coachman would not be easily captured. What if he rode back to London? She could not risk Gaston's life. She needed to buy some time and find out where he was held, if he had indeed been moved from her town house at all.

"Let's get your bloody spectacles and get on with this." He held her firmly as she led him into the yellow drawing room. The room where she'd first laid eyes on Gaston again. Where she had kissed him, so overjoyed by his return. Where she had thrown him out. She had wasted precious time with him. She swallowed the lump in her throat. If they survived, she would not waste another moment.

Luckily, she did own several pairs of spectacles. She pulled a set from a drawer, and he shoved the map in front of her. "Where to?"

She made a production of unfolding her spectacles and perched them on her nose, studying the map. "Yes, we start here," she said contemplatively, "and then go here."

"Where is here? What are those markings there?"

Sophia had no idea what the markings were, and she feared he would soon catch on that the map was useless. "I am truly famished." She rubbed her forehead. "And my head hurts." She looked to the window, where the drapes were drawn. "And it grows dark," she said as though she could see outside. "Can we not wait until morning?"

"No," he snapped, renewing his grip and dragging her back out of the drawing room and into the entrance hall. He fussed with something with his other hand, and she felt the press of metal into the base of her spine. "We do this now. Open the door."

Sophia did as told, yanking it open. She gasped, her knees weakening as she cried out in relief. Her *cavalerie* had arrived.

CHAPTER FIFTY-SEVEN

He says the best way out is always through.

—Robert Frost, "A Servant to Servants"

GASTON HAD BEEN ready to fire. His hand trembled slightly at his knowing he could have hurt Sophie, but he kept his gun raised anyway. The duke, standing behind Sophie, had a grip on her arm, and from this angle, Gaston could see the gun. He glanced at Laurence and down at Sophie's waist with a slight movement of his head, relieved when he could see Laurence understood the danger Sophie was in.

Gaston quickly inventoried Sophie. Her hair was in disarray, her clothing disheveled, dried blood staining her white gown. She should be terrified, but if she was, she didn't show it. Behind a pair of spectacles, her dark eyes were steady. His brave Sophie. He wanted to roar and charge, but he stood still, willing his hand to stop shaking.

The duke looked from Gaston to Laurence and back again, his customary disdainful arrogance unchanged. He appeared none the worse for wear, except his eyes were rheumy and red-rimmed.

"I should have killed you while I had the chance." The duke shook his head as though Gaston was a minor nuisance and not a genuine threat. "Where's Drake?"

"He's dead," Gaston said, which he assumed was entirely untrue. They'd left Drake under the supervision of the doctor but not before finding out the duke had been selling information to the French and was part of the plot to kill Liverpool. Worse, the aim was to create total chaos and the collapse of confidence in Britain, and to that end, the duke had been given another assignment—to assassinate the prince regent. High treason. If the duke realized they were aware of that, he would have nothing to lose. There would be no saving Sophie.

"Incompetent as always," the duke muttered. His eyes darted toward Laurence. "Who are you?"

"Put the gun down, Your Grace, and we'll talk about who I am."

The duke snorted, and Sophie winced as he wedged the gun more securely. "Quite the opposite, my boy. You put the gun down. Both of you. Then perhaps we'll talk."

Gaston would take no chances with Sophie. He lowered his gun, and he was relieved to see Laurence do the same.

"I said, down," the duke snapped, and Sophie flinched again.

They both set their weapons on the landing.

"Back up. Down a step."

They tried to separate, each taking one of the two sets of sweeping stairs on either side of the landing entrance.

"You take me for a fool? The same side." The duke shuffled forward with Sophie, both still out of arm's reach, and kicked each gun off the landing to the ground below.

"Now we're going on a little adventure. Back down slowly. One suspicious move and you can say goodbye to the countess."

It seemed ages before Gaston's foot hit the ground, his mind racing, trying to analyze the best way to disarm the duke without harming Sophie. The duke was tall and clearly strong. Sophie valiantly tried to trip and make him lose his grip, but he had no apparent issue holding firm.

"To the carriage. Backward. Slowly."

They shuffled back toward the carriage, stopping when they

were in the ring of lights of the oil lamps sitting on the ground. The duke tsk-tsked, shaking his head. "You shouldn't have done that to Spencer. Now one of you will have to do his work. Or I can let the countess get her pretty little hands dirty."

"I'll do it," Gaston said, perplexed that the duke continued to think there was truly a buried box.

"I thought you might. We don't need him." The duke looked at Laurence, then back at Gaston. "Get rid of him."

Sophie's eyes grew wide, and Laurence said nothing.

Gaston's head hummed, his gash pounding with his heartbeat. "I will not," he said calmly. "You can try to kill us all, but you won't succeed. Besides, where would that leave you financially?"

"Don't have the stomach for it, boy?" The duke shook his head in disgust. "Frenchmen," he said and spit to the side. "Knock him out. I don't care. But do it well, or we'll test your little theory of how many I can kill. I know for certain I can kill one." He set his chin on Sophie's shoulder and grinned, and Gaston knew why the duke was willing to go on this insane goose chase. Because he was an insane goose. *Mon Dieu!* It made his behavior too unpredictable. Gaston looked at Laurence apologetically.

Laurence held his stare and shrugged. "Do what you must."

Gaston grabbed the shovel lying beside the coachman. "Turn around." Laurence slowly turned his back to Gaston, and Gaston raised the shovel. He paused with it raised high, not wanting to do an innocent man harm, debating the wisdom of heading into the woods with a madman.

"Do it!" the duke shrieked in a high-pitched voice, and still Gaston hesitated, calculating whether he could swing around and move the few feet quickly enough to hit the duke with the shovel. But what if it landed on Sophie's head instead?

He caught the duke's movement out of the corner of his eye, and a shot rang out. But it wasn't Laurence who screamed in pain. Gaston swung around as the duke stumbled backward, holding his bloodied hand. Gaston lunged forward and pulled

Sophie away, and Laurence pounced like a cat on top of the duke.

Gaston embraced Sophie against his chest, holding her firmly, although he himself was unsteady with relief coursing through him. The duke moaned, rolling his head side to side.

"It's about time," Laurence said, still pinning the duke to the ground.

A man walked from the shadows, and Gaston had difficulty making sense of any of it.

"Stratton. Durand."

Sophie shifted in his arms and stiffened in surprise. "Bentley," she whispered.

"Indeed, Countess Tessaro," he said, bowing politely as though greeting them at an evening event. "It is I."

CHAPTER FIFTY-EIGHT

Who was witness of the crime?
Who shall now reveal it?

—Alfred Lord Tennyson, "Forlorn"

SOPHIA WAS WEAK-KNEED and grateful Gaston had his arms around her, holding her tight, pressing kisses to the top of her head. Laurence slowly got off the duke while Bentley kept the gun trained on the duke's head. He needn't have worried. The duke sat up and cradled his hand, rocking back and forth, weeping like a small child. She might feel sympathy had the man not meant such harm.

"You shot the gun out of his hand?" Sophia asked, still trying to make sense of what had happened in the last few minutes. She took off her blood-splattered glasses and wiped at her face. She clearly remembered the duke suddenly extending his hand under her armpit to shoot Laurence. The gun had been less than a foot from her. Chills raced down her spine as she pictured it. "I don't want to think of what would have happened had you missed."

"Best not to dwell on it," Bentley said. "Besides, I don't miss."

Gaston growled behind her, and she assumed it was because the full implication of Bentley's actions had registered with him as well.

"It's true," Laurence said, tying some rope around the duke's feet. "I've never seen him miss a target."

"See? I'm not simply another pretty face." Bentley grinned.

Once the duke was secured, they bound his coachman, putting them both in the carriage. A moan sounded from the other side. *Stefano!* Sophia broke from Gaston and ran to him, scanning his body for external wounds, running her hand over his head. She met a large, bloodied lump, and he moaned again but did not awaken.

Gaston joined her.

"Gaston, *per favore.*" Sophia felt like a helpless young girl.

Gaston knelt and carefully touched Stefano's head. "He will be fine, *mon amour.* There is a bump."

"And a bump is a good thing?"

"That is what the doctor told me," he said and touched his own head.

"Oh, my poor Gaston. You have been through much these last days, no?"

Still kneeling, he pulled her into his arms. "So have you, *ma chérie.*" She held on tightly as he whispered her name over and over into her hair.

"Let's take your reunion inside, shall we?" Bentley said, bending over and grabbing Stefano under the arms. "Along with this guy." Gaston took hold of Stefano's legs, and they hefted him as gently as they could. Laurence shouted from the box, and they waited as the duke's carriage pulled out.

"He is going back to London?" Sophie asked.

"No, to the stables." Bentley shifted Stefano's weight, and they began to walk with him across the courtyard. "The horses are too tired. As is Laurence. He'll keep the men locked in the carriage and watch them until I join him. When we're both rested, we'll take them directly to the Home Office. I should say, I will. Laurence will quietly disappear again when we get to London. We should be gone before daylight."

Sophia was speechless. Bentley knew all about Laurence's secret life. She could not fathom how he would.

"Somebody get down here and bloody well help, would you?" Bentley shouted at the trio of footmen and the cluster of maids huddled at the top of the stairs. They scuttled down the stairs, Patterson's large eyes darting among the men, Stefano's lifeless form, and her.

Sophia took charge. "You two, take him to his rooms and see one of the maids to his care. Patterson, you go to the village for Dr. Redding. Discretion, *s'il te plaît.*"

"Yes, my lady," they said in unison, and Patterson darted out of sight, while the other two took over from Gaston and Bentley.

"Where were they when you were in need?" Gaston scowled as he watched them carry Stefano up the stairs.

"When a duke tells you to stay away, you stay away," Sophia said, touching his arm. "It is the way of the world, no?"

Gaston grunted in response, and Bentley chuckled. They trailed the footmen into the manse, and Sophia gave the maids instruction, including an order for food. She led the three of them into the drawing room. She did not need to ask them if they would like a drink. She poured full glasses of cognac and served the men, grabbed her own, and sat on the sofa. Gaston sat beside her, and Bentley took the cozy armchair across from them. He sighed when he took his first sip, then set the glass on the side table.

"I assume you have a few questions?" Bentley raised an eyebrow, and a smile tugged at his mouth.

It was so normal and so entirely Bentley that Sophia laughed. And once she'd started, she couldn't stop. She laughed so hard tears rose, and once those overflowed, she couldn't stop crying. Gaston put his arm around her and pulled her to his chest, rubbing her back. It didn't matter how it had all come to pass. Gaston was alive. He was here. He was home.

CHAPTER FIFTY-NINE

Speak briefly then;
For we are peremptory to dispatch
This viperous traitor.

—Shakespeare, *Coriolanus*

W HEN SOPHIE CALMED, Gaston released his snug hold on her. He handed her his handkerchief, and she wiped her face, her fresh tears helping to remove some of the blood from her skin. Her beautiful face was lined with fatigue.

"Let's leave it until the morning, *ma chérie.* You should bathe and go to bed."

"*Non,*" she said, wiping at her eyes. "I will not sleep. Cannot. Not yet."

Gaston looked at Bentley. He'd thought the man a shallow dandy. This turn of events had undone that image, but his role in it remained perplexing. Gaston waved his glass at him in invitation.

Bentley shook his head. "I suspect the countess is more interested in your part of the story than mine. Tell your tale. I'll fill in any missing details."

Gaston held Bentley's good-natured gaze for a moment and decided not to argue. The man had saved Sophie. And, while Gaston's stomach flip-flopped when he thought of how easily the shot could have gone wrong, he would be eternally grateful.

"After you and the duke left, Drake lost his surety. I could tell he was not a man who would kill easily. So I began to probe. To question him. Hoping to find a way to get him to turn on the duke. I was thoroughly trussed and could not get out of my binds, and I was worried I would pass out from the exertion of trying."

Sophie touched his head gently. "Oh, *mon amour*," she said, tears glazing her eyes again. He took her hand, kissed it, and set it on her lap.

"*C'est correct*, Sophie. It is fine." In truth, it ached, but it did not matter now that she sat safely beside him. "Besides, nothing further happened. Your lake houseguest showed up."

"This I do not understand." Sophie scrunched her nose.

"Apparently, he had been suspicious of Drake for some time and had been following him. He—"

"But Laurence had gone to the continent? Stratton told me so," Sophie interrupted him, directing her question at Bentley.

"It was his intention, although he did not share his true reason with his father. He didn't want to alarm him unnecessarily. They are both incredibly fond of you, you know?"

Sophie nodded. "I still do not follow. Why was he going to the continent?"

"Mostly to find out more about this strange man who'd suddenly appeared in your life. A man who made you inordinately tense. Laurence reached out to some people he knew, and"— Bentley raised his glass toward Gaston—"he fit the description of a Frenchman who frequented the ports at Dunkirk and Gravelines." He looked back to Sophie. "Laurence was certain there was more going on than you realized, and he was determined to ensure you were safe. But he had a meeting with the Prime Minister before departing and was satisfied with what he learned so aborted his plans to head to the continent." He waved his glass at Gaston and grinned. "Continue."

Gaston stared at Bentley, legs casually crossed, sitting relaxed as though this was simply a normal visit. After all that had happened these past few days, the man could still present the air of a dandy.

"Gaston?" Sophie prompted.

Gaston shook his head and tried to refocus. "Stratton—"

"Let's stick with calling him by his Christian name, shall we? To preserve his identity should we ever be overheard. There are many Laurences, not so many Strattons. Do go on." Bentley waved his hand at Gaston.

"Laurence," Gaston said, retrieving the thoughts that had scattered with Bentley's interruption, "had watched Harris let Drake in and was waiting for him to come back out of your town house when the ducal carriage suddenly came out of the laneway. He couldn't see who was in it, as the windows were shuttered, but he sensed something was wrong. And when the postilions showed up with the post chaise and their knocking was ignored, he knew for sure something was off. He had the good sense to intercept them and ask them to wait. We could never have gotten here as quickly as we did had he not. Those men rode the horses like the devil himself was on their tails. My teeth are still rattling from the jostling in the post chaise." Laurence had not wanted witnesses to whatever lay ahead, so they'd left the two exhausted postilions behind at a nearby coaching house and continued on alone with fresh horses.

"*Dieu merci.*" Sophie touched his hand.

"*Oui,* thank God." He took a sip of the cognac, his mind racing through all that had happened the past two days, quickly sorting through what Sophie needed to know right now. "And I was correct about Drake. He was not meant for the role of villain. It was easy to get him to share all he knew."

"This is the part I want to hear," Bentley said and grinned. "I don't have all the pieces."

"Both Drake and the Duke of Salinger like to gamble."

"That I knew," Bentley said. "I might add it was not a well-kept secret."

"It would seem he became indebted to the wrong people. A

small group of Napoleon supporters."

Bentley leaned forward. "Who?"

"That I do not know. Only that one of them is French. An émigré, perhaps? The others are English."

Bentley harrumphed and sat back in his seat.

"This group offered Drake and the duke a way out. Find information to help their cause, and they'd forgive the debt. Once he'd given them some information, they had him cornered. Apparently, they both simultaneously blackmailed him and made it financially worth his while, giving him just enough to maintain the life to which he was accustomed. No doubt they were abetting his gambling problem to ensure he continued to be hungry for money."

"They definitely recognized his need *and* his greed," Bentley said.

"Or maybe they could see he was not well," Sophie said quietly, and Gaston worried about the hours she had been trapped alone with the duke. He squeezed her hand, and she gave him a small smile.

"Not well?" Bentley sat forward again.

"*Sì*, crazy. You did not see his behavior up close, but what sane man goes chasing across the country after buried treasure?"

"And what man in his right mind plots to assassinate the Prime Minister and the regent?" Gaston asked.

Bentley whistled under his breath. "I did not know about the regent."

A tap at the door interrupted them, and they waited as food was brought in. A maid also delivered a basin of water and some linen. Sophie washed while he and Bentley dug into the food, saving further conversation until she rejoined them.

She sat down, looking somewhat better, although her blood-spattered dress was a reminder to Gaston how close she had come to wearing her own blood. His anger rose, quick and unexpected, and he turned it on Bentley.

"And you...*merde*! What were you thinking? You could have

killed Sophie!"

Bentley seemed unfazed by the accusation. "No. The duke could have killed the countess. And that was a chance I was not willing to take."

Gaston swallowed the bile in his throat and washed the remnants down with cognac. He could see the truth of what Bentley said.

"But how did you come to be here? You were gone to the Newmarket races, no?" Sophie asked, relaxing back on the cushions, a piece of buttered bread in her hand.

"I was. But Laurence sent word. The messenger caught up with me at the first coaching inn where I was having dinner. Blasted good dinner I had to walk away from." He winked at Sophie.

While Gaston was happy to hear a light laugh from her, it still made no sense to him. "Why you?"

"Why me? Because we work together."

"*Non!*" Sophie said.

"*Mais oui,*" Bentley said. "I suppose I should be insulted by the disbelief on both your faces." He brushed at a crumb on his lapel. "The night of the masquerade, when you, Armand…yes, I now know your true name…knocked the countess over…beastly thing to do by the way." Gaston opened his mouth to speak, and Bentley waved his words away. "I know, I know, it was an accident. But considering your relationship, you could have stayed and let the countess know you lived. Cruel, that. Letting someone believe you're gone when you are not. I keep having a similar conversation with Laurence. To no avail, of course. He insists his sister cannot know. For her own safety. Perhaps he's right. You must agree with him, Countess, as you have never told Lady Walford." He tilted his head. "At least, I presume you haven't."

Sophie shook her head. "If he says it might put her in danger, then it is true. I do not question it. Better Catherine think her brother is somewhere fighting in the colonies than her, or the child, be harmed, no?"

"Yes, I suppose so. And Walford himself agrees. So there you have it. Laurence remains a ghost in our presence."

"For now. He has promised to return to the living when the war is over." Sophie popped a piece of bread in her mouth, chewing thoughtfully.

Gaston was not so easily sidetracked. "I have many questions," he said.

"I'm sure you do. I have some answers. Not all. And some things I can't share."

"Let's start with the message you received."

"Ah, yes." Bentley dug in his pocket, pulled out a small, folded piece of paper, and handed it to Gaston. "Told me everything I needed to know."

Gaston read it twice. *S has shed his robes. Taken our jewel to new château. Urgent.* He frowned at Bentley.

"Well, he couldn't simply write the duke has lost his cover and has kidnapped the countess and taken her to her residence, could he? What if someone intercepted? And trust me, Laurence only writes 'urgent' if it is indeed urgent. I did not hesitate."

"But how did you know it was the countess?"

Bentley's cheeks reddened, and he smiled almost bashfully. "It is what we call you. Our jewel."

Sophie's laugh tinkled lightly, and Gaston's tension began to melt away. He couldn't argue with Bentley, for she was a jewel. And the duke had certainly been disrobed. Gaston stiffened. The duke should never have been able to get ahold of Sophie in the first place. "If you both were aware the duke was covering something, why was he not being followed?"

"Oh, we were following him. Or I was. Remember those trips to Tattersall's?" Bentley asked. "I wasn't looking for company. I was trying to kill two birds with one stone. Find out exactly what your story was and keep an eye on the duke." He looked at Sophie. "And that rout? The duke was expected there. He was the man who didn't show up. Well, more the man who arrived too late for the meeting. Still, your eavesdropping was of great help. I believe the Prime Minister is suitably grateful."

"And yesterday?" Gaston prodded. "Why were you not on his heels yesterday?"

Bentley sighed heavily. "Yes, well that was a bit of a shambles, wasn't it? I watched the duke depart for what I thought was Newmarket. I rode on ahead to his usual inn. Less suspicious if I was there ahead of him. Of course, I now know he wasn't heading to Newmarket."

"You could not know," Sophie said. "What will happen to His Grace now?"

"It's hard to tell. Things are tricky when it's a peer. Especially a duke. Last year, Bellingham's trial occurred four days after he assassinated Prime Minister Perceval, and he hung three days later. But he murdered Perceval in clear sight of everyone. The duke was part of a plot not yet enacted. But there is the matter of plotting against the regent. That is something else entirely. It's high treason."

"I hope he hangs too," Gaston said, and he meant it. A peerage should not protect him from the consequences of his crimes. Gaston had seen people murdered for no reason other than they existed. It disgusted him to think a noble who acted without any honor, who had threatened Sophie's life, might walk free.

"Well, much will depend on what the prince regent says about it." Bentley stood and stretched. "Mind if I take the remainder of this"—he pointed to the platter of food—"and that"—he gestured to the decanter on the side table—"out to Laurence?"

"But of course," Sophie said, jumping to her feet. "I can get more."

"No need, although some water to wash wouldn't be turned away." He smiled and bowed to them both. "We'll be gone before you are awake, but I am sure I shall see you at the next soiree."

"Thank you," Sophie said, handing him the platter.

"It was my pleasure." Bentley grabbed the decanter and walked out of the drawing room.

Gaston could hear him talking with a footman, and then the entranceway fell silent. He watched the play of emotion on Sophie's face as she listened too. He worried she might collapse with fatigue. The pain in his head had not subsided with the drink, and he was glad the doctor had sent him with the tonic powder. He'd take some before going to sleep.

"It is all too much, no?" Sophie's eyes glazed.

"*Oui, c'est vrai.*" Gaston held out his hand, and Sophie put her hand in it. "Let's go to our bed, *mon amour,* and hold each other." He tugged her closer and kissed her forehead and her nose, then brushed the softest of kisses against her lips.

She leaned heavily on him as they climbed the stairs and stood numbly watching as he took his tonic. He walked to her and rubbed her shivering arms. He helped her undress, throwing her dress in a corner far from sight, and lifted her onto the bed. She lay watching him as he undressed, but her eyes grew heavy. He crawled in behind her and pulled her close.

"Go to sleep, *mon amour.* Let's leave all this behind and dream about the tomorrows that lie ahead."

She fell asleep quickly, her gentle, steady breathing a comfort. He'd been terrified that after all these years, after finally finding their way to each other, he was going to lose her again. This time forever.

But she was here. She was unharmed. It was over.

Sleep pulled, and he closed his eyes. A young girl in Paris, her hand held out. A young woman in *Venise,* offering her innocence. A strong woman, as bold as she was beautiful, head thrown back, turning on the dance floor. He smiled into the darkness and held her tighter. His Sophie.

"*Je t'aime,*" he whispered and did as he'd advised her to do—surrendered to his dreams of their tomorrows.

EPILOGUE

All is not lost that is delayed.

—French Proverb

CARA PINNED THE last flower onto Sophia's hair and stepped back, smiling at her handiwork.

"Sei bella, signora mia."

"Grazie, Cara. It is your effort that makes me beautiful."

They smiled at each other in the mirror. Sophia had once again offered a good pension to Cara, but she'd insisted she was not ready to sit in a rocking chair. Sophia did not argue. Cara knew who Sophia had been, who she'd become, and who she was now. It was a special connection, and she would have missed her dearly had she accepted.

"A few minutes alone, *per favore."*

"Of course, *signora mia."*

Sophia waited until Cara had left before pushing from the bench and strolling to the window. For late September, the gardens were stunning. Stefano and Raimondo had done a magnificent job maintaining their beauty. *Raimondo.* Sophia smiled. She'd asked him to take the role of her father today. He'd seemed so pleased she was convinced he had finally forgiven her for sending him away that day.

That day. She knew the memory of it would fade with time

as all wounds did, but though months had passed, the tumult of emotions had not. The duke had been declared criminally insane in the House of Lords and was sequestered at an undisclosed hospital outside of the city, awaiting the opening of the Bethlam Royal Hospital in Saint George's Fields. Lord Acherton had not stood trial at all. He had not been heard to agree with any plot, so it had been dismissed as hearsay. Drake had been remanded into the custody of his family but had been stripped of his property and rights. As no actual attempt had been made on the regent's life or the Prime Minister's, and the duke was incapable of naming Drake as an accomplice, Drake had not faced the noose for his participation in treason. Laurence continued to work with his covert squad so could not stand as witness to Drake's confession. Gaston could easily have testified to Drake's involvement but chose not to. He'd said, without Drake, they would not have evidence on the duke, and the man was no killer. Besides, losing his peerage was punishment enough. She loved Gaston all the more for his leniency.

Foiling a double assassination plot had its perks. Prime Minister Liverpool had waived all obligations, and Gaston was a free man. She and Gaston had decided they would still work for the cause, but it would be on their own terms. He'd asked for the favor of a special license, and they'd quietly married while the duke was on trial. Gaston had thought it too distasteful to celebrate during such a time.

Before taking their vows, Gaston had shared that Carmine had known Gaston lived, that the two had spoken when he'd come back for her all those years ago. She wondered what it would have changed had she known? She had already been married. Perhaps the burden of knowing he was alive and she could not be with him would have been too much? She was certain Carmine had done it out of caring, so she forgave his memory—which was easy to do with Gaston back in her life. Sophia was grateful he had searched her out one more time, even if his intent was originally to hurt her with a goodbye.

Gaston. She hugged herself and swayed happily. Only Jocelyne and Raimondo had stood as witnesses to their wedding. Which was why they would celebrate today. She had worried about waiting so late in the season, afraid the weather would be prohibitive for the outdoor celebration of her dreams. But Gaston had insisted on the delay, saying some things were worth waiting for. He'd wanted to tie up all loose ends and claimed autumn was his favorite season, although she'd always thought it was spring. He asked for little, so she did not argue. And it did not truly matter, for every day was a celebration with Gaston by her side as her husband.

Jocelyne had worked small miracles in the garden, draping chairs with cloth, weaving flowers into the arbor Sophia and Gaston would stand under to exchange vows in front of her friends. There would be no minister this time, as they were already legally wed. Instead, Stratton had agreed to officiate. Noise from her sitting room drew her attention from the gardens below, and her heart thumped excitedly as she turned from the window.

"*Mie amiche*," she said, clapping her hands as Elizabeth and Catherine entered her chambers. "I am so happy you are here!"

Catherine laughed. "You saw me last night," she said, kissing each of Sophia's proffered cheeks.

"It is true, but it was late when you arrived and you were tired. You have quite recovered, I think."

Catherine looked beautiful in a buttercup gown, her hair piled high with pearl pins to match the rest of her jewelry.

Sophia presented her cheeks to Elizabeth, who obliged and whispered, "You look beautiful," before she pulled away.

"And you are a princess, no?"

Elizabeth wore a shimmering pale-blue gown and a topaz-studded tiara.

Elizabeth touched her tiara. "Well, this is a special day, no?" she said, mimicking Sophia's accent.

"*Sì*, it is. And you are my special people."

They knew everything about her and Gaston now. They'd said there was no need for apologies, insisting Sophia had always been her genuine self even if she had not told them her whole truth. They had been filled with questions, and equal parts awe and dismay, as she'd shared the story of finding a young Gaston in front of the Bastille, of the rioters who'd taken her mother during the revolution, of losing both Gaston and her father after that. As she'd told Gaston later, they'd cried in all the right parts. That was the sign of true friendship.

"Let us go see our handsome men," Sophia said. They chatted happily as they made their way through her rooms and down the stairs. Elizabeth's four boys flew by without a glance, followed by their nanny and Miss Langdon, who was carrying young Daniel. She smiled at them but continued on toward the ballroom.

"It seems there are only little boys about," Sophia said, and both women apologized. "*Mie amiche*, do not apologize. They are children." While Sophia had no desire for children of her own, she did enjoy theirs. "And I am like their aunt, no?"

They hugged each other as one, then pulled away, laughing as they wiped at their eyes.

"And what do we have here?" Stratton's voice boomed in the large entrance. "The loveliest bouquet I have ever laid eyes upon."

After greetings were done, Sophia sent them on through the ballroom, to the garden, excusing herself. She needed a moment to get her rampant emotions under control. She stepped into the yellow drawing room. They had written their own vows to each other, and she worried she might forget what to say. She pulled out the paper from the side-table drawer, unfolding her spectacles and putting them on. She read the words softly to herself.

"Have I mentioned how adorable you look in those?" Butterflies still danced at the sight of Gaston. Dressed formally in black and white, he was as handsome as she'd ever seen him.

"I look like a grandmother, no?"

He walked toward her. "*Non.* You look beautiful. You will always look so. Even as a wizened old woman, you will be *magnifique.*" He kissed her on the nose, and she raised her lips for more, but he pulled away and walked to the window. "Ah, *finalement.*"

Sophia could hear the clatter of wheels in the courtyard. She'd thought all her guests had arrived. She walked toward him to see who it was.

"No, *mon amour*, there is no time. Come."

He grabbed her hand, pulled her to the front door and out onto the landing. The carriage was unmarked and shuttered. The coachman jumped to the ground and opened the door. There was a flourish of movement, and two men in top hats alighted, their faces shadowed by their brims. She looked at Gaston questioningly, but he simply squeezed her hand and urged her to the top of the stairs.

The taller of the two men looked up. Lord Liverpool? He smiled and tipped his hat. Liverpool leaned in to say something to the other man, who then looked up. Sophia stopped, and a tremor raced through her body. "*Non, ce n'est pas possible,*" she whispered to Gaston.

"*Oui,* it is him," he said quietly, his glazed eyes mirrors to hers.

She let go of his hand, and her legs found their strength as she flew down the remaining steps. "Papa!" she cried, bursting into tears as her father wrapped his arms around her.

"Sophie," he said gruffly, over and over into her hair.

Her mind was in turmoil, but her heart knew the truth. This was no fantasy. Her father had been returned to her. She pulled back and looked at him, and he wiped the tears from her cheeks.

"*Ma petite fille,*" he said, tears glistening on his face. "Though not so little anymore. You are a grown woman now, *non?*"

He was the same age as the duke but looked much older than him. And thinner. Gaunt, with hollowed cheeks and features too big for his face. But she could see her dear papa in his eyes and his smile.

"But how?" she asked, looking from him, to Gaston, to Lord Liverpool, who, hat in hand, looked exceedingly pleased with himself.

"It would seem your father is as resourceful as you," Lord Liverpool said. "But I will leave him to tell you his tale." He looked at Gaston. "My apologies for our delay. No doubt you have been stressed about it. The ship was late, and we had to get the man cleaned up and into some decent clothing. It is a wedding, after all." He returned his attention to Sophia and her father. "It was a pleasure to meet you, Monsieur Auclair. And to see you again, Countess Tessaro."

"Madame Armand," she corrected with a smile, still wiping at her eyes.

Lord Liverpool nodded in acknowledgment.

"You will, of course, join us."

"Unfortunately, it would not be wise." He put his hat on. "A seeming relationship between us would not benefit any future work you might consider."

Her father's arm still around her waist, Sophia leaned into him, unable to process it all. Gaston thrust out a hand. "We owe you a great debt, my lord."

"Not at all. You may have saved my life and that of the regent. We can call it even." Lord Liverpool shook Gaston's hand and her father's, bowing toward her before climbing into the carriage. The three of them stood side by side and watched the carriage roll away.

"I believe there is a wedding today, *non?*" Papa said.

"But I cannot grasp…I do not comprehend…how—"

"Sophie, you have not changed. You do not need to understand now. It is enough I am here." He looked fondly at Gaston. "That we are all here. There is plenty of time to share our stories later. Years, I hope." He leaned in and kissed each cheek.

She held a hand from each man as they climbed the stairs of Château Nouveau and entered the grand hall. Raimondo stood, as ever, waiting for her.

"Signore Auclair," he said, shaking her father's hand. "I will outline the plans for the ceremony."

"You knew?"

"I know everything," Raimondo said and winked at Gaston. Sophia's world had truly turned upside down. She said so to Gaston as Raimondo led her father into the receiving room.

Gaston pulled Sophia into the drawing room, closing the door behind them.

She turned on him. "How long have you known?"

"Liverpool had a lead on it when the duke was brought in, but he was not entirely sure if it was true, so I said nothing. I did not want to get your hopes up."

"Is it why you delayed this celebration?" Sophia's head was spinning, trying to sequence all that happened these past few months and make a single picture of it.

"*Oui*. I would have married you in front of everyone, the duke's trial be damned. But I thought if there was a chance for your father to be a part of it, the celebration could wait. On the other hand, you being officially my wife could not." Gaston tried to pull her close for a kiss, but she was not done.

"Where has he been?"

"It is a long story, and it is his to tell, but he escaped French Guiana with royalist Pichegru. They foolishly returned to France, hoping to make a difference, and he was imprisoned."

"*Non!*"

"*Oui.* He was the lucky one. Pichegru was executed."

"*Mon Dieu*," Sophia said quietly, grateful her father had been spared. "But how did Liverpool get him out of prison?"

"He was no longer in prison. They had discovered he could speak many languages, so they were using him as an interpreter on the eastern front." He tilted his head, holding her gaze. "Is it too much, Sophie? Should we not wed this day?" Gaston's eyes were dark with concern.

"It is too much," she said, filled with images of her father's life. But he was here now. It was all that mattered.

"He was supposed to arrive last night—"

Sophia pressed her fingers to his lips. "It is too much goodness. I don't know what to do with it."

He nodded solemnly, and she took her fingers away.

"So we will share it with our friends."

She loved the dawning realization and the slow smile lighting his face and warming his eyes. He picked her up and swung her around, and she laughed, letting joy override confusion and flow through her. Gaston set her on her feet with her back against the door.

He pressed his forehead to hers before pulling back and gazing directly into her eyes. "Will you marry me, Sophie Auclair Tessaro Armand?"

She adored that he now acknowledged all the pieces of her, for he had owned each and every part, even when he hadn't been there.

"*Sì*," she said, in the language of her mother, her heart aching a little, but she knew her mama would be so happy to know her dear papa was by Sophia's side once again. She kissed Gaston's nose.

"*Oui*," she said, in the language of their country, the language they shared. She kissed his cheek.

"Yes," she said, in the language of their new home, of their new family. She kissed Gaston's other cheek.

They looked into each other's eyes, Gaston's face blurring as happy tears threatened to spill. He leaned down, and they kissed.

Gently.

Slowly.

Lovingly.

Sealing the pledge to each other in the language of their hearts.

The End

About the Author

Rose Phillips has a BA, BEd, and an Advanced Degree in Educational Leadership—none of which led to her dream of being a romance writer, but they did help pay the bills. As an educator, she worked with at-risk adolescents, so writing young adult novels seemed a natural place to start. She has three novels published in that category. While she thoroughly enjoys writing for young adults, her true love has always been adult romance, especially historical.

Rose grew up in eastern Canada, on the island of Newfoundland. She now resides on the opposite side of the country, on Vancouver Island. She enjoys kayaking, hiking, playing pickleball, and visiting the many local wineries. She long ago found the love of her life, and he continues to be the reason she believes in happy ever afters.

Twitter: @roserambles1
Instagram: rosephillipsrambles
Blog: rosephillipsrambles.blogspot.com
Amazon: amazon.com/Rose-Phillips/e/B06XB1374P
Goodreads: goodreads.com/author/show/5976526.Rose_Phillips
Bookbub: bookbub.com/authors/rose-phillips

www.ingramcontent.com/pod-product-compliance
Lightning Source LLC
Chambersburg PA
CBHW052028220726

48293CB00015B/441